I0692300

Disclaimer: This novel is a work of fiction, except for the parts that aren't. Any similarities to real people or events is purely coincidental.

ISBN: 0-692-10920-X
ISBN-13: 978-0-692-10920-5

Dedication

I dedicate this novel to my daughter Maya and her boyfriend, Jared, for being a great example of what true love is. And to my love, and life partner Paul, who is always there to support me in every way, including my writing endeavors.

Out of the ruler's house a child will arise,

Part vampire and human, it's seen in his eyes.

From birth the conflict grows,

Exposing all enemies so that the vampire knows.

There are two that start a new race,

To bring order and slay enemies without a trace.

The time will be short before they are grown,

And then their full potential will be known.

Their abilities surpass by far,

The vampire and slayer to prevent war.

Chapter One
Rurik

"Adrian, you have to let him do this. He's almost sixteen, and is half human too." Mom's blue-green eyes flashed with determination. She was subconsciously standing on her tiptoes to make herself appear larger squaring off against Dad.

I sat on the edge of the kitchen counter with my roast beef sandwich, watching the scene develop with amusement. My Dad, Adrian, was trying to control his temper. If I hadn't seen this side of him many times over the years while growing up I would've been concerned. He was very effective at being intimidating. I supposed it was important since he was the ruler of this country for the secret vampire society. He was without a doubt a force to be reckoned with, not to mention over six feet tall and intimidatingly handsome. That was one aspect of my father that I did appreciate. I'd inherited his incredible looks.

It was hard to enjoy his amazing features at the moment while he stood there with boiling pools of lava churning under the surface of his black eyes. I felt a little sorry for my mom, Carmen. She always stood her ground with him, but she wasn't more than five feet four inches tops, and in my opinion didn't stand a chance. Don't get me wrong, she was a vampire too, and a slayer. I'd never seen a more lethal machine when she was fired up about something. But

I also knew that when it came to Dad, she was putty in his hands.

But, Mom was the only one I knew who would stand up to Dad when she felt she was in the right, no matter how frightening he could be.

"Carmen...." Dad paused for effect and sighed. "There's absolutely no way that Rurik is ever going to a public high school. It would be a security nightmare. That's final!"

I repositioned myself on my perch and took another bite of sandwich. This was just starting to get interesting. I wasn't worried…I knew that I would eventually get my way. If Mom lost this round she would subtly work on Dad until he agreed with us. He was always the hot headed stormy one in their relationship, but would calm down at some point and see the reasoning behind me going to a public school. I'd graduated with top grades in every category, and was bored to tears. I needed a little interaction with kids my own age…even if they were only human.

"Please, just think about it," Mom said in a soothing voice, trying a different approach. She could calm the savage beast in Dad unlike anyone else I'd ever seen. His eyes were already softening faintly in response to her quiet tone. I stayed out of the conversation, because I was way past the "thinking my dad was cool" stage. He and I disagreed constantly on every subject. I knew Mom was my best ally.

"He'll be running things at some point, and needs to know how to relate with humans," she went on. "You can't continue to keep him isolated from the world. How's Rurik ever supposed to rise up to become a great leader when you're afraid to let him interact with others?"

I stopped with the sandwich to my lips, hearing her regrettable use of words. Big oops; Mom should never have accused Dad of being afraid of anything. I could tell she realized her error and braced herself when Dad's eyes sparked angrily. I couldn't help involuntarily stiffening a little, and prepared myself for the onslaught I knew was now going to be unleashed.

"This has nothing to do with fear!" he shouted. "I'm in charge of this country. Don't you realize how detrimental it would be to the entire society for Rurik to ever show any signs of his abilities at a public school? It's ludicrous to even be standing here and having this conversation with you. There's no way I'm ever going to agree to this."

Mom stood there and took it like a trooper while Adrian Tallinn's wrath was rained upon her. She had guts; anyone else would have been cowering about now. She stood toe to toe with Dad and glared back up into his face. Dad glowered for several moments before he turned his attention to me, as if suddenly realizing that I was still there. I couldn't help bracing a little now that his full anger was aimed my direction.

"As for you, Rurik. Don't think just because you have Mom on your side in this makes any difference. Do you understand me?" His eyes narrowed while he waited for my response.

I was smart enough to know when dealing with Dad that increasing his temper was a really dumb thing to do at this point, so I only nodded my head in agreement.

"I make the final decisions around here when it comes to what's best for this family and the society. I'm still in charge. Don't ever forget that." His black eyes bore sternly into mine for a few moments, and then he turned back to Mom and gave her a look that could have wilted an entire garden before he turned around and left the room.

Mom sighed. It was obvious she'd been holding her breath. Then she turned to me and tried to smile. "I'm sorry, Rurik. I think I only made it worse."

She walked over and put her hand up and brushed the hair out of my eyes. She was constantly doing that. I liked my hair long in front, and it irritated her that it covered my "gorgeous brown eyes," as she referred to them.

"I'll work on him later, after he's calmed down a bit. He'll eventually see that he can't keep you hidden here forever."

I gave her a brilliant smile. "It's okay, Mom. Don't worry about it."

She sighed. "Your father and I have never seen eye to eye on the subject of you interacting with people. You're half human too." Mom had been human for the first several years they were married. I was around six years old when she was changed, and didn't really remember much about that side of her, only that even at that age I was concerned for her frail human body in comparison to our almost indestructible vampire ones. Mom never wanted to be a vampire, and only reluctantly became one when there was no other choice. I knew that sometimes she still, even now, missed being human. But she loved my dad unconditionally, and it was an inevitable consequence of choosing to be with him.

I grinned. "I'm not worried. You can manipulate Dad when you need to."

She smiled suddenly. "Don't ever let him hear you say that, or we'll never get our way again."

I raised my hand to my mouth and ran my finger across to indicate that my lips were sealed.

Mom patted my arm and then turned around and left the kitchen.

I finished my sandwich and then pulled my cell phone out to call Amy. Now there was a totally irritating girl if ever there was one. But at this point in time she was the only one my age I was allowed to associate with, and it was because she was the same as me, half vampire and half slayer. I shuddered when I remembered being told that she and I were supposedly going to marry someday and start a new super race of vampires. I wouldn't marry Amy if she was the last girl left on this planet. She was the biggest spoiled brat in all of creation.

"Hey," Amy answered the phone. "What're you up to?"

"Just watching the fireworks…Dad and Mom arguing again," I said with a grin. "You want to hang out this afternoon?"

"When are they not arguing?" Amy asked sarcastically. "Sure, I'd love to do a movie or something."

"Great, see you later."

I closed my phone and slid off the counter. I couldn't help grinning a little. Even though I despised Amy's spoiled, I'm so superior attitude, she was absolutely gorgeous. And I knew she liked me. She'd even let me hold her hand and kiss her once.

Girls were naturally attracted to me, with my good looks, thick, black wavy hair, and dark brown eyes. That was one of the reasons I couldn't wait to go to a public school…they wouldn't be able to resist me. But I could never tell Mom that, or she would be on Dad's side and I would be stuck in this prison forever.

#

"My mom and dad are so lame. At least you have this big house to live in," Amy commented, running her hand over the list of CD's on the shelf beside my stereo. Then she pulled one out and smiled. "Let's listen to this!"

I groaned. "Not Britney Stars again." I was going to have to remember to toss that one out. It had been given to me as a gift and I hated it. "You have a nice place too. Your parents bought that piece of property and built."

"Not nearly as awesome as yours," Amy complained. She popped the CD in, cranked up the volume, and plopped down beside me on the lounge. Then she took my hand and smiled up at me. She had the most beautiful blue eyes with thick lashes, her face framed by her long golden curls. Boys were helpless when they looked into her gaze. I was glad that it didn't have the same effect on me. I'd known her since we were born, our birthdays only a week apart. She was a little demon and got her way with everything, which irritated me enormously. I was always accused of picking on her every time she ran to our parents. They all seemed to be completely unaware of how manipulative she really could be. But

I smiled back. I knew she liked me, and that I could use that to my advantage.

"So what were your parents arguing about this time?" she asked.

I shrugged. "About me going to public high school. Dad doesn't seem to get why Mom and I think that I should."

Her eyes flew open wide. "Public school? Are you serious?"

I nodded.

"But why? You're half way through your college courses. Why would you want to go to high school?"

I gave her a look of annoyance. If anyone should understand, it was her. "Aren't you tired of being cooped up here like some freak lab experiment? I want to go out and experience a few things."

"Like what? There're only humans at a public school," she scoffed.

"I know," I emphasized with a smirk. "We'd be the top of everything we did there."

Her pouty frown slowly turned into a mischievous grin while she thought about my words. I knew if I could get Amy and her parents, Tony and Amanda, on me and Mom's side, Dad would soon crumble.

I smiled and said, "It would be fun to rule the school…wouldn't it?"

She smiled and nestled against my side. "I see your point. That could be a blast."

#

Mom eventually came through for me. I don't know how she managed with Dad being so dead set against the entire idea, but never underestimate the power of love and the enchanting abilities of a female. Mom may be putty in Dad's hands, but in a lot of ways, Dad was the same powerless mass when it came to Mom's charms.

**

I sat on the sofa and tried very hard to not get "a look" while I was read the entire rule book on how I was supposed to behave in public, and then heard all of the secret vampire society laws for the umpteenth time. I didn't want to blow it now by coming across as the smart mouthed teenager, and found myself trying to concentrate on anything dull and mundane to keep my features neutral, so I focused my attention at a spot on the wall.

"Are you even paying attention?" Dad suddenly asked, sounding a bit perturbed.

I looked up at him and tried to smile nicely. "Um…of course, Dad."

His eyes narrowed slightly, like he didn't quite believe me. "You know all of our rules by heart, but I want to emphasize the importance of not displaying any extra abilities while at school. Believe me, I know how tempting it'll be to control the humans around you, but you're only getting one shot at this. There are no second chances. Do you hear?"

I tried my best to nod sincerely and keep a straight face.

He stared at me doubtfully for a few moments before he continued. "I mean it, Rurik. You can't screw up in public. Ever."

"I completely understand Dad. Really."

"Don't patronize me. It may have been a few hundred years since I was a teenager, but that doesn't mean I don't remember how they think. For the life of me I can't figure out why you would want to go to high school in the first place. You're almost done with your college courses. It's not as if you're going to learn anything there."

"He just needs to get out of the house and interact with kids his own age," Mom interjected into the conversation.

Dad sighed. "Somehow that doesn't make me feel any better about this. I think this is a huge mistake I'm letting myself get talked into."

"I won't disappoint you," I said as sincerely as possible. "I mean it." And I did really mean it. I just wanted to have a little fun. It was impossible to do that at home with everyone watching everything I did constantly.

"He'll be fine, Adrian," Mom tried to reassure him.

"All right…. We'll try this for the first semester," Dad said slowly and carefully.

I grinned widely and couldn't help a little exclamation. "Yes!"

Dad stared at me darkly. "Only for a semester, and if there is any problem—at all—that is it. Understood?"

I nodded again and tried hard to control my enthusiasm. I was actually going to be allowed outside the house, into a public setting without constant supervision. It was unbelievable.

"The only reason I'm going for this in any way is because we've had no problems with our enemies in years now. Otherwise there would be no way I could let you go without a bodyguard."

Mom snickered slightly. "He can run circles around a bodyguard. His abilities surpassed any other vampire years ago."

I cringed. This wasn't the time to belittle Dad's remarks. I didn't want him to get mad and change his mind.

Dad looked acerbically at Mom. "I'm very aware of that, Carmen."

I held my breath while he stared at her with aggravation for a moment, and then he turned around without another word and walked out of the living area.

Mom gave me a wide grin, walked over, and put her arms around my neck. "I went out on a limb and promised your father that you'd never even consider causing any kind of stir at school. That you are just interested in getting to know the human side of you a little better. So make sure that I'm not eating my words."

"Thanks, Mom." I couldn't help grinning. "Don't worry, I promise to be good."

I couldn't wait until the following Monday to go to school. I was ecstatic about the idea, and was actually glad that Amy had decided she didn't want to go. She'd told me she was "so far beyond any of those immature teenagers" it would take all of her self-control to not want to just squash them."

#

When Monday arrived, Dad dropped me off in front of the high school in the limo. I cringed as every student standing around the front entrance stared at me when I got out. *What a way to make an entrance*, I thought with dismay. I'd already be pegged as weird just for pulling up to the school in a limousine.

A group of girls standing to one side stared when I walked past, so I flashed my brilliant smile. They almost looked thunderstruck, so I glanced quickly away and continued to the entrance. That was when I noticed a few guys glaring my direction. I could feel myself ruffling, and braced for a confrontation.

They were large and muscular…human jock types. The largest one appeared to be the leader and he eyed me hatefully, stepping directly in my path. Then he just stood there as if daring me to make him move.

I stopped and stood facing him for a moment, weighing my options. I knew my freedom would be short-lived if I were to put this punk in his place like I wanted to, so I took a deep breath and made myself smile.

"Excuse me," I said in an even tone.

The guy looked me up and down for a few moments before he gave me a disdainful grin, and then to my surprise stepped to the side and let me pass.

I grinned back and headed into the building, but heard them snicker behind me. One said, "He thinks he's something, doesn't he?"

"Yeah, we'll see about that. He looks like a total nerd to me."

The lady at the reception desk immediately looked up and said suspiciously, "Can I help you? Students aren't allowed inside the building till the buzzer rings." She was older and matronly looking, with her long graying hair in a ponytail and dark rimmed glasses. I gave her a charming smile and she was instantly drawn into my eyes. Her entire attitude relaxed and she smiled back.

"I'm Rurik Tallinn. This is my first day and I was told to come in and get my class schedule."

"Oh…that's right. I remember talking to your dad on the phone. Hold on, I think I have it here." She turned to a desk and picked up a couple pieces of paper and then handed them over. "This is the classes you have, and here's a map to get around the buildings."

I smiled and took them from her. "Thanks."

"If you have any questions at all, don't hesitate to ask me," she said kindly.

I nodded my head and turned around and headed back toward the front doors while I glanced over the sheet of classes.

"Wow, that's the friendliest I've seen Ms. Schwartz act to anyone. Ever."

I glanced up and a girl was standing just inside the door. She had long brown hair and large green eyes, with a cute turned up nose.

"She didn't seem that bad," I tried to say casually.

"Are you kidding? Everyone here dreads having to talk to Ms. Schwartz. What did you do to her?"

I was taken aback by her question. Had this girl seen me mesmerize the lady? I'd better be a little more discreet next time. "What do you mean?" I asked with suspicion.

She laughed. "Don't get all uptight, I didn't mean you really did anything to her."

I tried to relax, and brushed my bangs back out of my eyes and grinned.

"I'm Mindy." She smiled at me and I could tell that she was attracted to my good looks. The prey was always unwittingly drawn to the alluring qualities of the hunter. This was going to be a piece of cake.

"Hi, I'm Rurik," I returned.

Just then the buzzer rang and a hoard of students came rushing into the building, talking and laughing.

"Where's your first class?" Mindy shouted over the throng of kids.

"Um…I have science at the end of the hallway upstairs. Room 215. And then it's physical ed, and math after that, on the other side of campus."

She looked at me with amazement. "You memorized all of that already? You just glanced at your schedule and walked over here."

This girl was observant. I was going to have to be more careful around her. "I…have something of a photographic memory."

"Tight!" she exclaimed. "Well, maybe I'll see you at lunch. I have to go the opposite way. Nice to meet you, Rurik."

I grinned after her and then took off up the stairs to my first class.

It was pretty uneventful. I got curious stares from most of the students. No one said much to me, and I wondered if they were intimidated by my perfect features. I didn't have the awkward teenage look that most of them were still sporting. I'd never even had a pimple, or a bruise that lasted more than seconds.

When I arrived for my next class, gym, I noticed with dismay that the jocks that had confronted me outside the entrance this morning were there. The leader smirked when he saw me and slapped his buddy next to him, who stared my direction. I was afraid that there was an altercation coming, and I didn't have to wait long to find out.

It started in the locker room. The P.E. teacher, Mr. Scott, said to find an empty locker to put my clothes in and change. When I walked in, the group of trouble makers was already hanging out at one end of the bench and changing into their gym clothes. They watched me walk past them to the locker at the end. After changing, I put my things away and started back to the doorway when the largest of the group stepped in front of me again.

I stopped and stared him dead in the eye. He was every inch as tall as me, six feet with blond hair and brown eyes. I was even gladder at that moment that I'd inherited my dad's height instead of my mom's petite features.

My eyes glinted narrowly back into his, but I was trying hard not to glare and show my more intimidating expression. I wanted to avoid a fight with this kid. He had no idea what he was dealing with, and I didn't want to get kicked out of school on my first day. So I stood there, undecided as to what my best course of action should be, and it must have shown on my face.

He looked somewhat amused at my discomfort. "What's wrong?" he asked sarcastically. "Not so brave now that the teacher isn't around?"

"I just don't want to get kicked out of school my first day here for wiping the floor with you. That's all," I answered contemptuously.

I could see slight doubt flicker across his features. His three other buddies, who were standing at his side and completely blocking my exit, snickered.

"I think he's dissing you, Kayden," one of them said.

"I don't want a fight," I quickly answered.

"He's scared," the other boy said.

I was starting to get hot under the collar. "I'm not afraid of anything, and if you're smart, you'll move out of my way."

I stepped forward to brush past them and Kayden grabbed me by the arm and tried to pull me back. In an instant, I seized him by the shoulders and shoved him against the wall. His expression went from haughty to terrified in seconds. I could feel the vampire in me, and I had to restrain the urge to keep from pushing him through the wall. I clenched my teeth so I wouldn't growl and show my fangs. I close my eyes for a moment to regain control to keep them from glowing red, and when I opened them again, Kayden was still staring at me with a frightened expression.

I sighed, let my hands drop to my sides, and walked out into the gym.

Kayden and his buddies stayed away from me for the remainder of the class, although I got several angry glares. I could tell that they weren't going to drop it.

When I got to geometry, Mindy, the girl I'd met that morning, was there. She smiled and waved me over to the chair next to hers. "Hi, Rurik," she said.

I nodded and smiled back, taking the seat beside her. "I didn't know you were in geometry."

"Yeah, well. Don't tell everyone, but I'm good at math. My parents want me to go into computers."

"What's wrong with being good at math?" I asked, a little confused.

She looked at me like I was dumb. "Nobody wants to be pegged as the smart, nerdy type."

"Oh," I answered, still not understanding. *What's wrong with being smart?* I wondered.

I decided I'd better not tell her that I was way beyond geometry already. I was taking advanced calculus college courses.

By the end of class, I was surprised at how bright Mindy really was. Mom had repeatedly told me I was prejudiced against humans and that they were more intelligent than I thought but I'd always felt that she was just saying that because she still missed being human. I had to admit that being around mostly vampires my entire childhood had given me a rather biased opinion of humans.

Mindy answered the questions very quickly and she was right all the time. I couldn't help being a little impressed.

When class ended she asked me if I wanted to sit at the table with her friends for lunch, so I agreed and walked with her to the lunch room. Once I stood in line and got my meal, which looked like your basic spaghetti with Jell-O and vegetable, I walked over to where Mindy was already seated. She was deep in conversation with another girl, and didn't notice me until everyone at the table was staring in my direction. I felt a little awkward standing there with the lunch tray in my hand, being gawked at.

She finally looked up and smiled at me. "Oh…everyone, this is Rurik. He's new and I invited him to eat with us." She scooted her chair over. I put my tray of food down and pulled a chair up from an adjacent table.

"Hi," I nodded, and sat down.

"Hi Rurik, I'm Daniel," the kid on the end said. He was Asian, with a modern style chopped haircut. "And this is Kaylee, Mary, and Luke." He pointed to the others seated around me.

"Hey, aren't you the one who pulled up this morning in front of the school in a limo?" Luke asked. He peered at me through thick red hair and a face spattered with freckles.

Mindy gave him a dirty look and threw her napkin at him.

"What?" Luke asked. "What did I say?"

"Just ignore Luke, he's lame," she said to me.

Everyone chuckled.

I looked up across the room and saw Kayden and his friends eyeing me from where they were sitting. Daniel followed my gaze. "Don't mess with those three. They think they own this school. Kayden's dad is the principal."

I cringed. "Great, he's already decided that he doesn't like me."

"They think they can get away with everything. Kayden's the leader. Chase and Wyatt just follow him."

I was going to have to work harder at avoiding them. I could see them causing my early removal from school, sending me back into the confines of my prison life at the house.

Mindy looked across the room at them. "Yeah, those guys are real jerks. Kayden didn't seem bad at first, and I even went out on a couple of dates with him. But now he thinks he controls this school and everyone in it." She involuntarily crossed her arms while she talked about him. I could sense that she was almost afraid of the guy. "He wouldn't take no for an answer when I told him to leave me alone, I finally had to talk to his dad." She turned to me and smiled suddenly. "I started taking kick boxing a few months ago, so I have a few moves if he ever bothers me again."

I couldn't help smiling back…Mindy was spunky. And I was also aware of the fact that she was cute. Her features weren't perfect, like a vampire, and her nose was a little too turned up, but it was adorable with her perky personality and face. I found myself, to my surprise, liking her.

#

When I stepped out front at the end of the day, the limo was waiting again to pick me up. I grimaced at the stares all the students gave me when I walked over.

"See you tomorrow, Rurik!" I heard behind me. It was Mindy and I smiled and waved, opened the door, and scooted in.

Dad looked toward Mindy, who was getting on the bus. His eyes darkened slightly. "How was your first day?"

I grinned. "It was great, Dad."

"Any problems?"

"No, not a one." I didn't want to say anything to him about Kayden and his friends; he would immediately think the worst.

"Who's the girl?"

I tried extra hard not to stiffen and stay relaxed. I shrugged. "No one important, just a student." Then to change the subject, I nicely asked, "Could you please take me to school and pick me up in the Audi, instead of the limo?"

"What's wrong with the limo?" Dad asked.

I sighed. "I feel like everyone's staring at me. I'm trying to fit in and not stand out like a sore thumb. Arriving in a limo doesn't help."

Dad grinned. "All right, Rurik. I suppose it is a bit pretentious."

When I got home Mom was waiting at the door, practically bubbling with excitement. "How was your first day of school?"

I shrugged noncommittally. "It was okay." I suppose I should've been a little more enthusiastic after everything she'd gone through with Dad to get him to agree to let me go. I don't know what the deal was…I just suddenly didn't want her smothering me, being so motherly. It almost seemed like she was interfering in my personal business.

"Just okay?" She looked a little disappointed. "Did you have any problems? The other students not like you or something?" She was starting to get a worried look.

I decided that I couldn't torture her this way. "Mom, it's okay. Chill, everything was cool."

She breathed a sigh of relief.

"It was fun, really."

"Did you meet some nice kids?"

I suddenly thought of Mindy and didn't want to talk about the girl. "Yeah, some."

"Like who? Tell me all about them."

"Not much to say. Just kids." I tried to downplay it. "I've got some homework I have to do. I'll talk to you later." I used that as my excuse to make a quick exit, and ran upstairs to my room.

The next morning when Dad dropped me off in the Audi, Mindy was leaning against a post in front of the entrance. I couldn't help grinning slightly when she smiled at me.

"Hi, Rurik."

"Hey, Mindy." I was happy to see her. I stopped in front of her and absently ran my fingers through my thick bangs, and pushed them out of my face. I could hear her heartbeat speed up a little in response to my simple hand gesture, and it was surprisingly a pleasant thought. She definitely liked me.

Mindy suddenly looked a little shy and glanced away, then said, "Um…did you get your math homework done? Mrs. Broach sure knows how to pile it on. I was up late trying to figure out some of the formulas."

"Yeah, no problem," I answered back. I didn't want to tell her I was done in about fifteen minutes. "If you want to study together some time, I could help you. I'm really good at math."

She smiled. "Okay. I'd like that a lot."

"Great," I grinned.

Daniel came up and slapped me on the shoulder. "Hey dude."

I nodded back. The buzzer rang and everyone rapidly entered the building to get to their first class. I stopped at my locker to get my science book and was pushed forcibly from behind. I knew without even turning that it was Kayden. I closed my eyes for half a second to control my features, and then turned to face him.

"Rurik," Kayden said with a definite attitude.

I said nothing and stared back crossly.

"Just wanted to let you know that I can't wait to see you in P.E. again."

"Why?" I had to ask. "You like getting shoved into walls?"

He stiffened slightly in reference to our incident yesterday. Then he smiled and said, "We will see who does the shoving this time." He turned around and walked down the hall.

I watched him disappear around the corner before I went back to gathering my books for science class, and then sprinted up the stairs so I wouldn't be late.

When I walked into the locker room, Kayden and his thugs were sitting on the bench waiting for me, already dressed in their P.E. clothes. They watched me go over to the bench to get dressed without a word, but when I tried to step past them, they all stood up to face me.

I stopped and eyed them with annoyance. "I really don't want any trouble, Kayden," I said. "I'm just here to go to school."

"Really?" Kayden asked sarcastically. "You should have thought of that before you immediately zeroed in on my girlfriend."

I snickered. "That's not what Mindy told me. She doesn't want anything to do with you. It takes two to make a relationship. Did you miss that in sex ed class?"

He glared at me. "She's just confused at the moment, and having Mr. Pretty Boy suddenly show up on campus doesn't help. I'm warning you to back off now."

"You going to sic Daddy on me? Or can you handle your own battles?"

His jaw clenched. "Oh…I can definitely take care of a punk like you. Don't make me have to." Then he smiled and stepped aside for me to pass. The others moved slightly to make room for me, but continued to glare.

I quickly walked past them and into the gym.

"All right, what's the hold up?" Mr. Scott yelled when we all walked out to where the other students were already waiting. "If you guys can't get dressed and out here pronto, you'll be staying after school and cleaning the equipment. Got that, Mr. Tallinn?"

I nodded my head to Mr. Scott and stepped in line with the other students. Kayden smiled smugly at me, as if he liked the idea that I'd almost gotten in trouble because of him.

"Today we're going to start with running to get all of you softies in shape, so I want you to make three laps around the track. No walking, is that clear?!" We all nodded and he said, "Okay, get going."

I followed the other students outside and onto the dirt track. Kayden and his guys took off at a dead run and left everyone in the dust. I tried hard to stay in the middle of the group, but they seemed to be moving at a snail's pace. It was incredible to me that humans were so slow. After the first lap, some were already trailing behind and I easily caught up with Kayden's group. I noticed several were starting to pant heavily and I pretended to be tired also. It was difficult. I could have gone at this pace forever and never even gotten winded. By the time we'd done the three laps, I was in the lead and Mr. Scott was waiting for us at the end of the track.

"All right," he started as everyone straggled in. "We're going to be doing basketball today, so let's hop inside. Kayden, you and Rurik get the equipment out. You can show him where it's at."

I tried not to cringe; us being together alone was not a good idea. I followed Kayden down a hall and to a back closet. When we entered, I glanced around. It was a large storage room with every possible sports gear imaginable. Kayden headed over to a huge bin that held several basketballs and reached in and pulled one out. Then he unexpectedly threw it at me as hard as he could. I instinctively caught it easily without even flinching. My reflexes were faster than even the fastest vampires.

Kayden eyed me with suspicion. "What makes you so special?"

I smiled and shrugged without a word.

"The pump is over in the corner. Put air in them if they need it," he said roughly, and threw more balls in my direction.

I ruffled. I didn't like being told what to do by someone I considered little more than a meal. But I made myself relax and took the basketballs to the pump. If I let my vampire side take over, it would be detrimental to more than just me. The entire society relied on all of us being responsible members to keep our true identities secret.

In geometry, Mrs. Broach informed us that we were going to have a midterm test at the end of the week to see where everyone was at. Mindy winced noticeably at the idea. So I offered, "Would you like to study together, go over some of the notes?"

She smiled and nodded with enthusiasm. I couldn't help noticing how pretty her green eyes were when they sparkled happily my direction. Then Mindy frowned. "We can't do it at my place. My mom works nights, and doesn't allow anyone over after school."

"I'll have to get permission from my dad to invite you over. Dad and Mom…have a large business that requires a lot of time, so they aren't thrilled with people coming to our house either."

She looked disappointed, so I smiled and said, "Don't worry, we'll figure it out. It's important to get good grades, right? They should understand that." I didn't know if they would though. Dad and Mom ran the country for our society, and they didn't need me inviting people over to the house. It could present a problem.

After school, Dad was waiting with the Audi, which to my relief got less stares than the limo had. Mindy again waved and smiled when she got on the bus. I waved back.

Dad eyed me closely when I got in. "There something you want to tell me?"

"Like what?" I asked with surprise.

"Like who that girl is that keeps waving to you?"

I shrugged. "She's just a girl in some of my classes. I can't help that she likes me. I did inherit your amazing looks."

Dad tried to keep the corners of his mouth from turning up at my obvious attempt at buttering him up.

"What do you want?" Dad asked in a knowing tone.

"What do you mean?"

"You don't compliment your father these days unless there's something in it for you. I'm not stupid."

"I would never accuse you of being stupid, Dad. You're the smartest person I know."

"Okay, it's starting to get sickeningly sweet in here, Rurik. Out with it."

I sighed. "I would like to invite Mindy over to study for math. We're having a test on Friday."

"Since when have you ever needed to study?" he asked suspiciously.

"It's for Mindy. She just needs a little help going over some of the formulas. And since I'm so good at math, I offered to help."

Dad immediately tensed slightly. "Mindy? Is that her name? You don't need to be bringing people over to our house, especially a girl. That's not a good idea."

"We're just studying." I tried hard not to get defensive at his immediate no.

Dad sighed. "Rurik, if someone were to ever find out about our society it would be bad, mostly for them, because we wouldn't have any choice but to handle it. Don't you understand that?"

I nodded. "I know. I've had that pounded into my head for as long as I can remember."

His eyes narrowed. "Don't get smart mouthed. It isn't going to help you get your way."

"Sorry, Dad." I paused for effect. "Maybe Mindy's mom will let us study over at her house. Her mom works nights, so doesn't like people over, but we could go to Mindy's room. If we're quiet and kept the door closed, that might work."

Dad's eyes flashed angrily. "There's no way you're going over to a girl's house unsupervised." He sighed. "I guess it would be okay for her to come over here as long as you stayed out at the kitchen table…where I can keep an eye on you."

I smiled. "Thanks."

"Tell her I'll pick her up tomorrow after school. She can ride over with us and then I'll take her home after a couple of hours. That way I'll know where she lives."

I didn't like the look in his eyes when he said the last part. "She isn't going to be a problem, I promise. She's a nice girl."

He didn't appear to believe me, but said nothing.

#

I was excited about Mindy coming over to our house. No one was ever invited who wasn't part of the society. This was practically unprecedented.

Mom entered the kitchen that morning before school while I was eating my cereal. "So…who exactly is this girl?" she asked.

I shrugged. "Just a girl at school."

She eyed me carefully, making me feel like I was in front of a firing squad with the scrutiny she was giving me.

"She needs help with studying, and I'm good at math. I thought you wanted me to make friends, get to know my human side better."

"Of course. I just don't want you falling for a girl at school, that's all."

"It's not like that. She's just a friend."

"Are you sure, Rurik?" she asked with doubt.

"Mom, she's human. I'm not going to fall for some human," I said a little indignantly.

Mom bristled. "Your father did. Humans aren't all bad."

I sighed. "I know. I didn't mean it that way. I just like her as a friend, okay?"

She smiled. "All right, Rurik. I just don't want to see you get hurt."

I snorted. "You should know that you don't have to worry about that." I stood up with the bowl in my hand and walked over to the kitchen sink.

Mom came over to me and put her arms on my shoulders, and looked deep into my eyes. "I know that you're practically indestructible physically, Rurik. I'm not talking about that." She sighed and brushed my bangs out of my face. "I mean this." She reached out and put her hand over my heart. "I don't want you to fall for a girl that you can never be with."

I stiffened, suddenly feeling defensive. "Don't worry. I know what the prophecies say about me and Amy."

Mom leaned in and kissed me on the cheek. "You have a destiny to fulfill. You'll be a great leader, and you and Amy will eventually rule everything."

I tried not to recoil at the thought. I'd been spoon fed that line for as long as I can remember.

Mom gave me a hug and smiled. "I love you. See you after school with your friend Mindy."

"Love you too, Mom."

I grabbed my books and hopped in the car with Dad. Sometimes Mom was too serious. I had no plans at all to get involved with Mindy, other than maybe to have a little fun. After all, that was what I was going to school for.

#

I stood outside the front entrance and leaned casually against a post after school to wait for Mindy, since Dad hadn't arrived yet. Mindy walked out the front door and smiled widely at me about the same time that Dad pulled up.

"Ready?" I asked.

"Yeah," she grinned.

I walked over to the car with her and we both got into the backseat. Dad turned around to look at us when we scooted in.

"Hello, Mindy. I'm Rurik's dad."

Mindy was a bit taken back by Dad's good looks and perfect features. "Hi Mr. Tallinn, nice to meet you," she answered shyly.

"You can call me Adrian." He flashed his brilliant smile at her.

"Thanks for picking me up, and taking me home."

"My pleasure," Dad commented before turning back around in his seat and driving up the road.

Mindy turned to me and smiled. "I brought the list of study questions, and some of the formulas I've been having a hard time with."

"Great," I said. "It shouldn't take you too long to get the hang of it. You're pretty smart."

Mindy blushed slightly at my compliment and stared down at her books. I could see Dad watching our interaction in his rearview mirror while he drove, frowning.

Dad opened the gate with his remote, and Mindy's eyes widened a little. When we rounded the drive and the house came into view, she couldn't help taking in a sharp breath. We lived in a veritable castle, with a covered drive and columns larger than our car. The house was two and a half stories with a round turret and copper roof. The outside was made of large black, brown, and tan stones. The original structure had been in the family for well over a century, but the entire building had been refurbished and updated by Dad before he met Mom.

"Wow. This is nice," Mindy exclaimed.

I shrugged.

Once inside the entryway Mom was waiting with a big smile. She seemed very happy that I had a human friend. It was almost embarrassing the way she rushed up to introduce herself. "You must be Mindy. I'm Carmen, Rurik's mom. I'm happy to meet you."

"Hi," Mindy answered back, gawking about the entry. She was still ogling over the house. It was impressive, with its two and a half stories, travertine stone floors, and columns and archways leading into the interior. The stairway that led to the second floor was decorated by a hand carved mahogany railing.

"Come in and make yourself comfortable."

We followed Mom down the hall to the kitchen, and put our books on the small table by the window. "Would you like something to drink? A soda, milk…water?"

Mindy nodded. "Milk sounds good. Thanks."

We sat down at the table while Mom looked in the fridge. "Rurik, do you want something?"

"Sure," I answered. "I'll take a soda."

We spread our books out and opened them while Mom brought over the drinks. Then she stood and watched us. I knew it was making Mindy uncomfortable to have my mom hovering, and I looked up with a little irritation.

Mom got the hint. "Well, I'll leave you two to study. Yell if you need anything."

"Thanks," I said. Both Mindy and I watched Mom leave the room, and then turned to look at each other and couldn't help chuckling. "Sorry," I said. "We don't have a lot of people come to the house. Mom's just a little overly enthused."

We went over all the notes and the formulas, and as I thought, Mindy picked it up very quickly.

"Wow! Your garden is awesome!" Mindy exclaimed as we sat looking out at the back lawns through the French doors of the kitchen.

"Yeah," I said in a non-committal way. "I guess."

She stared at me with surprise. "You guess? You should see our small little backyard. You're lucky, Rurik. Not very many people live in a house like this."

I thought about that and realized she was right. I did take all of this for granted. Even Amy had commented more than once about how lucky I was. It just felt like a prison to me. Maybe an extra plush one, but still a prison. "Do you want to go for a walk? I'll show you around."

She perked up. "That would be great."

I stood up and opened the back patio door for her, and we stepped out. We walked down the stone pathways and into the trees away from the house, then past the fountains and the sculpture gardens, stopping at the entrance to the maze.

"You have a maze?" Her expression was dumbfounded.

I couldn't help smiling at her enthusiasm. "You want to see it?"

"Sure!"

We stepped inside and she followed me through the twists and turns of the hedging. I knew my way around by heart since I used to play in there all the time when I was little. There were sculptures of dragons and gargoyles, and benches to rest on.

"This is so tight," Mindy commented when we stopped to sit on a bench. She looked at her surroundings with wide eyes.

I couldn't help laughing.

"What?" she asked.

"You just seem so impressed, that's all."

"I am. You're the luckiest person to be able to live here."

I grimaced slightly. "I don't feel that lucky."

"Why?" she asked. "I would be so happy."

"It's not that great. It may be big, but it's very lonely. I had to almost beg to get my dad to let me go to a public school so I could be around kids my age." I sighed. "They have plans for my future and don't want anything messing them up. It's like a very big, very fancy jail to me."

"That sounds deep," Mindy commented.

"You have no idea. I didn't ask for any of this." I stared off at the large horse sculpture across from where we were sitting.

Mindy suddenly reached over and took my hand sympathetically, and I turned to her in surprise. Her eyes were warm and caring…she really did like me, I could tell. Her heartbeat sped up and her breathing quickened. We sat staring into each other's faces for a moment, and then I leaned over and very gently kissed her lips. It was the strangest sensation…her lips were so warm and vulnerable. The emotion I felt took me completely by surprise; I'd never experienced anything like it. I pulled back quickly and turned away, then stood up abruptly.

"I'm sorry. I shouldn't have done that," I said. "We'd better head back."

Mindy's expression was confused and hurt. She stood up and turned back the way we had come without a word. She kept her arms crossed while we walked up the path. Neither one of us said anything.

Finally, I couldn't stand the silence any longer and reached out and took her hand. "Hey," I said. "Are you mad at me?"

Mindy stopped and looked up into my eyes with her beautiful green ones, then shook her head sadly. "No, I'm not mad."

"What's the matter then?"

She sighed and turned away. "It's nothing."

"Tell me what's wrong, Mindy." I took hold of her shoulders and turned her to face me, and she gazed up into my eyes again. Her heart was beating irregularly and her pupils dilated. I wanted to kiss her, and I knew she wanted me to. I had to turn quickly from her. She groaned under her breath, pulled away from me, and stomped off up the path.

I ran up to her. "Mindy, tell me what's wrong with you."

"What's wrong with me?! What's wrong with you, Rurik?!" she practically yelled.

"What do you mean?"

"You…you keep somehow pulling me in with your eyes. I can tell you want to kiss me, and then you suddenly stop. Don't you like me?"

"It has nothing to do with that," I said quietly. *This is stupid. Isn't this what I wanted…to have fun with girls? Mindy wanted to kiss me…why was I hesitating?* I asked myself.

"Then, what's the problem?" She looked on the verge of tears.

I didn't know what to say to her because I didn't know what my problem was either. This was no time to develop a conscience. She wanted me to kiss her, but I didn't want to hurt her; she was too nice of a girl.

I hadn't planned on this. I hadn't thought I would end up feeling protective of her. I knew she liked me too much already, and I didn't want to harm her. I was crazy. "It's way too complicated to even begin to explain to you."

"Try," she said quietly.

I reached out and gently stroked her cheek and stared intently into her eyes. I could easily take her right there and then. I could mesmerize her and she would be all mine. But something in me knew it would be wrong. There was no way I could ever explain all of this to her, that I was a vampire…that she was my natural prey. That I was already promised to a beautiful but bratty girl vampire, and I had no choice in the matter. I was to rule all of this someday, and Amy was to be at my side.

"We need to just stay friends for…for a lot of reasons."

She looked angry and hurt at the same time staring back up into my face, and then she turned abruptly and walked back up the path. I followed her silently to the back patio and then inside the kitchen.

Dad was waiting for us. "There you are, Rurik. I was just going to go out looking for you. Are you all done studying?"

I nodded my head and Mindy gathered her things to leave. She looked up at me, her face unreadable. I could tell she was trying to protect her feelings, and I felt bad. "See you at school tomorrow, Rurik. Thanks for helping me study."

"Yeah, bye…see you tomorrow," I answered quietly.

I watched Mindy walk out the door with Dad and sat back down in the kitchen chair. That hadn't turned out as I'd planned at all. I could have easily had my way with Mindy while we were in the maze, but something held me back. I didn't understand why, but I felt protective of her.

Chapter Two
Mindy

The next day at school, when Dad dropped me off, I didn't see Mindy anywhere. I was beginning to wonder if she'd even come, but when I walked into geometry she was seated in her usual chair. She glanced up at me when I came in, but didn't smile.

I nodded her direction and sat down beside her. "I didn't see you this morning, I thought maybe you weren't at school today."

"I just had things to do," she answered aloofly.

I could tell I was getting the cold shoulder from her. This is what I'd wanted, I told myself, to back her off, but I wasn't happy about the fact that she was suddenly ignoring me. Anger and hurt welled up inside me and I couldn't help glaring at her. I knew my features could be intimidating...I'd inherited that from Dad too. But I couldn't keep myself from getting mad at Mindy for snubbing me, and I knew it showed on my face. I turned away and stared down at the book in front of me on my desk. Neither of us said a word the rest of class, and as soon as the bell rang she grabbed her things and rushed out the door.

I sighed as I watched her walk away. Girls were infuriating creatures. I'd thought it was just Amy, but maybe they were all that way. I stood up, gathered my books, and walked to my locker to drop them off before lunch.

By the time I got to the lunch room everyone was seated at the table where I normally ate, but I didn't feel welcome. I took my tray and sat down on the other side of the room by myself.

I noticed that Daniel kept glancing my way while I sat there and picked at the club sandwich. It wasn't long before he got up and came over. "Dude, what's the deal?"

"What do you mean?" I asked.

"How come you aren't sitting with us today?"

I glanced over to Mindy, who was looking my direction. When she saw me stare at her, she quickly turned her head away. "I'm just not feeling very welcome right now."

Daniel looked back at the group. "Oh…you and Mindy having a lover's fight?"

I snickered. "We aren't together. Mindy just seems mad about something. I think I'm safer here."

Daniel shrugged. "Suit yourself, dude." He walked back over to the group and sat down.

I watched them for a bit while I pushed my food around my plate; I just wasn't very hungry for some reason. Mindy seemed to be paying extra attention to Luke, and it was rapidly making me angry again. Then she laughed at something he said and leaned in and whispered in his ear. He smiled at her, and I wanted to go over and punch the guy out. This was ridiculous. I was the one who'd pushed her away, and now I was mad she was talking to another guy.

"Hi," I heard someone say. I glanced up and Tiffany, a girl in my history class, was standing beside my chair. She smiled when I looked up at her. "I'm Tiffany."

I didn't say anything, just sat there staring broodingly back. I wasn't in the best mood at the moment.

She seemed oblivious to my lack of feeling social and continued. "I'm in your history class. I've wanted to say hi to you, but you're usually hanging out with that other group."

I looked toward Mindy's table, and Luke was leaning over and put his hand casually on the back of her chair. I was practically livid now.

"Can I sit down?"

I tore my eyes away and glanced back up at Tiffany. She was very attractive, with her hair a perfectly groomed golden blonde that stopped at her shoulders. She had large blue eyes and her outfit was very cute.

I made myself smile. "Sure. Have a seat."

She sat down next to me and scooted in close. "Do you have a date for the dance Friday night? I was like, thinking about going. Someone else asked me, but I would rather not go with him."

She seemed to be rambling on, and I was having a hard time paying attention to what she was saying. I couldn't stop myself from continually glancing at Mindy and Luke. They were enjoying each other's company way too much, and it was infuriating me. I had to resist the urge to go over there and tell them both off.

Suddenly Tiffany put her hand on my arm and brought my attention back to her. Her hand was warm against my skin, and not unpleasant.

"What did you say?" I asked her.

She smiled when I looked into her eyes. "I wanted to know if you would like to go to the dance with me on Friday. Or...." She glanced over toward Mindy and then back to me. "Do you already have a date? I realize it's kind of like, last minute, since tomorrow's Friday."

"No, I don't have a date," I said, almost sourly. Tiffany sat there with expectation written on her face, waiting for me to answer her question. *Why not*, I thought? She was attractive, and Mindy was just another irritating girl. I gave her a wide grin. "Sure." Tiffany almost looked awestruck by my smile, but I didn't care. I was there to have some fun, and the attractive girl sitting next to me was fair game. "I'll meet you here at seven."

"Awesome," she said, almost in a daze. "See you tomorrow."

I couldn't wait until the end of the day to get out of school. I was in a bad mood the rest of the afternoon. When Dad met me out front I quickly scooted in beside him. He glanced toward the bus, like he was searching for Mindy, then to me questioningly, but didn't say anything. I sat in silence for a while next to him as we rode up the incline of hills back to our house.

"Dad, do you think it would be okay to go to the dance tomorrow at the school? It starts at seven."

He tensed. "I don't know, Rurik. I was thinking of having a family night together."

"Oh," I said, trying not to sound too disappointed. "I guess I can just tell Tiffany that we have other plans."

He perked up a bit. "Tiffany?"

"Yeah, she's the girl I was going to meet there."

"I just assumed you would be going with Mindy."

I stiffened. "No." We sat in silence for a few more minutes.

"Are you and Mindy not friends anymore?"

I shrugged. I didn't want to talk about this with him. "She's just irritating, that's all. Tiffany's in my history class, and is very pretty."

The corners of his mouth curved up. He seemed happy that I wasn't planning to go with Mindy.

"I suppose it would be okay for you to go for a few hours. There are teachers supervising, right?"

"Of course," I answered, and smiled at him.

#

Friday morning when I arrived at school, I glowered at the front entrance where Mindy was usually standing. She wasn't there.

When I went to the locker room to change, Kayden and his guys were waiting. Kayden looked at me self-importantly when I entered.

"Hey, Rurik. Happy to see you backed off of Mindy. That was a very smart thing to do."

I was definitely not in the mood to deal with him at the moment and glared back, but said nothing. He didn't seem to get the hint and went on.

"Now that we understand each other a little better, and who's really in charge here, maybe we'll get along."

I turned to face the lockers and ignored him while I changed. Then I threw my clothes in and slammed the locker closed. Kayden was still standing and staring arrogantly in my direction. He tried to step in my way when I passed by, but I swiftly maneuvered around him and purposely banged into his shoulder, knocking him against the wall.

"Watch it, Tallinn!" he yelled with anger.

I went out to the gym with him and the others following me. They all gave me self-important attitude.

In geometry, Mindy hardly even looked in my direction when I walked in and sat down next to her. I was glad; I didn't want to talk to any stupid girl anyway. Neither one of us spoke for the entire class. As soon as it was over, I stormed out and to the lunch room. I was sitting with my food already when Mindy, Kaylee, Luke, and Daniel came in. They glanced in my direction but didn't come over, and got their food and sat at their usual table.

It wasn't long before Tiffany showed up with a tray of food. "Can I sit with you?"

I nodded my head and smiled warmly at her. I glanced over to the other table and Mindy and Luke were deep in conversation again. I turned away with irritation and focused all of my attention on Tiffany. I concentrated on her and couldn't help mesmerizing her with my eyes. She was practically gushing with all the attention I was giving her, and rattled on about school and the dance incessantly. It was almost amusing. She was so pliable, so easy to manipulate. Maybe school would be enjoyable after all. I noticed Mindy glance in our direction a few times and she seemed upset…served her right.

When I left the school that afternoon Tiffany came running up and took my arm. "Hi, Rurik. See you here at seven for the dance."

"I'll be here," I answered with a grin. Dad was waiting out front and I smiled at Tiffany as I got into the Audi and we drove off.

"Is that Tiffany?" Dad asked.

"Yeah," I grinned.

"She's attractive."

I shrugged, not really wanting to talk about girls with my dad.

#

I dressed in black jeans and a silver shirt. I knew I looked great. Tiffany wouldn't stand a chance against me. I was actually looking forward to seeing her, and was in a surprisingly good mood when I hopped in the Audi and Dad drove me to school. He seemed like he had something on his mind, but never said anything the entire way.

"I'll pick you up out front at ten sharp," he commented when I got out. I nodded in his direction and then headed toward the entrance.

Tiffany was waiting. I caught my breath at how pretty she was standing there in the soft glow of the overhead lights. Her hair was pulled back from her face and she had on an amazing red dress that flowed around her incredible figure. She smiled widely at me and I grinned back.

"Hi," I said, and walked casually up and took her hand. Her heartbeat sped up when I touched her hand, and I smiled down at her. She was one of the most beautiful girls in this school, and I knew a lot of boys would be jealous of me tonight.

There were already several students milling about and dancing when we entered the cafeteria area where the dance was set up. Some trendy music was playing as a DJ on the stage kept the songs flowing. Tiffany and I danced through several songs, and I had to admit that I was thoroughly enjoying myself. I got several stares from girls who couldn't keep their eyes off me, and from jealous boys.

Things were fun until I saw Mindy walk in with Luke. I could feel myself tense up and I scowled in their direction. I stopped dancing, walked back over to the table, and sat down.

Tiffany followed me over. "Rurik, what's wrong?"

"Not a thing," I answered with irritation. "I was just tired of dancing."

She sighed and sat down beside me. Neither of us talked for awhile; she could tell my mood was dark. I glared at Mindy and Luke as they swayed around the dance floor, and suddenly the entire night seemed to be a bore.

Tiffany finally reached over and took my hand when she noticed me frowning at Mindy. "You want to take a walk?" she asked provocatively.

Mindy and Luke went back over to a table and sat down. I saw that Luke had his hand on her knee and I was getting riled again. "Sure," I said irritably, and stood up. I walked quickly out front, and Tiffany practically had to run to keep up with me.

"Hey, slow down a little!"

I stopped and waited for her. "Sorry."

She came up and took my hand, and we went around to the side of the building into the shadows. We stopped and I looked down into her face. She was very pretty.

"Rurik, I really like…like you," she said, and smiled up into my eyes.

I was still in a dark mood but sighed and pushed her against the wall; she was gorgeous and willing. I knew I wasn't the first to have had her and that I could have my way with her without having to mesmerize her…she had a reputation around the school. I brought my lips down to hers and completely consumed her with my kiss. She was so easy. The adrenaline rush was trying to take over. It was more than just the fact that she was a beautiful girl, and that I was a sixteen year old boy. It was the hunter in me, subduing the prey. The feeling was overwhelmingly enjoyable.

I took her hand and led her into the trees and the bushes, where I lay her on the ground. Several times I almost stepped over the line and drank her blood. It was so tempting in the heat of passion to want to take her completely and devour her. I'd always killed just for food, but this went beyond that and was way more pleasurable. We stayed there for a while before we finally got dressed and headed back into the dance. One of the teachers glanced our way when we entered, but no one seemed to notice that we'd been gone for well over an hour.

The rest of the evening Tiffany hung on my arm at the table if we weren't dancing. I found myself watching the clock; I was ready to leave and tired of being there. When ten o'clock came I walked out holding Tiffany's hand and took her over to her car. She looked up at me and I knew she wanted to kiss me, that she liked me too much. I leaned down and quickly kissed her lips, and then turned around without a word and walked back to where Dad was waiting.

His eyes narrowed as he watched me get in. "How was the dance?"

I shrugged. "It was okay."

"Looks like Tiffany and you got along."

"Yeah, she's all right."

We sat in silence for a while as we drove back to the house. I could tell something was on Dad's mind, but he didn't bring it up until we'd stopped under the covered drive.

"Rurik, I think we need to have a discussion about girls."

I couldn't help snorting under my breath.

Dad's eyes glinted and he continued. "You're very attractive, and girls will be falling all over you. You're going to have to be careful, and use a little restraint."

I sighed. "Do we have to talk about this now?"

His eyes flashed angrily. "Yes Rurik, we do!" He paused and eyed me for a moment. "You're a very powerful vampire, and prey doesn't stand a chance against you. I remember being a teenager and all the girls that liked me. How easy it was to have my way with most of them."

"I understand," I groaned.

He went on. "I wasn't a vampire at that time, like you are. I didn't have to worry about them ending up dead…like you do."

"Dad, I do have a little restraint. I can control that part of it."

"So it's as I thought…you have already being having relations with girls?"

I tried not to moan…this was more than painful.

"Answer me, Rurik." His tone was quiet, but deadly serious.

I sighed. "Okay, yes. I have with Tiffany."

Dad's eyes turned coal black and sparked with red at the centers. "That's a very dangerous game you're playing. She was obviously already head over heels for you. I could tell when I picked you up tonight."

"Dad, it's no big deal. She's slept with half the guys at school."

"You're not half the guys at that school!" he yelled angrily. I couldn't help flinching. His voice reverberated around the car. "You're a vampire! You aren't the average guy anywhere, and a lot of girls won't be able to resist you!"

"I realize that," I answered evenly.

"And you are marrying Amy someday. You need to think about your future before you get involved with a human girl."

I was starting to get angry. "Maybe I don't want to marry Amy! She's a spoiled brat. I wouldn't marry her if she was the last girl left on this planet!" I glared angrily at Dad for a moment and then opened the door, hopped out, and slammed it so hard behind me it was amazing it didn't break off its hinges. Then I exploded into the house.

Mom was standing in the entry, and when she saw my cross look the smile went immediately off her face. "What's wrong, Rurik?"

"Everything!" I yelled back, and then ran up the stairs to my room and slammed the door behind me.

#

Adrian walked into the house.

Carmen was still standing and looking up the stairs where Rurik had disappeared. "What's going on, Adrian?"

Adrian sighed. "Rurik's getting too involved with girls, that's what."

Carmen looked slightly shocked, and then said, "Oh."

"This is exactly why I didn't want him going to a public school. I knew there would be no way to curb his appetite, and with all of those willing girls…he's going to get himself into trouble."

They walked down the hall and to the sitting room at the end by the kitchen. Carmen scooted in close to Adrian and took his hand, and sighed. "Well, Rurik does have your handsome looks. Maybe it was inevitable."

Adrian frowned back. "I think we should take him out of school."

"He's only been there for a week. You said you would give him to the end of the semester."

"Yes, Carmen. It's only been a week and he's already sleeping with a girl. What if she or another girl gets killed? He could easily lose control, you know that."

Carmen sighed. "It would totally crush him to take him out of school at this point. You have to give him a chance."

"It's not worth risking the entire society for him to stretch his wings," Adrian said dryly.

"I understand that, but Rurik's important too. He'll be one of our greatest rulers one day." She sighed. "Let me talk to him, okay? Sometimes he takes things better from me right now than you."

"All right," Adrian answered doubtfully.

#

I heard a knock at the door and braced myself, I didn't want another confrontation. "Come in."

Mom opened the door and walked into the room. "Hi."

"Hi," I returned.

She came over and sat on the edge of the bed, and reached out and took my hand. I sighed heavily as I looked back into her face.

"Rurik, I'm worried about you. Are you all right?"

"Yeah, Mom."

"Anything you need to talk about?"

I frowned. "Why does life have to be so complicated? Why can't it just be fun?"

"What's troubling you?" she asked with sympathy.

I clenched my jaw and stared across the room. Then I turned back to her. "I suddenly have all these girls that like me."

She smiled slightly. "And what's wrong with that?"

"It isn't the right one."

"Oh," she answered. "Mindy."

I didn't say anything back to her and stared down at our hands.

"Rurik, you know that you and Mindy can never happen."

I pulled my hand out of hers and flopped back against the headboard, but didn't say anything.

"She's human, you're a vampire."

I looked at her crossly. "That didn't stop you and Dad."

Her expression was almost sad. "That was the exception rather than the rule. Most vampire human relationships don't end well."

"It's not fair," I stated. "How come I can't choose who I want to be with? Why does it have to be Amy?"

"I can't answer that. I don't know why, that's just the way it is."

"But I don't love Amy…I don't even like her most of the time."

Mom smiled wistfully at me. "That doesn't mean that eventually you won't fall in love with her. You're only sixteen."

We both sat in silence for several minutes.

"Your father's worried about you. He thinks he should take you out of school already."

I stiffened. "No, Mom. Please don't let him do that. I can't go back to being cooped up here twenty-four hours a day again."

She sighed and brushed her hand lightly over my arm. "I can't really disagree with him, Rurik. You've only been there a week and you're already involved with a couple of girls. It's way too dangerous to let you continue."

I was starting to get desperate at the thought of being stuck there without any freedom again…the idea was very claustrophobic. "I promise that I'll be good. Don't let him take me out of school." My eyes filled up with tears. I felt stupid. I was an almost sixteen year old boy, practically a man. I hadn't cried in years, and I suddenly felt on the verge.

Mom sighed and reached in and hugged me. "I love you, Rurik. You're more important than anything to us. We just want what's best for you."

"I can control myself, Mom. It isn't just the girls...I need to get out and interact with others my age. I have some friends there now...I think it's important to get to know my human side." I almost felt like I was begging, but I couldn't stand the thought of not going to school now that I'd started. "Give me another chance...please.'

She stared into my face sympathetically. "All right, Rurik. I'll see what I can do. But if Dad goes for it, this is it...it'll be your last chance. You know that."

I breathed a sigh of relief. "Thanks, Mom."

She smiled and stood up to leave. "Thank me later, nothing's happened yet."

#

I was given one final chance, and I'd better "toe the line" was the way Dad put it. I was so relieved that I was still going to be allowed to go. I enjoyed my freedom and getting out of the house for a few hours, but I knew the biggest reason I was glad to be going back to school Monday morning was because I would be able to see Mindy. Even if she wasn't talking to me, I still wanted to be around her.

Dad dropped me off out front and Tiffany was waiting. She smiled widely and rushed up.

"Hi, Rurik!" She took my arm and held onto it. "I thought you would call this weekend. I was disappointed that you didn't."

I smiled distractedly at her and tried to step away. I was suddenly feeling like she was smothering me. "I was busy."

She frowned at my obvious aloofness, but then she smiled and stood on tiptoes to whisper in my ear. "You were amazing on Friday. When can we get together again?"

I thought about our little rendezvous on the side of the building and couldn't help smiling…the thought was pleasant. Then I saw Mindy walk by, and she barely even turned in my direction. Tiffany reached up and put her arms around my neck, and I was suddenly in a very bad mood.

"Tiffany!" I yelled. "Stop it!" I pulled her arms from around my neck and glared down at her. I knew I was unleashing my darker side on her, but I didn't care at the moment.

She looked into my eyes with genuine fear and stepped back. "Okay," she said in a small voice.

I sighed, stared into her frightened expression, and then turned away from her without a word and went inside the building.

Gym was almost torture. Kayden and his friends decided that since I'd backed down to him that I must be a coward, and they took every opportunity to taunt me. I was in such a bad mood that I could have happily killed every one of them and not cared what the consequences were, so I tried extra hard to avoid them. I was thinking about geometry and Mindy. I wanted to somehow make up with her, so we could be friends again. If Dad and Mom made me leave school permanently, I might not see her anymore.

When I walked into class, she was sitting at her chair already. She glanced up at me absently and I smiled my warmest, most charming smile possible.

She looked surprised, then glared at me before she lowered her head to the paper in front of her again.

I sat down and took a breath. "Hi Mindy," I said pleasantly enough.

She raised her head and gave me a seething look. "What do you want, Rurik?"

I was taken back a little by her anger toward me. I was used to getting my way with my charms and mesmerizing abilities. "Nothing," I said flatly. "I just wanted to say hi."

She stared at me caustically for a moment, sighed, and lowered her head back to her work. She completely ignored me for the remainder of the class. When the bell rang, she jumped up to leave.

"Hey," I said, and grabbed her arm.

She turned to me heatedly. "What do you want from me?!"

"I just wanted to say that I was sorry, for hurting your feelings. I want to be friends, to sit together at lunch like we use to."

She chuckled sarcastically. "Why don't you just go sit with your friend Tiffany?"

"I don't want to sit with her, I want to sit with you," I said quietly.

Her eyes softened a bit as she looked back into mine. Then they got angry again and she said, "Well, you sure couldn't tell that Friday at the dance!" Then she turned around and walked quickly out the door and started down the hall.

"Hey, Mindy! Wait up." I ran up to her and took her arm again. She turned to me, and she looked like she was trying hard not to start crying.

"Are you okay?" I asked gently.

Her eyes softened gazing into my face, and then turned dark and angry again.

"Uhhgg! You are such a devil, Rurik!" she shouted angrily. "You twist my emotions with just a look, or a word!"

I was surprised at her outburst. "I'm sorry, Mindy. I'm trying to apologize." I sighed. "I don't want to sit with Tiffany. I only went out with her because I was mad at you."

She looked at me questioningly. "You're the one who said we had to just be friends."

Kids were walking all around us toward the lunch room as we stood there in the middle of the hallway and talked, so I led her over against the wall. I nodded my head. "I know that's what I said, but…it wasn't what I meant." She stared intently into my face. "What I mean is…I want us to be friends again. I mean…." Why was this so hard to say? I was the powerful hunter vampire, but when she stood there staring up into my face with her beautiful, soft green eyes I couldn't seem to think clearly. "I...like you, Mindy. I'm sorry I told you I just wanted us to be friends." I took a deep breath. "I want more than that."

Mindy looked at me with surprise. "You sure have a funny way of showing it."

I sighed. "I know. There's just so much you don't know, that I can't tell you. I really wish I could." I looked deep into her eyes. I could tell that she liked me…her heart and breathing had sped up again. "Can we just go in the lunchroom and sit down?"

She smiled and nodded her head.

I walked in with Mindy. Daniel, Kaylee, and Luke looked over at us with surprise. Tiffany was sitting at the table where I'd sat with her the last couple days, and she stared at me with a crushed expression on her face. I almost felt sorry for her.

Mindy and I got our lunch trays and food.

"Why don't we sit by ourselves today so we can talk?" I suggested.

"Okay," she answered shyly.

We went over to a table by the window while everybody watched. Every person at Mindy's usual table stared at us. Kayden and his friends glared hatefully, and Tiffany sat by herself, looking like she was about to burst into tears any moment.

Mindy and I sat and chatted about her mom and how her parents had divorced when she was little. Her dad had moved out of state and didn't keep in contact with her. We talked about movies, food, and music. She was a lot of fun to be around; it was amazing that I felt this comfortable with her, like I'd known her my whole life.

"Do you want to come over after school today?" I asked.

She nodded her head. "That would be awesome. Will it be okay with your dad? It's not like we have to study for a test."

I frowned. Dad could be a problem, and he and Mom had just given me the whole "don't get involved with girls" lecture. I shrugged. "Maybe we better bring a few books home, just to make it look like we're studying."

She grinned. "Okay."

Mindy walked out with me after school and up to Dad's Audi. I opened the door and stuck my head in. "Hey Dad. We have a quiz tomorrow that the teacher just told us about. Do you think Mindy could come over to study a little?"

Dad stared back darkly. "What about our conversation the other day? Did you forget that already?"

"No. We just want to hang out to go over the questions."

He looked at me with doubt, and then back to Mindy's hopeful expression. "Okay, for a few hours and that's it."

Mindy smiled happily as we hopped in the backseat together. I could hear Mindy's heart thumping next to me. I hoped Dad didn't notice…it was so obvious that she liked me.

"What's the test about?" Dad suddenly asked, staring at us through the rearview mirror.

"Um…." I looked down at my lap and noticed that Mindy had a book. I grabbed it. "It's a book report on *War and Peace*. We have a lot of reading to do."

"Okay," Dad said, and I breathed a sigh of relief.

Mom was surprised to see Mindy when we walked in. I'd told her that I liked Mindy, so I hoped she believed our excuse of having to study. We put our books on the table in the kitchen, got drinks, and sat down. We read a little in the book, but it wasn't long before Mom got tired of listening and went off to do other things.

I smiled at Mindy. "Would you like to take a walk?"

Mindy nodded and we went out the back door and down the path. I almost forgot the book and had to go back and retrieve it. We were supposed to look like we were studying.

Once we were out of sight of the house, I reached over and took her hand. She smiled and blushed. Her hand was so warm and soft, and I could feel her pulse racing in her wrist. I couldn't wait to kiss her again. I slowed down our pace and stopped, turning her to face me. Her eyes looked up into mine longingly and I pulled her to me. She gasped with excitement when I brought my lips down to hers.

Mindy's arms wrapped around my neck and her heart beat wildly in her chest. I wanted all of her. "Oh, Mindy," I whispered softly in her ear.

I lowered her to the ground and her breath was short and sporadic. I gently caressed her curves with my hand.

Suddenly she pushed against me. "Rurik…," she said softly. "Rurik, stop."

I didn't want to; I was consumed with wanting her. I kissed her deeply and started to unbutton her top.

"Rurik, don't…," she barely whispered. "I'm not ready."

I stopped with my hand on her top and looked down at her with surprise.

Her eyes were warm and smoldering from our passionate kiss. "I…can't. I haven't ever…. I…." She almost looked like she was going to burst into tears suddenly.

I brushed her face lightly with my fingertips and stared down at her. "Are you telling me that you've never been with a guy?"

She nodded and blushed.

I sat up. "Oh…I just assumed that since you had dated Kayden that…I'm sorry, Mindy. I didn't realize that you'd never done it before."

She sat up and buttoned her blouse. "I'm sorry too. I know lots of girls do, but…I'm just not ready."

"It's okay."

She looked sad. "Are you mad at me?"

"No, why would I be mad?"

She stared down at the ground in front of her. "Because, I'm not experienced. Because I haven't—"

I put my hand up to her lips. "Shhh…that doesn't matter to me. I like you. We can take our time." I pushed her back down onto the ground and looked into her eyes. They were so warm and tender and vulnerable, I couldn't help feeling protective again. I leaned down and very gently kissed her lips. When I drew back she sighed happily, and I pulled her to me and held her in my arms. We stayed that way for a long time, but I knew my parents would be getting suspicious with how long we'd been gone.

"We better head back," I reluctantly said.

"Okay," she answered. I stood up and reached my hand out and pulled her up off the ground.

When we got to the house, Dad was standing in the kitchen and he didn't look happy. "Where have you two been?" His eyes were intimidating and black.

Mindy looked immediately nervous at his harsh expression.

"We just went for a walk," I answered defensively.

He didn't look like he completely believed me. "Is that all?"

"Of course." I was a little indignant at his implied accusation.

He stared harshly at us. "Your mother's taking Mindy home. I want you to stay here. So we can talk."

I didn't like the tone or the look he was giving me. Mom came into the room and was hurrying Mindy out.

"See you tomorrow at school, Rurik," Mindy said nervously.

I tried to give her a reassuring smile. "Okay, Mindy. See you then."

As soon as Mom and Mindy left the room, Dad turned to me. "Didn't we just have this conversation about girls?"

"Nothing happened," I answered.

"You expect me to believe that you went off into the trees alone with that girl and nothing happened?"

"Yes." He stood staring at me for several moments, not saying anything, so I continued. "Mindy's a nice girl…she's not like that. She doesn't sleep around with guys."

"How do you know?"

I stood silently for several moments. I realized that I'd walked right into this one. If I said she'd told me, then he would know we were talking intimately.

If I said I didn't know, then he would assume that we'd been doing something, and that I was lying. I knew he had me either way, so I opted for the truth.

I took a deep breath. "She told me that she's never been with a guy before, okay?" His face softened and he looked like he believed me. "She's really nice, Dad. You'd like her if you would give her a chance."

"This has nothing to do with her being nice. You have other plans for your future and don't need to get involved with a human. You're getting too attached to that girl." He sighed. "I'm not going to allow you to see her anymore."

"What?!" I practically yelled. "That's not fair!"

"I'm sorry to be so mean about this, but it's my responsibility as your father and the leader of our society to do what's best for you, whether you see it now or not."

"Dad, please," I started. "I really like Mindy. Don't do this."

"It's just a crush, Rurik; you'll get over it."

I couldn't believe it. The thought of never seeing Mindy again was unbearable. I cared about her a lot. "Maybe if you got to know her a little better, maybe if—"

"Stop it, Rurik! I said no and that's final!" His black eyes flashed with annoyance.

I gave him a cross look, but I knew it was useless to argue at this point. I stared his direction for a moment, and then turned around and stormed out of the kitchen and up to my room. I slammed the door and flopped down on my bed. It was so unfair, I hated them all! I picked up my clock beside my bed and threw it furiously against the opposite wall with all my might. It splintered into a thousand tiny pieces that scattered throughout the entire room.

#

When Carmen arrived home, she found Adrian in a chair in the sitting room. He watched her walk over with his black eyes, and he didn't look happy. He sighed deeply. "I'm afraid that I've made Rurik hate me. I told him he isn't allowed to see Mindy anymore."

"Poor Rurik. I wish there was something we could do to make this easier for him."

Adrian pulled Carmen over and she sat down in his lap. "I know. I feel bad being so strict about this. Rurik's right, Mindy's an angel." He sighed and looked into Carmen's face and stroked her cheek. "She reminds me so much of you when I first met you, so young and innocent in a lot of ways."

Carmen smiled and leaned down and kissed Adrian softly on his lips, then pulled back and stared into his face with a solemn expression. "It's hard sometimes to be the parent. And it's especially hard on Rurik because he has such an important destiny…his life isn't his own."

"I can't allow him to get involved with a girl when his future's with Amy."

Carmen sighed. "I told Mindy that Rurik was promised to another girl."

"You did? How did she take it?"

"She was crushed, I think she really loves Rurik. I felt awful doing that to the poor girl. I'm sorry I talked you into letting Rurik go to school in the first place."

"Well, it's done now, he'll get over it. Most people don't end up with their first love. It's part of growing up."

"I hope so," Carmen said. "I'm just lucky I ended up with you."

Adrian smiled wistfully. "Even after everything you went through and all you've given up?"

"I would never change anything. You're worth all of it."

"I just hope that Rurik will feel that way about Amy someday," Adrian sighed.

#

In the morning I sat next to Dad without a word on the way to school. He stared straight ahead saying nothing…he really could be cold and heartless sometimes. I didn't know if I would ever forgive him for not letting me see Mindy. I sighed; at least I could see her at school. When I hopped out of the car in front of the school, I tried hard to be casual about scouring the kids for any sign of Mindy. I didn't see her anywhere.

My first class of the day was science. It was uneventful…we had a test. Dad and Mom had both warned me against answering every question correctly all the time, so I missed a few here and there on purpose. I also tried to slow down, not to be finished way before the other students. I was glad the monotony was over when the bell rang and I was off to P.E. I was counting the minutes to third period geometry, when I would be able to see Mindy.

I walked into the locker room to get changed for P.E. lost in my thoughts, thinking about Mindy and our kiss yesterday. Kayden stepped up to me and grasped me roughly around my shirt collar. I immediately tensed up and had to force myself to not throw him across the room as he pushed me back against the wall.

"I'm tired of you messing with my girlfriend!" he said irately.

I couldn't help smirking smugly at him. "Mindy might have something to say about which one of us is her boyfriend. She didn't seem to be thinking about you at all last night when we were kissing."

Kayden was furious. "I ought to punch you right in the nose, Tallinn! I'm not going to warn you again to stay away from her. She's mine!"

I reached my hands up and grabbed both of his wrists tightly, applied just enough pressure to be excruciatingly painful without breaking any bones, and pushed him back against the opposite wall and stared into his face. He screamed from the pain...he was such a baby.

"No, Kayden," I said slowly. "I'm not going to warn you again. Stay away from me and Mindy, or you'll be sorry. Is that understood?" I glared into his eyes with my black intimidating expression. I knew I was showing him the monster in me; I could tell by his terrified look. I didn't care...I wanted him to be afraid. I'd had enough of him.

Kayden nodded meekly. He was almost crying, and cowered from the pain and fear. I smiled coldly and released him, letting him fall to the floor in a heap. I turned around and walked out into the gym. He stayed away from me the rest of the hour.

I was so anxious to get to geometry to see Mindy that I was the first one there. I sat and waited while other students filtered in, and then the tardy bell rang. She never showed up. I was suddenly worried about her. Where was she? It was hard to sit in class and listen to the teacher droning on. When it was finally finished and I got to the lunchroom, Mindy was nowhere to be seen. I saw Daniel and Luke and went over.

"Hey guys, has either of you seen Mindy today?"

They shook their heads. "I don't think she's here. I have a class with her first hour and she wasn't in that either," Daniel said.

I was dark and brooding the rest of the day. All I could think about was Mindy, wondering where she was and why she wasn't at school. I couldn't wait to call her when I got home.

When Dad picked me up in front of the school, I tried hard not to glare at him. I couldn't help thinking that he might have something to do with why Mindy wasn't at school today.

"How was your day?" Dad asked when I got in the passenger seat beside him.

I shrugged. "Okay, I guess." I wasn't in the mood to talk to him, and he must have realized it because he didn't say anything else the entire way home. Once I was up in my room, I grabbed my cell phone and called Mindy's number.

"Hello?"

I couldn't help breathing a sigh of relief at hearing her voice. "Hi Mindy, it's Rurik."

There was silence on the other end.

"Are you there?"

"Yeah, I'm here," she said quietly. Her voice sounded strained.

"What's wrong? Why weren't you at school today? I missed you."

She sighed. "Don't, Rurik. Don't say stuff you don't mean." Her voice broke a little, like she was trying hard not to cry.

"What? Of course I mean it. I told you already that I like you."

There was silence again.

"Mindy? Say something. What're you thinking?"

"I...I know that you're engaged to someone else, Rurik," she finally said. "Your mom told me."

I clenched my teeth. My parents had no right to interfere in my life like this.

"Is it true?" she whispered.

"Mindy...." I started. "That's what my parents want...not me."

"So...you aren't engaged?" she asked.

I sighed. "She's who I'm supposed to marry, but I don't want to."

"This is a free country, Rurik. You don't have to marry anyone you don't want to."

"It's a little more complicated than that," I said sarcastically.

She was silent for a moment. "Explain it to me...I'm listening."

I closed my eyes and sighed. "There's no way I can tell you what I have to on the phone. Can I see you?"

"Okay. When? Where?"

"Later tonight. My parents have a meeting that they need to attend at midnight. They won't miss me if I'm gone then."

"That's a weird time for a meeting. Where do you want to meet? My mom works nights, so you could come over here."

"Okay, I'll be there shortly after midnight."

Chapter Three

Amy

I spent the rest of the afternoon nervously considering what I was going to say to Mindy. I didn't want to blow her out of the water with the whole horrible reality all at once. I thought about what I could tell her without having to disclose everything. What if she wanted nothing more to do with me after she heard what I had to say? I paced nervously around the house. I could hardly even eat any dinner.

Mom kept eyeing me carefully. She came over when I was in the kitchen eating a sandwich. "Are you going to be okay?"

I tried hard not to glare. I was so mad at her and Dad for pushing Mindy away. I couldn't help stiffening and saying with sarcasm, "What do you care?"

Her expression saddened. "I do care. I love you, more than anything."

I snickered. "You have a strange way of showing it, Mom."

"I know you don't understand, but eventually, someday, you will."

"Oh, I understand. The society has always been all that matters. I knew Dad had that attitude, but I thought you were different. That you actually had feelings."

Her eyes filled with tears at my words. I knew it was a low blow on my part. She'd always been very emotional, especially as a human, and once she became a vampire, it had changed only minimally. Mom had commented more than once that vampires could have a cold, unemotional side to them, and she hoped that she was never that way. I'd just accused her of acting exactly like one of the things she disliked most about vampires.

"I do have feelings, Rurik. And right now my heart's breaking for you, for what you're going through with Mindy." She paused and looked deep into my eyes. "But that doesn't change the fact that Mindy is not what you need. There's no way she could help like Amy will be able to with your future."

"Maybe I don't want that future!" I couldn't help yelling. "Maybe I don't want to be some great leader, the new direction for vampires! Did you and Dad ever think about that?!" I looked at her furiously as she stood there staring back at me without a word. I continued in a calmer tone. "You can't make me be what I don't want to be." I glared at her and she physically flinched. I knew that I'd never given her a look like that before…I'd never felt so much animosity toward my parents as I did at that moment. I turned around, walked out, and went up to my room.

I sat there the rest of the evening. I just wanted time to pass so I could see Mindy. A little before midnight, Mom came up and softly knocked on the door.

"Come in," I said.

Mom walked in and over to the bed where I was sitting. She looked questioningly into my face. "I just wanted to let you know that we're going to our meeting at the building. We won't be back till morning, probably."

"Okay, Mom, see you later," I looked at her with emotionless, cold black eyes. I was over my hate of her for the moment, although I had no fond feelings either.

She leaned down and kissed the top of my head, then turned around and walked out of the room. I couldn't help sighing. How had life gotten so complicated?

Shortly after they left, I climbed out my window and then down the side of the building to the back trees. I easily scrambled over the chain link fencing and took off swiftly to Mindy's house. Vampires are incredible, fast, and powerful beings, and since no one was around to see, I took advantage of racing at the speeds I enjoyed most. I stayed in the dark shadows, and was so fleeting that if anyone happened to be looking my direction as I went by, they would have seen nothing but a quickly moving blur and wondered if they'd been imagining things.

It took me only about ten minutes to get to Mindy's house as the crow flies; a car would have taken closer to half an hour. She lived in a small suburban neighborhood, where all the houses looked virtually the same. The only distinguishing features were the colors the siding was painted, or the landscaping and lawn ornaments. I walked silently up to her house and knocked on the door. I heard soft steps approaching and then saw her peek through the drapes before she took the deadbolt off the door and opened it for me.

Mindy looked questioningly into my face, and I had to hold back the desire to take her into my arms and embrace her. I smiled instead.

"Hi," she said shyly, and smiled back. "Come in."

She opened the door wider and I stepped into her tiny living room. It was clean and cute, but the furniture was old and worn. Blankets had been put over the threadbare sections to help them appear more appealing. There was a small kitchen to one side, and Mindy went to the refrigerator and opened it.

"Do you want something to drink?"

"Sure," I answered, and walked over. She had her head in the fridge looking for something, and when she turned to face me she jumped, startled. "I didn't hear you walk over...you scared me."

"Sorry," I grinned. "I do have a very light step."

"Do you want soda?"

"That sounds great."

Mindy handed me a soda and asked, "Should we sit out here, or would you rather go to my room?"

"Let's go to your room," I suggested. I was curious to see what it looked like, the things that she was interested in.

I followed her down a hallway to a room at the end. There was a twin bed with a white painted headboard against one wall, and a small futon along another side with a desk and computer. She sat down on the futon and I glanced around as I entered. She had pictures of horses and kittens, and a shelf with what I assumed were some of her favorite stuffed animals from when she was younger. There was also a bookshelf with several books and CD's on it, along with a boom box.

I sat down beside her and took her hand. Her expression turned serious and she stared back into my face. I took a deep breath, trying to think how to start.

"Mindy," I finally began. "My family's not how they appear to be to the outside world. We belong to part of a secret organization…a society. We have our own rules and laws. Dad and Mom run this country."

She was watching my face intently while I spoke.

"I can't explain everything to you, but I'm part of a group that's supposed to change things in our society for the better." I paused, trying to think what to say next.

"What does this have to do with you being engaged to this girl?"

I sighed. "I'm not engaged to her. It was foretold a long time ago that a new breed would rise up and become the rulers of the society. I'm that new breed."

"What do you mean, Rurik? I don't understand."

"My mom and dad married and had me. I'm different…faster and better in every way. Amy, the girl I'm supposed to marry, is the same. There are prophecies about us becoming great leaders and starting a new race together." I looked at her questioningly. "Do you understand? They expect me to marry Amy because it was prophesied a long time ago, but that doesn't mean I want to."

She was shaking her head. "This doesn't make any sense. How are you different, better? What kind of society is this? It sounds like science fiction."

"I can't explain it all to you, but I can tell you that I ran here from my house in less than ten minutes."

She stared at me with disbelief. "That's impossible. It takes at least half an hour in a car."

"I know. All of us are incredibly fast and powerful compared to humans. But Amy and I are the fastest and strongest of any of us."

"Compared to humans? Are you telling me you aren't human, Rurik? What are you…an alien?"

I grinned slightly. "No, not aliens. We've always been here, alongside of humans. We've just kept our society secret to protect ourselves."

She shook her head again, "I'm sorry, but I don't believe this. It all sounds too crazy."

"I can prove it to you," I said quietly. I stood up and held out my hand to her.

She sat motionless, looking at me. Her face was almost afraid, like she didn't want to find out I was telling the truth.

I gazed into her eyes and said as gently as I could. "It's okay, Mindy. I won't ever hurt you."

She laughed nervously, took my hand, and stood up. I held her hand and we walked outside into her subdivision. There was utter silence…no one was around. I glanced up and down the dark street, looking for anything to use to illustrate my point. I saw a very large eighteen wheeler at the end of the road and walked toward it. When we stopped, I let go of Mindy's hand and she suddenly looked concerned.

"What are you going to do? You don't have to prove anything to me. I don't want you to get hurt."

"It's okay. It takes a lot to hurt me," I tried to reassure her.

I stepped in front of the truck, bent down, and picked up the end of the cab easily. Mindy gasped and backed away.

"How can you do that?!" she exclaimed. "Is this some kind of trick?"

I sat the truck down. "It isn't a trick. I'm very strong." I took a breath and then raced down to the other end of the block.

Mindy shouted. "Rurik, where are you? Where did you go?!"

"I'm down here!" I yelled back. When she turned with astonishment and looked down the street in my direction, I waved. And then I raced back to where she was standing in about half a second.

She stared at me with wide eyes, her face very pale.

"Are you all right?" I asked with concern.

She nodded. "I'm just a little dizzy." Then she collapsed in my arms. I carried her back into her house and placed her carefully on the couch. She slowly opened her eyes. When she saw me, she flinched back.

"It's okay, Mindy. I'm not going to hurt you."

"What are you, Rurik?" she asked quietly as she stared up into my face.

I gently brushed her hair out of her eyes. "That's not important. What is…is that I like you. I want to be able to keep seeing you…. If I didn't just scare you off."

She sat up, and I could tell from her expression that she was trying to get a grip on everything that I'd just told her. What she'd just seen. "What about your parents? They want you to marry this other girl, Amy."

I sighed. "They'll eventually come around. We don't have to tell anyone right now. I can see you in secret. Your mom works nights, my parents are busy a lot of nights with the society. I can come over here."

She sat quietly for a few minutes. I was suddenly terrified that she didn't want to see me. I waited with nervous anticipation for her to say something, anything. I felt my happiness was in the hands of this petite human who had somehow managed to capture my heart.

"That is…if you still want me to come over," I said uncertainly. I took her hand and stared carefully into her face. "Do you?"

She smiled and nodded her head.

I couldn't help breathing a huge sigh of relief. I pulled her to me and hugged her. "I was so afraid for a moment that you were going to tell me that you didn't want to see me anymore."

She looked longingly into my eyes and I gently bent down to her and kissed her lips. She melted willingly into my embrace. We snuggled on her couch for a long time, and talked and laughed as if we'd known each other for years. I could have stayed there forever with her, but I wanted to make sure I was home before my parents got back.

I stood up and pulled Mindy to her feet, and hugged her one last time. "I should go. I don't want my parents finding out and ruining this."

Her eyes were so soft and tender staring back up at me. "See you at school." She stood on her tiptoes and pressed her lips to mine.

I drew her firmly to me and kissed her hungrily. When I finally stepped away I could feel her being drawn into my powerful mesmerizing eyes. I desperately wanted all of her…it was a completely overwhelming feeling. I had to physically tear my eyes from hers.

"Goodbye," I managed to whisper. And then I turned quickly and walked out the door.

#

I was downstairs in the kitchen eating a large bowl of cereal when my parents came in. I had my appetite back and was starving. I tried to not seem as cheerful as I felt. I knew they expected me to still be angry with them, and I was. But the thought of being able to see Mindy, of kissing her and holding her in my arms, was such euphoria it was difficult to be ticked off at anyone at the moment.

When I arrived at school Mindy looked tired in geometry class.

"Are you all right?" I asked, and sat down beside her.

She smiled at me and then nodded. "I'm just tired. We were up most of the night."

"Oh, I forget sometimes about that. I don't need much sleep."

She looked at me with amazement. We walked from geometry class to her locker to put our books up, and then to the lunch room, and sat at our regular table.

"Hey," Daniel grinned. "Are we actually being graced by your presence?"

I smirked. "Very funny." I sat down next to Mindy with my tray of food, and protectively put my arm around the back of her chair. "We just had a few things we needed to talk about and work out."

"There's a Halloween mall crawl in a couple weeks. I think we should all dress up as ghosts, goblins, or vampires and go," Kaylee said enthusiastically. "What d'ya say?"

Luke laughed. "Vampires are so last year. How about zombies? They're always attacking the malls."

"I know, right?" Kaylee commented.

I shrugged. "I've always liked vampires. What do you think, Mindy?"

Mindy smiled. "Vampires are cool."

I couldn't help grinning to myself, enjoying my own private joke.

After lunch I walked Mindy back to her locker to retrieve our books. I leaned in close to her face, and her heart immediately sped up and her breath quickened. I enjoyed the obvious effect I had on her. "Will I see you tonight?"

She smiled widely. "I'd like that, Rurik."

"Great, my parents have their monthly council meeting to attend, so they'll be busy again." I ran my fingers up her arm and looked deeply into her eyes. "See you then," I said softly, and turned to go to my next class.

#

When I arrived at Mindy's, she opened the door up and leapt into my arms. I grinned and kissed her. We closed the door and went into her room, where I lay on the bed and looked up at the ceiling while she propped herself up on her elbow and softly ran her fingers up and down my arm. The feeling was incredible.

"What're you thinking about?" she asked after a while.

I glanced over to her. "How happy I am here with you. How much I like being around you."

She smiled shyly at my words and glanced down at the bedspread. I reached my hand out and turned her face to mine.

"I don't ever want to be anywhere else but here with you," I said honestly, and gazed into her eyes.

"I feel the same way."

"You're so sweet, Mindy. I don't know if bringing you into my world is fair to you."

"I don't care about any of that, as long as we can be together."

I tried not to grimace...she had no idea what I even was. What my parents and the society consisted of, that we were all vampires and consumed human blood. People who came across our paths died regularly. If she knew all of that about me, she would run away as fast as she could. I reached over and stroked the soft skin on her cheek.

"You're so kind and beautiful," I said with sadness in my voice.

"What's wrong?" she asked, picking up on my sudden mood change.

I sighed. "I just can't bear the thought of losing you."

"I'm not going anywhere."

"You will when you find out the truth about me."

"I don't believe you," she said, almost angrily. "You should have more faith in me than that. There's nothing that you could ever tell me that would change the way I feel."

"Even if I'm your worst nightmare?"

"Very funny," she said crossly, and slapped my arm. "Like you could ever be my worst nightmare. You're my best dream."

I had to grin at her analogy, and reached up and pulled her down on top of me. I stroked her face and she leaned in and kissed me. I pulled her to me and quickly flipped her over until I was on top of her. She giggled and I bent down and kissed her, and then looked into her eyes. She was completely powerless under me. I had an almost uncontrollable desire to take her, and then to drink her blood. The thought scared me as I realized how exciting it would be.

"Rurik, what's wrong?" Mindy suddenly asked. She was staring into my face with concern.

That brought me out of my thoughts, and I swiftly got up and walked to the other side of the room. I stood and stared out the window, trying to regain control of the beast in me that wanted to hurt the girl that I loved.

"Are you okay?" she asked.

I glanced over to her and nodded. "Yeah, I'm fine." I smiled and sat down on the chair in front of her desk, at a safer distance from her. "I should go…you need to get some sleep." She looked disappointed, but I could tell that she was so tired she was having a hard time staying awake. I walked slowly over and bent down and quickly kissed her. "I'll let myself out." Then I turned and left. I knew I needed to get out of there before I did something that I would regret.

I walked out into the quiet dark street and slid stealthily into the trees, moving without a sound. I listened keenly with my vampire senses, and tested the gentle breeze that wafted by for any scents. A faint almost indiscernible smell tickled my nostrils, and I headed in the direction it was emanating from. I occasionally checked the air to make sure I was advancing toward my mark. The scent grew stronger with every step.

My mouth was starting to water at the thought, and my breath quickened with anticipation. There was a park up ahead, and I moved silently forward until I saw what I was looking for. Stopping, I surveyed my surroundings.

It was the center of the playground, and swing sets moved almost eerily in the gentle breeze, as if pushed by a small invisible child. On the other side of the clearing was a fountain that sprayed up into the air, and then fell like soft rain back down into the clam shaped bowls beneath it. I listened. The only sounds were the creaking of the rusty swing sets and the spattering of water from the fountain. No one was in sight, no one except for me and the man lying asleep on the bench.

I stepped over to him and looked down. He was in a deep sleep, with an empty bottle on the ground under the bench. I could smell the alcohol, but it wasn't important. The alcohol in his bloodstream would have no effect on me. It would, however, act as a sedative to make him easier to take without much, if any, struggle. He was surprisingly well dressed for sleeping on a bench in a park; he didn't look homeless. I noticed a cell phone lying beside him, and realized that he had gone out and drunk himself into a stupor for some reason. It didn't really matter, but it was his misfortune to have picked this night and this bench.

I leaned down to him, my eyes starting to glow as the vampire side in me took control. At that very moment he opened his eyes. He stared at me, as if not comprehending what he was seeing at first, then the horrible reality sank in and he opened his mouth to scream. He never even got the chance.

I stood up and moved quietly into the trees and back toward my house. My thirst had been satiated. I was only half vampire, so I didn't need to drink as often and regularly as other vampires did…it was a regular ritual for them. For me it was more of a craving. I enjoyed the blood, but didn't require it to survive.

#

When the weekend came I was looking forward to being able to spend Saturday night with Mindy without having to leave early because she needed her sleep for school. She would be able to sleep in. But instead, to my chagrin, Mom and Dad invited Amy over for the weekend with her parents, Tony and Amanda. I tried hard not to scowl when Mom told me in the kitchen with a smile on her face. She could play innocent all she wanted, but I knew exactly what her and Dad were up to. They were making sure that I spent time with Amy, with less time to think about anyone else who might be on my mind.

"Hi, Rurik." Amy smiled widely and sauntered into the entry.

I grinned back halfheartedly and obediently stood there while her parents entered.   Mom hugged Amanda, Amy's mom. They'd been best friends forever, even when they were still human.

After the initial greetings, Amy and I went up to my room to listen to music. Normally Mom and Dad would give me a "you better behave yourselves look" when we headed up to my room, but this time they actually looked happy about the idea.

Amy immediately zeroed in on the stereo with the CD collection and started thumbing through the lists of albums. I watched with a sense of satisfaction while she went through the entire list twice. I knew she was looking for Britney Stars, and I'd made sure that it was out with the trash that morning. It was bad enough I had to spend the entire weekend with her, but Britney Stars would have just added insult to injury. She finally picked a different one out of the stack and put it in the player, then came over and sat beside me on the lounge.

"Are you tired of playing high school yet?" she asked, with a mischievous smile.

I shrugged. "I'm still liking it at the moment. It's entertaining."

She wrinkled up her adorable nose. "What could possibly be fun about hanging out with food all day?"

I tried not to stiffen at her insult to the humans at the school. I'd had that attitude not too long ago. "You're half human too."

She looked at me with disgust. "Excuse me? Half slayer…there is a difference."

"Maybe."

She smiled suddenly. "I've been thinking about joining you at your school. It's been boring here without you."

That was the last thing I needed right now…a spy for Mom and Dad as to who I hung out with and everything I did at school. "You wouldn't like it," I tried to say casually.

"Why not? You seem to."

"Believe me, I know you, and it would be way boring for you."

She sighed, "You're probably right."

I tried not to breathe a sigh of relief and smiled. "There is, however, a mall crawl for Halloween next weekend that we're thinking about going to. It could be fun." I knew my parents would never let me go with the kids at school, but if Amy went, that would be a whole different story.

"Who's we?" she asked.

"The kids I hang out with at school."

"Oh yeah? That might be cool."

"It's a costume thing, so you'll have to dress up."

"As what?"

I shrugged. "A zombie, or you could go as a vampire."

She laughed. "Should I wear my fangs?" Then she smiled widely and showed me her long fangs.

They were impressive if she opened her mouth wide, but were set back far enough to not be noticeable during normal conversation. Humans always assumed vampires had long pointed fangs on the canines, but in actuality they were set back farther, on the bicuspids, and weren't discernible unless necessary. If we all ran around with pointy teeth in the front of our mouths, it would be difficult to blend in with society.

I grinned back. "I'm planning to sport mine. Maybe I'll wear a cape, too."

She shuddered. "That is so Goth."

"I know, but it's what humans expect us to look like."

"What're your friends going as?"

"Some said they were going to be vampires, some zombies, or ghosts."

"If anyone shows up with plastic fangs and white sparkly make up, I'm gonna puke."

I couldn't help laughing. I was actually enjoying hanging out with Amy...I didn't have to hide the real me when I was around her. She liked me the way I was, because she and I were the same. I'd forgotten how extraordinarily beautiful she was. I'd been looking at nothing but humans lately with their too big noses, or derrieres, and their adolescent lanky awkwardness.

Amy was beyond stunning; every feature that she had was perfectly proportioned. So it was no surprise that when she took my hand and smiled up into my eyes I had to kiss her. I could tell she wanted me to, and I leaned down and pulled her to me. She willingly and fervently kissed me back. It took me by surprise how enjoyable it was. She wasn't soft and warm and vulnerable like Mindy, but she was exciting. I could almost feel the sparks flying between us.

I finally broke our embrace and tried to get a grip on my emotions. I wanted her, and I could tell she was willing. I sighed and turned away, got up off the sofa, and walked to the other side of the room to look at the CD's, pretending to pick out a new selection to listen to. But I wasn't even paying attention to what it was that I opened and slid into the player. My mind was numb. This was a complication I never would have expected. I was attracted to Amy.

The weekend was way more enjoyable than I'd thought it would be. Since we rarely slept, Amy and I were together almost constantly. I didn't even have a chance to call Mindy. I didn't want to risk texting her because that would be proof on my phone that I was seeing her. I thought about her often and wondered how her weekend was going, and was looking forward to Monday morning and seeing her when Dad dropped me off in front of the school again.

Mindy was standing out front when I walked up, and she smiled in my direction.

"Hi," I grinned.

Her eyes looked a little concerned. "I thought you would come over this weekend, or call."

"Yeah, sorry. We had company all weekend and I couldn't." I almost felt guilty, like I'd been cheating on her, because it wasn't like the weekend had sucked...I'd had fun. And it was with Amy, who I was supposed to marry. Amy, who I'd told Mindy I couldn't stand, and what did I do this weekend? I kissed Amy and liked it. What kind of low life was I?

Mindy smiled. "That's okay. I just missed you."

I softly ran my fingertips up her arm and stared intently into her face. She was drawn into my eyes almost immediately. Her breath quickened and her heart sped up. I couldn't help smiling slightly. Then the buzzer rang and broke our trance.

"See you in geometry," I said, and took off in the opposite direction to science class.

I wondered what it was about humans that made them so dense sometimes. Kayden seemed to have already forgotten the almost broken bones he'd received by my hands only a week ago. When I walked into the locker room, he was waiting with a smug superior attitude written all over his face. When I walked past and to my locker, he didn't make a move, just sat and watched me. It wasn't until I was dressed and putting my clothes away that he decided to speak.

"You know, Tallinn," he started. "My dad's the principal. I could make your life here a living hell."

I smiled, although I knew my eyes were deadly and dark. "I figured that eventually you would turn to Daddy to fight your battles for you, Kayden."

He glowered hatefully at me. "I don't need anyone's help to take you on. You're asking for trouble if you continue down your current path."

"I thought you would have learned your lesson about threatening me," I said, and glanced down expressively at his wrists. "Or have you forgotten already?"

He tensed and his hand went subconsciously to his arm and rubbed it. So he did remember. I slowly walked forward, and he involuntarily backed up against the locker he was leaning against while he sat on the bench.

"I'm just saying. You better watch your back, or something's going to happen when you least expect it," he said.

I stood in front of him and looked down for a moment. There was fear in his eyes as he stared up at me, but there was also a stubborn, *I'm used to being in charge and I call the shots* look. I smiled maliciously and then walked out into the gym. As I said earlier, some humans were just dense.

The week went quickly by, and I managed to sneak out to see Mindy a few times. It was Thursday already, and the mall crawl for Halloween was tomorrow night. I hadn't told Mindy that Amy was going to come yet. I didn't know why. Actually, I did know why. Mindy would be totally uncomfortable around Amy. It was supposed to be a night out with my friends from school, and I'd invited Amy, the "I'm so perfect and superior" attitude queen. The complete opposite of Mindy. I knew I had to tell her when I saw her tonight.

Mindy answered the door and smiled widely. Her eyes sparkled with excitement as she pulled me into the house and down the hall to her bedroom, then led me over to the futon.

"Okay, sit here," she grinned enthusiastically.

"What're you up to?" I couldn't help smiling back. She was cute when she was excited about something.

"I have a surprise. Sit here and don't move, I'll be back in a couple of minutes." Then she turned around with one more smile and left the room.

I could hear her down the hall in the bathroom, moving things around as I sat and waited.

"Are you done yet? I'm tired of sitting here all by myself."

"Hold on!" I heard her yell down the hall. "Don't you dare come out here."

"I won't, just hurry. I came here to see you tonight, not scream down the hall at each other."

I heard the bathroom door open and soft footsteps. "Close your eyes."

"Oh, come on Mindy!" I complained, half joking.

"No, not until you close your eyes."

I sighed dramatically, then shut my eyes. "Okay, they're closed."

"For real?"

"Yes, now will you get in here?!" I yelled good-naturedly.

I heard her walk in and stop in front of where I was sitting. She took a breath and then said, "Okay, open them."

I opened my eyes and stared at her with surprise. She was standing in front of me in a short, bright pink dress. It came to just below what would be considered decent, and she wore spiked high heels with hose. It was very alluring.

"Wow!" I couldn't help exclaiming.

She blushed slightly. "Do you like it? It's my costume for tomorrow night."

"You look amazing, Mindy," I said, and I meant it. I always knew she was pretty, in a conservative sort of way, but this really showed off her figure. I reached up and pulled her down onto my lap. Her eyes immediately took on that soft pliable look, and I kissed her. "I better keep an eye on you tomorrow night. I'll have to fight the boys off."

"Oh stop!" she said with a shy smile. "I'm not interested in anyone but you."

"That's a good thing, because I'm very jealous," I teased.

"Tomorrow's going to be so much fun. I can't wait to hang out with everyone."

I stiffened slightly. I knew this was my cue to tell her about Amy. "Yeah, well, I wanted to talk to you about that."

She could instantly tell by my tone that she wasn't going to like what I said. "You're going, aren't you?" she asked disappointedly.

"Yeah, of course I'm going, but...." I hesitated, and she stared back at me. "I already told you that I would have to meet you guys at the mall, right?"

She nodded.

"Well, the only way my parents would agree to let me go was if I brought someone with me."

She tensed up. "Who?"

I grimaced. "Amy."

"Oh," she answered quietly. "Like a date?"

I could tell she was trying hard not to get emotional, but her eyes were filling with tears.

"No, not like that. Amy and I don't date, we just hang out together. We have since we were babies."

She breathed a slight sigh of relief. "Oh."

I hugged her against me. "I have to keep things copasetic with my parents. If they knew how much I liked you, it would mess up everything. So we just have to keep it casual tomorrow night. That's all."

"All right," Mindy reluctantly answered.

#

When I got home from school on Friday Amy was waiting in her costume, and she was the definition of Venus. There could not have ever been a more perfect female creature on this planet, ever. She had on a dazzling short scarlet dress with a red and black sequined cape that stopped at her waist. The skintight slinky outfit showed off her voluptuous figure to a T. Her gorgeous blonde curls cascaded down around her shoulders, and she'd applied the brightest shade of cherry lipstick I'd ever seen.

"So…what do you think? Do I look okay?" she asked, putting her hands on her hips and twirling around.

I smiled and almost laughed. She already knew that she looked totally amazing. "The guys won't stand a chance against you."

Amy grinned mischievously. "That's what I'm hoping. This might actually be fun. The one night of the year I can run around telling everyone that I'm a vampire and get away with it."

"I'll be down in a few," I said, and leaped up the stairs several at a time to my room to change. I put on the black cape and dark slacks with a ruffled white shirt. Then I combed my bangs back with a little bit of hair gel, and I was ready to go. When I went downstairs, Amy was sitting at the table in the kitchen chatting with Mom.

Amy turned to look at me and laughed. "You've got to be kidding me. You look like Dracula."

I couldn't help smiling. "Well, some vampires do still wear capes."

"Only the creepy ones," she answered with a grin.

Dad came in with an amused smile on his face at our costumes. "Ready to go?"

"We're ready," Amy said enthusiastically. "Bring on the humans."

Dad didn't quite appreciate her humor and frowned. "Same rules as always still apply. Don't get carried away."

"We know, Dad," I answered, and took Amy's arm and walked out the door.

"Have fun!" Mom yelled after us.

Dad dropped us off in front of the food court. We were supposed to meet the others right inside. We got several stares when we entered the mall. I was sure we looked incredible.

I glanced around and saw Luke, Daniel, and Mindy standing by the fountain. Mindy saw me first and smiled widely, but when she saw Amy the smile fell from her face. Luke turned in the direction Mindy was staring and waved. His mouth physically dropped open as he watched Amy saunter over.

"Hi guys," I said casually. "Um...everyone, this is my friend Amy."

Daniel stepped up quickly. "Hi Amy, I'm Daniel. And this is Luke."

Amy smiled warmly at them. "Hi, Daniel, hi Luke. Nice to meet you." She was purposely pulling them in with her eyes…she was such a tease.

I couldn't help rolling my eyes at her. "Amy, this is Mindy."

Mindy looked at Amy and tried to smile, but I could tell she was feeling completely inadequate next to this goddess standing by my side. Amy nodded at Mindy but hardly paid her any attention; she was focused on Daniel at the moment. I went over and casually took Mindy's arm. "You look great," I said, and smiled down at her.

She didn't appear happy while she stared back at Amy. Luke and Daniel were giving Amy their undivided attention, and I knew Amy would hardly pay me and Mindy any mind at the moment.

"We're going to go get a soda. Do you want to meet back here in an hour or so?" I asked.

Luke's eyes widened at the thought that I was going to leave them with Amy, and he quickly answered, "That'd be awesome. See you in a couple of hours."

We headed off to the fast food burger joint to get a drink. Once we had our soda and found a seat in a corner, away from the crowd, I leaned across and took Mindy's hand. She was still being very quiet and wasn't smiling.

"You look totally amazing, Mindy," I said.

She smiled, but there was doubt in her expression.

"What's wrong?"

She sighed. "How can I compete with that…that…Amy? She's gorgeous." Her eyes filled with tears.

"You don't have to compete with her, Mindy. You're the one I like, not Amy."

She snorted under her breath. "Why? Why do you want me when you can have her?"

"She doesn't have anything on you," I answered. "You're caring and beautiful."

"Beautiful? Amy is way prettier than me."

I squeezed her hand. "She's not human, Mindy. She may look perfect, but that doesn't make her better. I like you…you're warm and real."

She stared at me intently. "What does that mean…*not* human? How are you *not* human?"

I sighed and pulled my hand away from hers, sitting up straighter. My eyes narrowed. "You really don't want to know. Some of the most beautiful things in this world are the deadliest."

"Are you trying to tell me that you're dangerous?"

I stared back into her face without commenting.

"I don't believe you, Rurik. You'd never hurt me."

"No, you're right. I would never intentionally hurt you…I care about you too much," I sighed. But unintentionally, I'd wanted to drink her blood the other night. Could I control the vampire in me around her? I smiled suddenly and stood up. "Let's go check out some of the other costumes."

She grinned. "Okay."

We walked through the mall hand in hand and looked at all of the costumes. It was like an elaborate, macabre circus of sorts. There was every ghost, goblin, ghoul, and monster imaginable. Then the flip side was the fairies, princesses, animals, knights, and presidents. Practically anything imaginable was represented in some form of costume. After we'd walked a loop around the mall and done a little window shopping, I pulled Mindy toward a back exit. I wanted a few minutes alone with her where we wouldn't be seen.

I opened the door and we stepped out into the cool night. It was a small alcove area where trucks could back up and unload, and was secluded from view.

I pushed her against the wall of the building and held her in my arms and kissed her, while she willingly melted against my embrace. She was incredibly vulnerable, and the knowledge that I was so much more powerful than her heightened my senses. I couldn't help but be aware of her rapidly beating heart and the blood coursing through her veins. I ran my mouth down to her throat and her pulse quivered nervously against my lips. I growled under my breath, the vampire in me starting to consume me. My lips turned to ice against her flesh.

She suddenly pushed against me. "Rurik, what are you doing? Stop…you're scaring me." She squirmed out from against me and moved away.

But I didn't want to stop. I grabbed her by the arm and pushed her back against the wall again.

"Stop it, Rurik!" she yelled a little more insistently. "This isn't funny!"

Just then the back door opened and a man peeked his head out. "Hey! You kids aren't supposed to be back here!"

That brought me to my senses and I looked down at Mindy. She was staring into my face with a mixture of anger, fear, and concern. "Come on," I said abruptly, and took her arm and we went inside.

Amy, Luke, and Daniel strolled over. "There you are. We've been looking everywhere for you two. Where have you been?"

Mindy was still breathing rapidly, her heart pounding while she stared back into my face.

I tore my eyes away from hers and looked at the group. "Um…we were just walking around and got hot, so we thought we would step outside for a moment to get some fresh air." I glanced toward Amy and she was frowning, watching Mindy's expression intently. I knew Amy could hear Mindy's heart wildly beating and see the dilated pupils of her eyes. She could tell that Mindy was trying to regain her composure.

"Yeah, I'll bet you got hot," Amy stated a bit sarcastically. "We need to go out front. Your dad is going to be here any minute."

I nodded and glanced down at Mindy again. I didn't want to leave her here like this, but I didn't have any choice. I could tell she was still trying to recover from our incident in the alley…there was still concern in her eyes.

"All right." Then I turned to Mindy and squeezed her hand. "I'll talk to you later."

Mindy nodded her head and walked away with Daniel and Luke without a word. I was almost desperate to go after her, to stop her. But I couldn't. Amy was staring at me keenly, and she looked mad.

When we stepped out front to wait for Dad, she hissed under her breath. "What were you doing? Are you crazy?!"

"Nothing happened, Amy," I tried to say calmly.

"She likes you, Rurik, it's obvious. And it was also pretty obvious that she was scared."

I tried not to cringe. The last thing I ever wanted to do was hurt Mindy, or make her afraid of me.

Just then I saw Dad pull up in the Audi. We hopped in the backseat and took off down the road.

"You kids have fun?"

I nodded my head and tried to smile. Amy just sat looking straight ahead angrily and didn't say anything. Dad frowned and watched our expressions and body language while we sat in the back, not talking and staring out the windows on the opposite sides of the car. I was glad when we got back to the house that Tony was there waiting to pick up Amy. I didn't want to have to try to explain things to her. I was more concerned about Mindy at the moment.

I made my excuse that I had a couple of essays to do and went up to my room. Mom and Dad were busy doing things in Dad's office, and they looked like they would be occupied for a while. I quickly changed and climbed out my back window.

When I got to Mindy's door, I braced myself and knocked. At first I didn't hear anything at all, and then there was the slightest rustling noise behind the door.

"Mindy, it's me, Rurik!" I yelled. I waited but there was no response. "Mindy, please open the door."

I stood silently outside and waited. I could easily break the door handle off in my hand, but I didn't want to scare her any more than she was. I could hear her on the other side of the door, and it sounded like she was crying. "I promise I'm not going to hurt you," I said gently. "I'm sorry that I scared you. Please, Mindy, let me in so we can talk."

I heard movement, and then the deadbolt clicked off and the door slowly opened. I was shocked at what I saw. Mindy was standing in the entry with tears running down her face, her dress torn in several places, and she had blood on her lip.

Chapter Four
Kayden

"Mindy! What happened?!" I pulled her close and held her tightly. She sobbed uncontrollably while I directed her over to the couch, where we sat down. Then I lifted her face to mine. "Are you okay? Tell me who did this?" I was livid studying her shattered expression.

"It was Kayden," she finally said through sobs. "He came here and knocked. I...I thought it was you. I didn't look and opened the door. He was so angry, and pushed his way in. He...he.... I fought him, but he was so strong. I finally was able to get a hold of my mom's vase and smashed it against his nose." She suddenly looked mad and almost laughed. "There was so much blood, and he left."

I glanced around the living room. The vase pieces were scattered about the floor amid blood droplets.

"Are you okay, Mindy? He...he didn't do anything to you, did he?" I was burning with rage that was welling up in me at the thought. I wanted to kill Kayden slowly and tortuously.

She stared up into my face and shook her head. "He tried, but I fought him. It was a good thing I'd been taking kick boxing lessons. I kicked him good." She laughed shakily. "I don't think he'll be trying anything with any girl for a while. But he was so mad, and he hit me. I grabbed the vase to defend myself."

I pulled Mindy close and held her for several minutes. She went into the bathroom and took a shower while I cleaned up the mess in the living area. She entered the living room in robe and slippers with wet hair, and I walked over, bent down, and gently kissed her lips with a determined countenance. I knew what I needed to do.

"Lock up after me, I need to go out." I was trying to control my expression for her sake. I didn't want to terrify her further, but I was beyond furious.

"Where're you going?" she asked with concern.

"I have to take care of Kayden, so he won't ever try to hurt you again."

She could see the deadly expression on my face. "No, Rurik. He's not worth it…you'll get in trouble. I don't want anything happening to you."

I gazed down into her troubled face. "It's okay, Mindy. Don't worry, I'll be fine."

"Please don't," she pleaded, and grabbed my arm.

I smiled reassuringly. "I have to take care of this. Lock the door after me." Then I opened the door and walked out. I heard Mindy lock and deadbolt it as I disappeared into the darkness.

Kayden hadn't left too long ago, and his scent was still lingering strongly in the air. There were also blood drops forming a trail in the direction of his retreat. The absolute furious rage I felt was almost overwhelming. I couldn't wait to get my hands on him. Mindy was the sweetest girl, and she didn't deserve any of this.

The blood trail continued for almost a mile. Mindy must have clobbered him good. The thought was amusing…I hoped he was in agonizing pain. Suddenly I heard noise in the trees up ahead and slowed down my pace, listening carefully. I stealthily approached and peered into the brush.

Kayden was sitting on the ground, and had removed his shirt and held it up to his nose, which was still bleeding profusely. He was cussing under his breath. "That stupid girl is going to pay for this. She broke my f----g nose! When I get my hands on her, she's gonna be so sorry."

I stepped into the small clearing and stood there, just watching him.

Kayden seemed to slowly become aware of my presence and looked up. At first he appeared puzzled as to why I would be there and stared blankly back, but it didn't take him too long to realize that I must have come from Mindy's from the look in my dark expression.

"What do you want?!" he yelled.

"You're going to pay for what you did to Mindy, you low life slime."

He groaned. It was obvious he wasn't in the mood for any more fighting. "Go away, Tallinn! I'm the one who got the worst of it."

I glared at him and stepped menacingly closer.

Kayden stood up to face me; he could tell that I wasn't going to let him go. We slowly circled each other a couple of times.

I smiled maliciously at him. "I'm going to kill you, Kayden. You've lived way too long already."

He chuckled slightly, but when he saw the deadly look in my eyes, his expression grew serious. "You don't want to mess with me, Rurik. I'll kick your butt."

I growled viciously and advanced. My eyes started to glow and I bared my fangs.

His expression changed to one of horror. "What the hell are you?!" he screamed. And then he turned around and ran.

He didn't get more than two steps before I leaped on top of him. Normally I would subdue and kill my prey quickly, before they had time to struggle or scream. But I wanted to play with Kayden a little before I ended his life. He didn't deserve a speedy death after what he'd done to Mindy. He let out a blood curdling cry as I sank my teeth into the back of his neck. He struggled with all of his might. I let him free and he ran hysterically into the brush, while I methodically pursued him.

Kayden was beside himself with terror. He stumbled and fell continually, and kept looking behind him as I advanced, reducing the distance between us steadily. I wasn't in a rush; I could smell and taste his fear. I was like a cat playing with my meal before I ate it. Once he'd run himself down to the dead end of an alley, he turned to face me with absolute panic in his eyes. I walked slowly closer. He shook uncontrollably with fear.

"Not so big and tough now, are you, Kayden? Did you enjoy beating up Mindy…someone half your size?"

"No!" he yelled. "I'm sorry, I didn't mean it!"

I stopped and stared into his eyes with disgust. "Yes you did, you piece of scum. You meant to do what you did to her, and you planned to do more!"

Kayden sank to his knees in front of me and started bawling like a baby. "Pleeaazzz, don't kill me…," he blubbered. "I'm sorry."

I smiled. I had no sympathy for him at all. "I'm not going to kill you."

His face washed over with such relief he looked like he was going to pass out.

"Until I drink your blood…then I'm going to kill you."

He collapsed in a heap on the ground at my words and I slowly walked forward, stopping and looking down. He was such a pathetic excuse for a human.

I grabbed him by the collar of his shirt, lifted him to his feet, and held him to the wall. His body shook, and he gasped and cried when my eyes turned red as I exposed my fangs and brought them down to his neck. He screamed bloody murder at the top of his lungs. I could have drained him in seconds, but I wasn't in any hurry.

His struggles became weaker and weaker, his existence slowly ebbing away, until he was limp in my grasp. The plan was to drink his blood to the last drop and then rip his throat out to keep him from changing into a vampire, but there was a sudden noise behind me.

"Rurik?" It was Mindy's voice.

I turned abruptly and she was standing there staring at me with utter horror in her expression. I knew my eyes were still glowing and that I had Kayden's blood at the corners of my mouth.

She backed away and shook her head with disbelief.

"Mindy, you shouldn't be here."

She continued to retreat. The fear on her face was ripping my heart out.

I let Kayden's body fall to the ground, wiped my face, and took a step toward her. "Mindy, it's okay," I tried to say soothingly. I was trying desperately to calm the vampire in me, to stop my eyes from glowing.

"Don't come any closer, Rurik," she said in no more than a whisper, her eyes wide with fear.

I stopped. "It's all right…I'm not going to hurt you."

She was still shaking her head, tears streaming down her cheeks. "What kind of monster are you?"

I cringed at her words. "Mindy, please…. I love you."

She turned on her heels and ran away from me down the street.

I looked down at Kayden. It was important to finish him off, or he would become a vampire within twenty four hours. But I needed to go after Mindy, and was only indecisive for a moment…Kayden would wait. He wasn't going anywhere.

I ran out of the alley and after Mindy, catching her as she was rounding the next corner. I grabbed her by the arm and turned her to face me. Her expression hysterical, she screamed and tried to hit me, crying and yelling. I held her close, trying to comfort her. "It's okay, Mindy, everything's going to be okay," I said over and over.

After several minutes she finally stopped struggling, but was still shaking horribly. I picked her up in my arms and carried her back to her house.

We sat on the couch for hours with me cradling her against me, while she stared straight ahead and said nothing. She wasn't crying or hysterical anymore, she was just silent, which almost seemed worse. Eventually she fell asleep from the emotional trauma, and I carried her down the hall and lay her gently in her bed, covering her with a blanket and standing over her for a long time, watching her fitful sleep, I hated to leave, but if I didn't go back and take care of Kayden's body, he would become a vampire.

Finally deciding there was no other choice, I reluctantly left Mindy's house and went as quickly as possible back to where I'd left Kayden's body and walked down the alley. To my disbelief he was gone. I looked up and down in both directions. He'd definitely been dead when I left...there was no way he could have gotten up, but the body wasn't here. This didn't make any sense. Disheartened, I walked out of the alley and headed back to Mindy's so I would be there before she woke up.

#

Chase and Wyatt sat at the end of the dirt road in the back of the pickup. They stared disbelievingly at the body wrapped in the tarp. It was almost morning, and the sun was just starting to peek over the horizon.

"Come on," Chase said, suddenly getting up and hopping out of the truck bed. "Let's get this over with."

Wyatt stared at Chase with doubt. "I still don't understand why we didn't just go to the police, bro. Why do we have to get rid of the body?"

"I've already told you," Chase said irritably. He sighed and then continued. "We don't know what happened to Kayden. How he ended up dead. All we know is that he called us last night on his cell and wanted us to pick him up, and then go over with him to that girl Mindy's house to take care of her. Something happened to him after he called. It could have been Mindy, or her new boyfriend, or someone else. We got to figure this out and get even. If the cops are snooping around, we won't be able to." He rattled this story off like he was trying to explain something simple to a five year old for the tenth time. "Kayden would want us to take care of whoever did this to him. Got it?"

Wyatt smiled. "Yeah, I'd love to take care of Mindy and that jerk Rurik. Especially Mindy."

Chase nodded his head in agreement. "That's why we have to hide the body out here, where no one will ever find it. If anyone asks us, Kayden ran off to Las Vegas, as far as we know. That ought to keep them busy looking elsewhere long enough for us to get even with whoever did this to him." He grabbed the end of the now stiff corpse and started to pull it out of the truck bed. "Help me with this, and then come back and grab the shovels."

#

I sat beside Mindy's bed and watched her toss and turn in her sleep; she was obviously not sleeping peacefully. I sighed sadly. This was why I hadn't wanted to tell her what I was. She was a nice girl and didn't belong in my world. I felt bad…if I'd just left her alone in the first place maybe none of this would've happened. But it probably wouldn't have mattered with Kayden being so fixated on her. He'd have eventually, at one point or another, tried to force himself on her. At least it was a good thing that I was there to take care of Kayden so he could never hurt Mindy again.

But Mindy wasn't supposed to see me do it, and the look on her face had been one of terror. This was exactly what I'd been dreading, knowing that at some point in time the sweet, loving, trusting look in Mindy's eyes would be replaced by horror and fear when she looked at me. I reached over and sadly stroked her cheek. She was starting to stir.

Mindy opened her eyes, and then sat up with a start and backed away from me. The expression in her face was painful for me…the terrified look I was expecting.

I sat very still and tried to smile gently at her. "Hi," I said softly.

She didn't say anything, just stared suspiciously.

"Mindy, please say something." I sighed. "I'm really sorry that you saw me do…that. I never wanted you to be hurt…or scared, or to know what I am."

"What you are?" Mindy asked quietly. "What you are doesn't exist."

"We do exist. We've just always hidden our true identities so we can live among humans undetected. It works better this way…for us and humans."

She shook her head incredulously. "So you're telling me that…that…you have always been here? How many of you are there?"

"Vampires. You can say it. That's what we are, and yes…we've always been here, and there are a lot of us."

She stared at me like a deer in headlights.

"Are you going to be okay? I have to get back to my house before my parents find out that I'm gone."

"So…your parents, and Amy…they're…vampires too?"

I nodded.

I could see her trying to comprehend all of this while she sat on the bed and stared at me without saying anything. I leaned forward to take her hand. Surprisingly she let me, and then she stared down at our hands as if it was a dream she was still trying to wake from.

"I need to go. I'll come back and check on you later, okay?" I gently caressed the skin of her hand with my fingertips, and then stood up and looked down at her. She still just sat and stared at me with an almost puzzled expression, so I slowly and carefully bent down to her and kissed her lips. She didn't flinch, or react in any way. I sighed. "I'll have my cell phone; call if you need anything at all…all right?"

She nodded her head very subtly, and then I turned and left. It was almost morning, and I knew it would be a miracle if my parents hadn't noticed me missing yet. I also had no idea what I was going to do about Kayden's body being gone. I closed the door and locked the latch to Mindy's house behind me, then raced as fast as possible back to my place.

I climbed in my window and sat at my desk to think things through. I only had about twelve hours to find Kayden's body before he became a vampire. I didn't want to think about the ramifications if that were to happen and Dad found out. It was strictly against the rules of our society to bring anyone new into our organization without permission. There were a large number of vampires already, and not allowing anyone else to become one unless they had permission helped to insure that we didn't become overpopulated and adversely affect our food supply.

I was worried about Mindy also. She was completely hysterical when she found out what I was, but by the time I left her house she was acting like she was in shock and not any emotion at all. I didn't know how she was going to react, or if she would try to tell anyone. If Dad found out that she knew about our society, it could be very bad. The society had never been lenient at all with outsiders knowing about us.

There was a knock at my door and it startled me out of my thoughts. "Come in."

The door opened and Dad walked in. I didn't know if he knew that I'd snuck out last night and braced myself for the worst, while I tried to act completely casual.

He nodded my direction. "I just came in to check on you. You've been in here all night." His eyes looked concerned. "Are you doing all right? Amy didn't seem to be very happy last evening when I picked you two up at the mall."

I nodded. "I'm okay, Dad. Just a lot on my mind." I sighed. "Amy's spoiled. If she doesn't get everything her way she's a brat about it."

He grinned slightly and sat down on the edge of the bed across from me. He didn't look like he disagreed with me. "Anything you want to talk about?"

I shook my head. "No. I just need to think things through, that's all." I couldn't tell him what was really on my mind...Mindy, and Kayden's body. "I think I just need some time to myself."

"All right, Rurik. If you ever need to talk, your mother and I are here for you. I realize you are going through an awful lot lately. A normal teenager with hormones and girl challenges is hard enough. But with you being a vampire...that makes the whole thing trickier." His eyes turned contemplative and his expression serious. "You need to be especially careful around human girls."

I sighed. "I know."

"I mean it. They'll be very attracted to you, not just because of your good looks, either. You're the most lethal predator alive. You can draw them in very easily, but that's when it gets dangerous. Your instincts to subdue them and drink their blood will try to kick in."

I thought about that with Mindy. I loved her, but I'd already had more than one occasion where I had an almost overpowering urge to take her. I couldn't help sighing. "What do you do about it?" I asked him.

"That's the twenty four karat question. When your mother was human I was on guard constantly around her. It never goes away…that's what we are, and is the natural course of hunter versus prey. The best thing is to avoid them as much as possible in a one on one situation, until you grow through this and develop a little restraint." He stood up. "That's why, as irritating as Amy can be sometimes, she's the girl you need to be hanging out with. She's your equal. Someone like Mindy is just liable to get hurt…or killed." He reached over and patted my shoulder lightly. "I'll leave you to your thoughts for now. Your mother and I need to go out for the afternoon, and then we have another meeting with the council members tonight. We may not be back for a while."

"All right, Dad," I answered. I tried not to look too relieved.

"Call on my cell if anything comes up."

#

As soon as I was sure my parents were gone I snuck out the back again. I had to find Kayden's body quickly. It was late afternoon and would be dark in a few hours. Kayden would be waking in the early evening if I didn't find him first. He would rise as one of us, the undead creatures of the night, and be famished. He wouldn't have any desire except to feed, and I knew that he wouldn't care who it was.

I went back to the alley where I'd left his body and searched carefully for any clues. There was a little blood on the ground where Kayden had lain. I noticed fresh tire marks from a vehicle, as if someone had pulled up to the body and then put it in their vehicle and left. But who? And why? I was stumped. This was when I knew that I should go to Dad, tell him what happened, and face the consequences before anything worse occurred. But I knew what the cost would be, that I would never see Mindy again, ever, and I couldn't live with that. The thought was so far beyond painful that I decided I had to figure out a way to handle all of this myself. Keeping Mindy was the highest priority.

So I left the alley and went over to Mindy's house. I hoped she was okay…it had been several hours since I was there that morning. I knocked on her door and waited. I could hear her inside.

"Mindy, it's me. Please let me in."

There was no answer.

"Mindy, I know you're there. I'm not leaving…open the door."

"Go away, Rurik. I don't want to see you."

I closed my eyes and leaned my head against the door frame. "Mindy," I said as softly and gently as I could. "I can't leave you like this…please open the door."

I could hear her trying hard to not cry.

"I can easily break this door down, you know that…but I don't want to. Please, Mindy."

She sighed and then slowly unlocked the latch. I stood back while she opened the door and faced me. Her eyes were red and puffy from crying, and she stared in my direction suspiciously.

"Can I come in?"

She nodded her head and then stood to the side. I walked into the living room and she closed the door behind us, then gestured with her hand for me to sit down on the couch while she sat on the opposite end from me. Her face was incredibly sad, and I wanted desperately to hold her and make everything better.

"Tell me what you're thinking," I said softly.

Her eyes were filling with tears again, and her lower lip quivered. "I don't know what to think, Rurik," she said quietly. "This is all just so incredible...so horrible." She grabbed a tissue off the table and wiped her eyes. "I know you warned me that it was awful, that I didn't want to know what you are. I love you, but...how can I deal with THAT?"

I breathed a sigh of relief to hear that she loved me still. "I love you too, Mindy, more than anything. I didn't want you to find out what I was, especially that way." I tentatively reached over and took her hand. She didn't pull away from me or protest, although her eyes widened and I could hear her heart pounding nervously.

"I'm sorry it happened this way," I said quietly. I scooted over next to her and slowly put my arm around her shoulder. She was trembling with fear, but she didn't try to retreat. "I never wanted you to be afraid of me." I pulled her against me and hugged her. Her body was tense, but after a bit she relaxed in my arms. "Are you going to be okay?"

She stared up into my face for a few moments, and then slowly said, "I don't know...I ...I...."

I bent down and gently kissed her lips, and she immediately melted into my embrace and sighed. I felt protective of her, holding her in my arms. She was delicate and fragile, an angel in a lot of ways, the complete opposite of my dark side. "Oh Mindy," I whispered. "I love you so much."

Her eyes softened and she stared up into my face. "I love you too, Rurik."

#

It was dark, damp, and cold with a musty dirt smell when Kayden slowly opened his eyes. Everything was pitch black, his arms and legs immobilized. Where was he? He tried to move his head and couldn't. Something was very wrong. Then he vaguely remembered Rurik attacking him, his glowing red eyes and horrible long teeth. Rurik bringing his fangs down to his neck and drinking his blood. The pain was excruciating, and the terror unimaginable. Rurik! He sat up with a start and dirt flew everywhere. What the hell was going on? He was sitting half buried in the ground in the middle of a field. There was nothing in any direction except grassland, weeds, and a few trees. He pulled himself up out of the hole he was in and stood up, brushing the dirt from his clothes.

Kayden felt great, all of his senses alert. The smells were incredible, and even though he knew that it was night, he could see clearly for long distances in every direction. He realized that he was close to Chase's house, and set off that way. He had no idea how he ended up in this field in the middle of nowhere, but all he could think about was exacting revenge on Rurik for what he'd tried to do to him, and then they would take care of Mindy.

He moved amazingly fast toward the subdivision on the other side. Chase's house was just down at the end of the first street. Kayden walked up and pounded loudly on the door. It opened abruptly and Chase stood staring back, with complete shock written across his features.

"Well, are you going to invite me in? Don't just stand there like you've seen a ghost. I've had a hell of a day already," Kayden barked.

"Wha…? You…," Chase tried to say. He dumbly nodded his head and uttered a few unintelligible sounds, while Kayden brushed past him.

"I just woke up buried in a field. When I find out who the fool is that did that to me, I'm gonna kill him."

Chase found his voice. "You were dead…. We buried you because you were dead."

"What?! You stupid idiot, do I look dead to you?"

"I swear, Kayden. You didn't have a pulse, your eyes were staring blankly ahead. And you…you were stiff as a board. You had to be dead."

"Well, obviously I wasn't. Maybe I was in a coma or something. Didn't you morons think of that?"

"I'm sorry, bro. We could've sworn you weren't breathing."

"I ought to punch you right in the mouth! How stupid can you be?!" Kayden sat down at the kitchen table and glanced around. "Your parents still out of town till the end of the week?"

Chase nodded. "Yeah, they won't be home till late on Friday."

"Good," Kayden grinned. "That should give us time to take care of a few lowlifes. I'm starving. You got anything to eat in this house?"

"I'm sure we have something," Chase answered. He walked over to the refrigerator and shuffled through the shelves, then grabbed a box and pulled it out. "We got some leftover pizza, does that sound good?" Chase turned to look at Kayden, who was suddenly standing on the other side of the door to the refrigerator. "Boy, you got over here quick. I didn't even hear ya."

Kayden stood smiling back; his eyes had a dark menacing quality to them.

"What're you looking at me like that for? I told you I was sorry…we really thought you were dead," Chase reiterated nervously.

Kayden didn't say a word and slowly stepped closer to Chase.

"What the hell is wrong with you, Kayden?!"

Kayden continued to move threateningly closer without a sound.

Chase was backed into a corner now, and was starting to feel trapped. "Hey, get a grip. Chill. Eat some pizza and relax, man!"

Chase watched with horror as Kayden's eyes started to glow and he growled evilly. Chase screamed bloody murder and tried desperately to get around Kayden, who grabbed him in one swift move and slammed him against the wall. The box fell to the floor and pizza scattered everywhere. Then Kayden opened his mouth wide, brought his fangs down to Chase's throat, and cruelly sank his teeth into Chase's neck, drinking hungrily. Then Kayden let go of Chase's body and it slid to the floor. Chase stared blankly up at him with a horrified expression on his face.

Kayden felt so alive and energized. He lifted his head toward the ceiling and howled, satisfied completely. Never in his life had he felt this great before. He was going to have to thank Rurik for turning him into a vampire before he killed him, he thought while heading down the street and back to his house to think things over…it was almost morning and instinctively he knew that he shouldn't be out when the sun came up. A plan needed to be made on how he wanted to get revenge against Rurik.

When Kayden walked into his house, his mother came out of a back room in her robe and slippers. "Kayden? Is that you?"

"Yeah, Mom," Kayden replied with irritation.

She put her hands on her hips and glared at him. "Where have you been, young man? We've been worried sick about you!"

"I was out with some friends, all right? Chill!"

Kayden's dad came out, rubbing his eyes sleepily. "Don't talk to your mother that way, or you'll be grounded!"

Kayden's eyes gleamed hatefully. "I'm not in the mood for this, I'm going up to my room." He tried to brush past his dad to head up the stairs, and his dad grabbed his shoulder.

"Just a minute, we aren't done with this discussion yet!"

Kayden grabbed his dad's arm and twisted it painfully behind his back, and stared down with anger into his dad's suddenly concerned face. "Yes we are!" he shouted. "I've had a rough twenty four hours, and I don't need you two hassling me!" His eyes were dark and threatening, his parents' faces totally shocked. "Got it?" He eyed them irately, and then suddenly grinned and let go of his dad's arm. "Good. I'm glad we understand each other." He turned around and left his dumbfounded parents staring after him, and headed up to his room.

#

That evening Mindy called my cell and said that her mom was off for the evening, so I couldn't come over.

"All right," I replied. "If you need anything at all, I'll have my phone with me at all times. Okay?" I didn't want to worry her, but I was concerned about Kayden, and him showing up at her house. I had to go out and see if I could find him. It had been one heck of a weekend, and tomorrow was Monday already.

When I climbed back in my window in the morning, Dad was sitting on my bed waiting for me with a frown on his face. "Get in here and sit down."

I swallowed apprehensively. Had he found out about Mindy and that I'd been sneaking out to see her? It would be ironic if I got in trouble tonight when I didn't actually go to see her. Or worse, did Kayden do something really stupid already and Dad knew there was a rogue vampire running around? I sat down in the chair at my desk, afraid to get too close with the look he was giving me.

"Where've you been?" Dad asked angrily.

"I...I went out. I was hungry."

"Is that all?" he asked skeptically.

"Of course."

"You didn't see a certain girl while you were out, did you?"

I tensed, wondering if he suspected or if Amy had said something. I would get even with her if she had. I was relieved that he was only asking me about this night, and I could honestly say, "No, Dad. I promise, I didn't go see Mindy."

His face relaxed a bit; he looked as if he believed me, so I went on to drive my point in. "In fact, Amy came over yesterday while you and Mom were at your meeting."

He seemed to like that. "Okay, Rurik. I hate to treat you like the inquisition, but I need to make sure. Our society has strict rules for a very good reason. Make sure you let us know if you need to go out in the future. Call my cell if you have to."

I tried to smile. "I understand."

He stood up to leave. "Better get ready for school."

#

I was not prepared at all for what school had in store for me that day.

Mindy stood out front at the entrance as usual and smiled timidly at me. I went up and put my arm around her. "How are you doing?" I wished she would look at me like she used to, before she found out I was a vampire. Now there was definite caution behind her shy smile.

She nodded her head. "I'm fine, I think...."

I smiled at her, then the buzzer rang. "See you in third period."

First period, science, droned along till it was finally time for P.E. I was in a pretty good mood thinking about seeing Mindy in geometry and lunch hour. I would be extra gentle and caring with her, and she would get over the trauma of this weekend, I was sure. I smiled to myself rounding the corner into the locker room, glanced up, and came to an abrupt stop.

Sitting on the bench, dressed and ready for gym, was Kayden.

"Well, it's Mr. Tallinn," he smugly said. "I've been looking forward to seeing you." He stood up and strolled slowly over.

Chase was standing by the benches and watched me with a dark, sinister expression. It was obvious that he was now a vampire too.

Kayden stopped when he was a foot in front of me. "I just wanted to thank you for including me in your club. I'm thoroughly enjoying this. I have to admit I feel beyond great. If I'd known, I may have joined without any protest." I glared at him without a word, and he smiled back and continued. "Now I can see why it is that Mindy is so attracted to you. As strong and powerful as vampires are, you could really give her something to remember, huh Tallinn? I can't wait for my turn with her."

I grabbed him by the scruff of the neck and pushed him against the wall. "I'm warning you. We're not finished. You come anywhere near Mindy and you'll be permanently dead next time. You hear me?!"

He put his arms up and shoved me off of him, and I slammed into the back wall. My eyes started to glow and I had to force them to stop. I could not afford to rile him at school…it would cause such a mess of casualties that Dad would probably be forced to execute us all. I straightened up and gave him a lethal stare. "We'll settle this later, Kayden." Then I walked out into the gymnasium.

When I arrived at geometry class, Mindy could immediately see in my expression that there was something very wrong. "What's the matter?" she whispered.

I glanced around to make sure no one else was listening, and leaned in close to her ear. "Kayden's here."

Her eyes widened and her face went pale. "What!?" she practically shouted. "How can that be?!"

I put my hand up to her mouth when several students in the room turned to stare at us. "Shhh, keep your voice down."

"Sorry," she answered sheepishly. "What're we going to do?"

I shook my head. "I can't start anything with him here. My dad would literally kill me, if he doesn't already for what's happened."

She looked at me with concern. "I'm sorry, Rurik."

"How is this your fault?"

"If you'd never gotten involved with me, then you wouldn't have ended up in the middle of this with Kayden."

"Yeah," I said angrily. "And he may have finished what he started with you. I'm not sorry at all that you are in my life, Mindy, and that I'm here to protect you." I knew my expression was dark and intimidating when I looked into her eyes and thought about Kayden and what I wanted to do to him. She subconsciously scooted back in her chair to get a little further from me.

"Mr. Tallinn," the teacher suddenly said loudly. We stopped our conversation and stared in her direction. "Do you and Mindy have something you would like to share?"

I shook my head. "No."

"All right then, please be quiet. You can have your conversation during lunch. Just because both of you are

<u>A</u> students doesn't mean you can get away with not paying attention and disrupting the class. Is that clear to you as well, Mindy?"

"Yes, Mrs. Broach," she said, and then blushed while everyone stared at us.

Once geometry was over, I took Mindy's arm and walked her to her locker to drop off our books for lunch. Mindy's face looked frightened. "I'm scared. That means that Kayden's a vampire too, doesn't it?"

I glanced about me to make sure no one was in human earshot, and then nodded. "He's very riled up and dangerous, Chase too. Whatever you do, don't provoke him here at school. He won't care who he hurts, and my dad could have a serious mess to try to cover up. I'll have to take care of them tonight."

Mindy nodded meekly and took my arm; she was stiff and trying hard not to look petrified. We walked into the lunchroom together, and I stopped and stared at our usual table in disbelief and alarm. Sitting between Daniel and Luke, and thoroughly enjoying herself, was Amy. She saw me at the same time that our eyes fixed on her, and she waved and smiled coyly.

I walked straight over to the table and stood staring down at her. "What're you doing here?" I asked crossly.

She smiled pleasantly. "Hi, Rurik. It's nice to see you, too." Then she turned to Mindy and gave her a warm smile. "You too, Mindy."

Mindy bleakly smiled back. "Hi Amy," she managed.

"You didn't answer my question," I said angrily.

She gave me an irritated look. "I enrolled this morning. My parents thought it would be good for me to get out of the house." She turned to Daniel and smiled. "Interact with kids my own age more."

I heard a commotion on the other side of the cafeteria and turned to see Kayden and Chase harassing one of the other students, Oliver, who looked almost beside himself. Kayden held his sack lunch up just out of reach and taunted him. Oliver was almost on the verge of tears.

"Friends of yours?" Amy asked meaningfully. She could tell they were vampires.

I gave her a seething glare and said nothing.

"Aren't you going to do anything about it?" Mindy asked.

I stared painfully in her direction. I didn't need to get into a fight with Kayden in the middle of the lunchroom, but Mindy stood staring back at me accusingly, like it was my fault Kayden was now this out of control monster that was picking on a poor hapless kid.

"No," I said adamantly.

"Why not?" Mindy asked. She was getting mad at me.

"Yeah, Rurik," Amy agreed. "Why not?"

I gave Amy a "mind your own business" glare. She knew she was being the instigator, trying to cause a fight. She didn't care at all about the kid who was being tortured.

I stood and looked at them both with exasperation for a few moments while they stared accusingly back. Then I took a deep breath, sighed, and stomped over to Kayden.

Kayden turned to me with surprise. "What do you want, Tallinn?"

"Give the kid his lunch back," I said in an even tone.

He snickered. "What do you care?"

Mindy came over and glared at him. "Give Oliver his lunch, Kayden!" She looked impressively angry, and Kayden was taken back at her expression and scowled.

Amy stood beside Mindy and me, and crossed her arms and stared in his direction also.

"Well hello, beautiful," Kayden said to her. "How come I haven't seen you around before?"

Amy smiled warmly at him, then said with sarcasm, "Maybe because I don't reside in the same cesspool you just crawled out of."

Kayden's eyes glinted with anger. Then to my surprise he grinned and abruptly threw the sack lunch at the feet of Oliver, who quickly snatched it up and retreated. Kayden smiled and said, "Can't wait to catch up with you later, Rurik. And, I'll be looking forward to where I left off with Mindy the other day."

Mindy stiffened, her expression scared.

I took a menacing step toward him and Amy quickly grabbed my arm. "Rurik," she hissed. "You do not want to get into it with this jerk here, understand?"

I made myself stop and nodded in reluctant agreement with her before I turned to Kayden. "Catch you later," I said in a threatening tone.

We went back to our table to eat lunch. There were no further incidents, but Kayden watched us the remainder of the hour with a smug, arrogant expression.

#

After school Amy ran up and took my arm while I walked over to Dad's car. "Hey, I'm coming over to your house with you."

I scowled at her. "No you're not."

She stared at me with resolve. "I need you to fill me in on how Kayden and his friend became vampires so we can figure out what to do about it…unless you're planning to tell your dad."

I glanced toward Dad's car. He was looking in our direction, so I stopped and turned to Amy. "All right, you can come over, but I'm warning you not to say anything."

She smiled. "Of course not, Rurik. We just need to make a plan, that's all."

I groaned to myself and walked over to the car with Amy on my arm, opened the door, and we scooted in. "Hi, Dad. Amy's coming over for a bit, if that's okay."

Dad grinned widely. "Of course. How was your first day of school, Amy?"

"Oh, it was fun. I'm so glad I decided to come here and get out of the house a little. I've already met some of Rurik's friends." She smiled coyly at me and held onto my arm.

I couldn't help rolling my eyes.

Once we were in my room, I closed the door and turned to Amy. She casually looked through the CDs and put one in the player, and then went over to my computer and started messing with it. "I'm so happy I decided to go to school. It really was fun to meet all of those humans and hang out together today. What do you think we'll be doing tomorrow?"

I gave her a humorless look. "Cut the crap, Amy. Get to the point."

She looked mockingly surprised for a moment, and then said, "I want to know how Kayden and his friend became vampires. What happened to all those years of having the society rules pounded into our heads? You go to school for a few months and suddenly you forget, or what?"

I sighed. "It wasn't my intention to turn Kayden into a vampire. I…was interrupted in the middle of feeding, and didn't get a chance to finish him off. And I had nothing to do with Chase…Kayden must've done it."

Amy squinted her eyes thoughtfully. "Why did you suddenly want to kill him? If students at the school are going to start ending up missing and dead, didn't it occur to you that your dad may become suspicious? You know we're not supposed to take anyone who can be linked back to us."

"Yes…I know. But he deserved to die," I stated angrily.

Amy looked at me with almost awe at the dark expression that went across my features. "Wow. I don't think I've ever seen you this angry before. What did he do?"

"He attacked Mindy and tried to rape her."

"Oh," Amy answered. "How come you didn't make sure the amoeba was dead?"

"Mindy came up behind me and…and saw me draining Kayden. She ran off. I had to go after her. I thought I could just come back and take care of Kayden later, but his body was gone." I sighed. "I guess his friends came and took it, and he became a vampire."

Amy smiled and chuckled. I glared back. There wasn't anything funny about any of this.

"Boy, Rurik, you sure know how to do it good when you decide to screw up, don't you?" She paused for meaning before she continued. "How many laws have you broken now? Um…killing a student at school, turning him into a vampire. Oh…and telling an outsider about our organization. You'll be lucky if your dad doesn't flog all the hide off of you."

"I'm glad you find it funny that my father may kill me. Are you going to help me take care of those jerks, or not?"

She shrugged. "What's in it for me?"

My eyes narrowed suspiciously. "What do you want?"

She smiled slyly. "I don't know, I'll have to think about it."

"Well, don't get carried away. It would be nice to have your help, but I can do it on my own if I have to. Either way it needs to get handled quickly, before they turn half this town into vampires. If Dad finds out, you're right…a serious flogging will be the least of my worries."

Chapter Five
Face-Off

Amy and I agreed to meet up later that evening to try and handle Kayden and Chase. We figured they would be anxious to fight us, but must have instinctively realized that we were more powerful and experienced than them. They did a good job of eluding us. After going to Kayden's house and then Chase's, we decided to hang outside of Mindy's to make sure they didn't show up there. We sat quietly in the shadows for hours.

"This is really boring," Amy complained after a few hours. "You're going to owe me big time."

"Have you thought about what you want?"

She grinned mischievously. "I've been thinking about it all day, and I'd like you to take me to the homecoming dance."

I grimaced. Mindy and I had made plans to meet there. "I already kind of had plans for that."

She frowned. "With who?" I didn't answer right away, and she said indignantly, "I should have known you'd be going with Mindy."

I sighed. "I don't want to get into this right now, Amy."

"I just don't understand the attraction there. I'm so much prettier and smarter."

"Change the subject. I'm not talking about Mindy with you."

She sat silently for a moment. "Well, that's what I want. You'll just have to explain it to her."

"Anything else but that," I commented dryly.

Amy's bottom lip protruded and stiffened in an obvious pout. I resisted the urge to grin at her moping, stood up, and stretched. "I'm going to go in and see Mindy for a little bit. Give a yell if someone shows up."

Her back straightened with anger. "I have to sit out here while you go in and cuddle, or…whatever it is that you do?"

"I just need to make sure Mindy's doing okay. She's had a couple of shocks this last week. I promise to make it up to you when Kayden and Chase are dead."

"The list just keeps getting longer," she said with irritation, resting her chin on her knees and glowering up at me.

I walked up to the house, knocked, and Mindy answered the door, smiling widely.

"Can I come in?"

She nodded and I stepped into the house. As soon as Mindy closed the door, I wrapped my arms around her, took her hand, and led her over to the couch, where we sat down. We chatted about inconsequential things for a while, just to keep it light.

"Mindy, I love you so much. I just want things to be the way they were with us before you found out what I was."

"I love you too, Rurik. But, I just can't help thinking about seeing you with Kayden." She shuddered at the thought and her face took on a serious expression. Then she studied our hands as we held each other's before she shifted her focus to me again. "I'm just trying to understand. What's it like to be a vampire?"

I shrugged and thought about how to explain it. "Well, I was born the way I am, so I don't really have anything different to compare it to. We're stronger and faster than humans, and don't sleep much. We also have to eat. I eat regular food also, being half human, but other vampires don't."

We sat lost in our thoughts for a few minutes, and then there was a sudden knocking at the door, exploding the quiet between us. Mindy jumped.

I sighed with exasperation and stood up. "It's Amy," I said reassuringly, and walked over to the door.

"What's she doing here?"

"Well, we thought we should keep an eye on your house with Kayden running around." I opened the door and Amy was standing there with an annoyed expression.

"Come in, Amy," I said with irritation.

She strolled in and glanced around the tiny living area. "I was getting very bored sitting outside by myself, so I thought I'd come visit you two. I'm also thirsty."

"I told you that I wouldn't be long," I remarked dryly.

"Oh, am I interrupting?" she asked sarcastically.

Mindy stood up. "No, it's fine. Come in and sit down, Amy. Um…do you want something to drink? I mean, from the fridge…I have soda. Are you like Rurik? Do you drink…other stuff besides…?" Mindy stood there with a mortified look on her face, and Amy seemed amused at her discomfort.

"Don't worry, I'm not going to attack you and drink your blood," Amy answered. "Milk's fine."

Mindy, visibly relieved, headed over to the fridge to retrieve it. "Do you want one, Rurik?"

"Yeah, sure," I answered, and we all sat back down with drinks in hand.

There was awkward silence for several minutes.

Amy was glancing around Mindy's small house. "So, this is how the other half lives," she finally said.

I cringed. "Don't be rude, Amy…if it's possible."

"I wasn't meaning to be. I was just commenting."

"It's okay, Rurik," Mindy answered.

Amy smiled with satisfaction that Mindy was defending her.

"Amy needs to learn to keep her mouth shut sometimes. Right, Amy?" I glared.

She shrugged. "Whatever. I just tell it like I see it." Then to change the subject, she asked, "What are we going to do about Kayden?"

"I don't know. He and Chase did a good job of avoiding us tonight, but he can't hide forever. Eventually he'll have to face us."

But it seemed that Kayden was able to remain hidden. We only saw him at school, and we didn't dare fight him there. Amy and I managed to go out every night during the week to try and take care of him. It was frustrating. I only spent snippets of time with Mindy in between scouring the area with Amy, who was enjoying having all of my attention for a change. Mindy was trying to keep up the brave front, but I knew she was afraid of Kayden and his threats. And I could tell that me spending so much time with Amy, and so little time with her, was making her very insecure.

\#

"Will you shut up?!" Kayden yelled with irritation at Chase. "Anyone within a mile from here can hear you whistling."

Chase gave Kayden a caustic glare. "How much longer do we have to stand here and be quiet? I want to have some fun...go hunting and eat. I'm starving."

Kayden growled. "We're waitin' for Wyatt to get home from detention for skipping school the last couple of days."

` "Yeah. Yeah, I know," Chase mumbled.

Kayden couldn't help smirking to himself. "The fool has no clue that I'm alive. Or that we are vampires. He's gonna mess his pants."

Chase laughed loudly at the thought, and Kayden turned to him furiously. "You make another noise and I'm gonna scatter you across the pavement!" He grabbed Chase by the shoulders and pushed him roughly against the brick wall behind him. Chase's face turned to terror staring back into Kayden's glare.

Just then they heard Wyatt approaching from the end of the street. Kayden grinned with mischievousness and stepped back against the wall to wait for Wyatt. Chase fell in beside Kayden and rubbed his sore shoulder with his hand. They could hear Wyatt's steady footsteps approaching. The second that he walked around the corner of the building, Kayden stepped out into his path.

Wyatt stopped dead in his tracks and stared, openmouthed, at Kayden.

"Hey, Wyatt," Kayden said with a cocky grin. Chase came up beside Kayden and nodded his head.

Wyatt continued to gawk at them both with a blank stare.

"Aren't you gonna say somethin'?" Kayden asked.

Wyatt found his voice and fearfully replied, "Kayden. What're you doing here, dude? You're supposed to be dead."

"Well, I ain't," Kayden answered mordantly. "No thanks to you and Chase here, burying me up to my eyeballs in dirt."

"Sorry about that, dude," Wyatt replied, and shifted nervously from foot to foot. "We thought you were a goner. Didn't we, Chase?" He turned imploringly to Chase for support.

Chase said nothing, his eyes narrow slits.

Kayden shrugged indifferently. "That doesn't matter now. We're planning to get even with Rurik for what he did to me. You want in?"

Wyatt looked relieved that Kayden didn't seem to be angry, and grinned. "Sure thing."

Kayden's eyes sparked with red and he showed his fangs. "We thought you might want to join our gang."

Wyatt shook his head in disbelief and backed away. "What happened to you?"

Chase smiled. "We're vampires now. It's great. Wait till you try it."

Wyatt's expression was terror struck, and he continued to shake his head while he stepped slowly away from them.

Kayden edged in Wyatt's direction. "Come on, Wyatt. You'll like it. I swear, you ain't never felt this good."

Chase's eyes turned red and started to glow, and he licked his lips with hungry anticipation. He could hear Wyatt's heart pounding and smell his fear…it excited his senses. His mouth watered.

Wyatt spun on his heels and took off down the road, and Chase leaped on top of him and sank his teeth into the back of Wyatt's neck. Wyatt screamed and clawed at the ground in front of him. He pulled up huge handfuls of grass in his desperate attempt to escape the onslaught.

Kayden grabbed Chase by the shoulders, pulled him off of Wyatt, and flung him back several feet. "Get off him! He's my meal!"

Chase careened backward before recovering his footing and glaring. "I'm starving, Kayden...you always get first blood," he complained.

"That's cuz I'm in charge, moron," Kayden answered with disdain.

Wyatt scrambled to his feet with his hand held to his neck. Blood flowed freely out between his fingers. He stumbled, and then turned around and raced up the street. Chase was on him in a second, and they tumbled to the ground again.

Kayden grabbed Chase and pulled him off Wyatt a second time. "Get away from my dinner!" he growled.

"No!" Chase yelled at Kayden with vehemence, "I'm eating first this time!"

They rolled across the pavement consumed with rage, snapping and gnawing at each other. It quickly became apparent that Kayden was far superior in strength. Chase realized his error in attacking Kayden, and started to whimper as Kayden tore into him. "I'm sorry man...don't kill me, Kayden. Please...I was desperate for blood...I lost my cool."

Kayden halted his onslaught and glared down at Chase, who shook cowardly, staring into Kayden's evil countenance. "Don't ever cross me again, Chase. *Next time I will kill you.* You got it?"

Chase nodded wholeheartedly in agreement, absolutely relieved that he wasn't going to be killed.

"I'm…I'm sorry, man. I promise. I won't ever do that again."

Kayden stood up and pulled Chase to his feet, and then glanced around. "Where did my dinner go?" He stared off toward the highway, cursed loudly, and took off running.

Chase watched Kayden race away at tremendous speed, staring at the scene in front of him.

Wyatt had blood running down the entire front of his shirt and soaking his clothes. His eyes were glazed over, and he stumbled blindly toward the highway, staggering into the street. He seemed unaware of the traffic, and stepped off the grass and onto the paved road. For a moment Chase thought that Kayden would reach Wyatt in time. But without warning there was the loud honking of a semi-truck and squealing brakes, followed immediately by a heavy thud, and Wyatt's body took the full force of the blow from the speeding vehicle.

Kayden stopped abruptly, cursing loudly and stomping the ground with his feet several times, watching the semi and Wyatt's body continue for several more yards before they finally came to a stop. Kayden turned disgustedly back to Chase, who had genuine fear on his face when Kayden walked up. Kayden's mouth was a grim line, and his eyes were red with fury.

Chase thought he may die for ruining Kayden's meal plans after all. He stood staring and trembling, waiting for Kayden to say or do something.

Suddenly Kayden grinned and laughed loudly. "I guess Wyatt won't be joining our club after all."

Chase snorted and tried hard to force a laugh, nervous relief washing over his features.

#

I'd been so preoccupied with the hunt for Kayden and Chase, and the concern of my dad finding out, that when my parents came up into my room Friday morning with severe expressions, I was prepared for the worst.

I sat on the end of the bed, waiting with apprehension while they both stood without a word in front of me. I tried to prepare myself for whatever horrible consequences and pain I would endure for breaking several rules of our society. I knew Dad wouldn't make any exceptions for me because I was his son. That would be favoritism, and was frowned upon by the other members. There was a long, heavy silence while we sat and stared into each other's eyes. Just when I thought I couldn't endure the unspoken torture any more, to my shock and amazement they both grinned.

"Rurik," Mom said at long last. "We have a surprise for you downstairs for your birthday."

I was so relieved that I couldn't stop myself from breathing a huge sigh, laughing shakily. "I thought I was in trouble, the way you two were staring at me." It had been so crazy lately that I'd totally forgotten about my birthday.

"Sorry about that," Dad replied. "We were just building the suspense."

I followed them down the stairs and to the front entry.

Dad grinned broadly and said, "Open the door."

I opened it. Sitting under the covered porch was a brand new Camaro! And it was my favorite colors, black with a red racing stripe down the middle.

"For real? It's for me?!"

Both nodded enthusiastically, and Dad handed me keys. "We knew you'd want to drive it to school today and show off."

I went out, opened the driver's door, and sat in the seat, running my hands over the dashboard and the instrument panel. It had a very impressive stereo system, and the interior was black leather. I was thrilled. "Thanks, Mom and Dad," I grinned. "This car rocks."

Dad turned to me with a serious expression. "I realize with your fast reflexes you'll want to speed, but don't try it. If you get a ticket, the car will be taken away. Is that understood?"

I nodded enthusiastically.

"We mean it Rurik," Mom reiterated. "No speeding."

"All right, Mom, I know." I resisted the urge to say, "I heard you the first time, it's not like I'm a two year old." But, I didn't want to ruin the moment with a smart mouth remark, so I bit my tongue and kept quiet.

I left early for school that morning, anticipating showing off my new car to Mindy. When I pulled up in front of the school she was just getting off the bus. I honked the horn and waved. When she turned around, at first she didn't recognize it was me, but then her eyes flew open wide and she ran over.

I lowered the passenger window. "Hi," I grinned.

"Wow! This is sick!" Mindy exclaimed, looking the car over inside and out.

"Get in," I said. "I'll take you for a ride. It's still fifteen minutes till school starts."

"Okay," she exclaimed, and hopped into the passenger seat beside me.

Dad and Mom were right, it was so tempting to speed when I took off with Mindy by my side. I had to really resist the urge. I pulled back into the student parking lot, parked, and beamed at Mindy. "What do you think?"

Her green eyes sparkled. "It's a beautiful car, Rurik."

"Now we'll have a little more freedom…to go places and be alone together." I leaned toward her and gently kissed her soft lips.

She blushed slightly. "Do you think you can come over tomorrow night? I have a gift for you…for your birthday too."

"I'll find a way to sneak out."

She smiled and put her arms around my neck. "I truly do love you."

"I love you too, Mindy." We gazed into each other's eyes, and I could feel her being captivated by my trance. The sensation was amazing, and I couldn't seem to resist drawing her in. This beautiful, fragile creature sitting next to me really loved me.

The school bell rang and brought us out of our daze. I glanced toward the school. "We'd better get to class."

I hopped out, came around, and opened Mindy's door for her. She smiled; I could tell she appreciated the chivalry.

We parted ways at the front entrance. "See you third period," I said.

Kayden and Chase were waiting for me when I entered the locker room to change for gym class. They had a cocky, confident attitude, and I couldn't help feeling they were up to something.

"Hey, Rurik," Kayden glowered.

"You know," I had to say while I slipped my gym clothes on. "You can't avoid a confrontation with me forever, guys. It'll eventually happen."

Kayden's eyes were evil black slits. "I'm not avoiding anything. I'm just choosing the time and the place that I will take you down and make Mindy mine."

I glared back at him. "You just don't know when you're being rejected, do you, Kayden? She doesn't want anything to do with you."

He shrugged. "That doesn't matter. She'll be mine and will learn to love me."

"You're delusional." I shook my head disgustedly and walked out into the gym with the rest of the class.

#

At lunch when Mindy and I entered the cafeteria, I could immediately sense Amy's anxiety. She shifted her eyes to a large table in the corner, where Kayden was standing and talking loudly, Chase standing beside him. But what was alarming was that there were four other students sitting at the table also. It was evident to Amy and me that those four other students were vampires. Two of them were boys I'd seen around campus, Bret and Ryan. The other two caught me by surprise.

Oliver, the nerdy kid they'd been taunting the other day, was standing at the other end looking completely confident and full of himself. He was no longer wearing glasses, and his hair was parted on the side, instead of the middle, changing the entire shape of his face. He actually wasn't bad looking.

The other one, to my shock and dismay, was Tiffany. Her eyes bore into mine while she sat in the chair next to Kayden, and I could see real hate in them. I could tell she wanted to get even with me for using and then dumping her. Kayden glanced my direction and saw the exchange between Tiffany and me. He leaned down, pulling Tiffany brusquely to himself. He kissed her and glared back at me, his eyes sparking with fiery embers.

Tiffany didn't protest at all, but I could tell she was just tolerating Kayden's advances because she didn't have any choice. She sat there with no real emotion in her eyes while he casually sat beside her and draped his arm over her shoulder. I couldn't help feeling a little sorry for her.

I stood in line with Mindy, got lunch, and then we walked over to our table. I sat next to Amy to talk, with Mindy seated on my other side. Kaylee, Daniel, and Luke were across the table, and seemed deep in conversation at the moment.

Amy leaned over and whispered, "What're we going to do…there's six of them already? It's only been a week."

"I don't know. This is getting out of hand. We have to destroy them or they're going to take over this whole town."

Mindy overheard our conversation. "Six what?" she asked, and then saw us glancing at the table on the other side of the lunchroom. Recognition came into her eyes, and her face paled. "Oh…they're all…?"

I nodded to her, and put my hand over hers at the fearful expression that went across her features.

"We have to tell your father," Amy hissed.

"Are you crazy?!" I practically shouted. People turned and stared, so I lowered my voice and continued softly, "*He will literally kill us.* That is not an option."

Amy looked indignant. "You're just worried about what will happen to Mindy if your dad finds out."

I gave her a dirty look. "You know as well as I what the rules and the punishments are. There's no way we can go to my parents!"

"We can't take on six. There are too many of them, even if we are stronger."

"There's no choice. Period." I gave her a look that clearly said going to Dad was never going to happen. We finished our food without another word about it. I could see the worry in Amy's eyes, and I couldn't blame her. I was having a hard time dealing with the thought of taking on six vampires myself.

#

Saturday morning my cell phone rang, and it was a number that I didn't recognize. "Hello?"

There was silence for a moment, and then I heard, "Hi, Rurik. It's Tiffany."

"Oh, hi Tiffany," I responded cautiously.

"Um…," she started, and then paused.

I heard Kayden yell in the background. "Tell him!"

"Um…,"she said again. "Kayden wants you to meet us at the school parking lot at one Monday morning. Okay?"

"All right. We'll be there."

I closed my phone. Kayden was confident that he had enough cohorts to take us on now. It would be two to six, but what they didn't realize was that Amy and I were the strongest, the fastest of our kind. It wasn't going to be as lopsided of a fight as he was hoping.

#

I didn't get a chance to sneak out till after one in the morning Sunday. I knew Mindy was probably anxious about whether I was going to make it. I had my doubts too, as Dad went over the monthly meeting for our area that I was required to attend with all of the local vampires. It seemed to go on and on, while I sat there trying hard not to glance at the time on my phone every couple of minutes. Once the meeting was finally over and everyone was mingling and chatting, I made my excuse of homework and left.

It was such a relief when I was at Mindy's door knocking. There were a few moments of silence, and I was just getting ready to knock again when I heard her soft footsteps approaching. She removed the deadbolt and slowly opened it. I stared with surprise; she bashfully gazed back into my eyes. She looked like she'd fallen asleep and was still trying to wake up. Her hair was slightly disheveled, and she rubbed her eyes sleepily. But that wasn't what caught my attention. What she was wearing did.

An exquisitely beautiful white silk flowing nightgown, with lace and small pink rosebuds around the swooping neckline, the sleeves a delicate stitching of flowers that intertwined along the full length of her arms. The garment was covered with a sheer fabric and Mindy wore the most delectable honey and vanilla scent imaginable. She was captivating.

I took a deep breath while she stood there gazing up into my face, her eyes soft and questioning at the same time.

I stepped into her house and closed the door behind us. "You're absolutely stunning, Mindy. Amy has nothing on you."

She smiled and blushed at my words.

"What is all this?" I asked softly. I put my arms around her waist and stared down into her face.

She was flushed with excitement, and I could hear her heart nervously beating in her chest. "It's my birthday present to you," she almost whispered. "I...I want you to make love to me."

My breath caught, staring into her dazzling emerald eyes. I lightly clasped her hands and led her down the hall to her bedroom. We sat on the edge of the bed and I looked tenderly into her face. She was gorgeous, and all of my senses flamed with desire. I could tell she was more than nervous; her heart beat wildly, and her breath came in short gasps when I leaned in and very gently kissed her lips. I lay her back against the pillows, and stroked her face and hair softly with my fingertips as she looked up into my eyes.

She was trembling with excitement and fear. Fear of the unknown, and fear of what I was. I wanted her desperately. The thought was almost unbearable, but I took a deep breath and said quietly, "I really think we should wait."

Complete surprise crossed her features. Then she recovered enough to ask, "Why?" with a look of confusion.

I sighed and gently caressed her face and shoulders, letting my fingertips run soothingly across her arms while she quivered at my touch. It was almost torture to have her lying there under me so vulnerable, and easily mine. I had to take a deep breath to steady my own nerves. "I...just don't think you're really ready for this. I don't want to rush you."

Her expression was relieved, but hurt at the same time. She blinked her eyes rapidly, and I could see her trying to hold back the tears. "Don't you want to?" she finally asked.

"Believe me, I want you more than anything in the world right now. I'm having a very hard time restraining. You're too beautiful for words."

"I...I don't understand," she said quietly.

I sighed. "This is a very big step, and I think you're just trying to give me what you think I want, rather than what's right for you. I know it's been hard for you with me spending so much time with Amy lately." I paused. "What you're willing to give to me is also very precious. I just don't want to see you offering yourself for the wrong reasons." I couldn't believe that I was sitting there, with this lovely creature willing to let me take her, and I was trying to talk her out of it.

It was an amazing revelation. I realized as I stared into her sweet face, her lying there totally vulnerable to me, that this was what true love was all about, wholly unselfish acts. She was willing to give herself to me completely because she loved me. And I was trying to talk her out of it, because in my heart I knew she wasn't ready. Each of us wanted to do the unselfish and loving thing in the relationship. The love I felt for her at that moment was the most overpowering emotion I could ever remember experiencing.

I scooped her into my arms and held her for a long time. It was unbelievably moving. We kissed and cuddled for hours. I could tell she was relieved that it went no further than that. And I was amazed at the restraint I was able to maintain with her soft, warm body in my embrace.

Complete and selfless love is a powerful motivator. She curled up in my embrace and drifted off to sleep. I gazed down at her with amazement and wonder that this precious, delicate human had chosen me, out of all others, to give her heart to. The feelings of protectiveness and adoration I felt for her were unequaled.

#

All day on Sunday I was uneasy. I tried to tell myself that Amy and I were far more powerful beings, but two against six was still steep odds. And we were only teenagers, just starting to realize our potentials and places in this society. We knew the prophecies about us, that we were the new super-race of vampires that had been prophesied about centuries earlier, greater than vampire or slayer. But neither of us could bring ourselves to be totally confident about what was going to transpire in a few hours.

Mindy desperately wanted to come with us…she felt somewhat responsible for the whole situation. Amy and I sat at her house while we waited till it was time to meet with Kayden and the others.

"Mindy, it'll be way too dangerous for you," I tried to reason.

"I'm going to go crazy sitting around here wondering if you and Amy are okay. I need to be there," she said earnestly.

"You're a fragile human, and could easily get in the crossfire and be killed."

Her eyes filled with tears, and she got to her feet determinedly and crossed her arms. "You can't make me stay here…I'm going."

I turned to Amy with frustration. "Will you please help me explain this to her?"

"Rurik's right, Mindy," Amy stated. "You'd just be in the way. If you go he's more likely to get hurt worrying about you. You need to stay here."

That seemed to make sense to Mindy. "Oh," she reluctantly agreed. "I just wish I could be more help."

I put my arms around her and held her. "It'll be a help knowing that you're safe here. "

She sighed with resignation and nodded.

It was about time to leave, and I tenderly kissed her lips and then had to pull her arms from around my neck and sit her down on the couch. I looked gently into her sad expression. "I'll be fine. I promise."

Amy and I turned without another word and left her house.

Neither of us said a thing on the way to the school; there wasn't anything important to talk about at the moment while we concentrated on the coming events. When we pulled into the parking lot, it was deserted except for a couple of vehicles down at the opposite end. I recognized the pickup immediately as Chase's…he drove it to school regularly. I assumed the small car next to it was Kayden's, because he was sitting on the front hood with Tiffany standing next to his side and Bret and Ryan by the passenger door. I pulled up and parked across the lot, about fifty yards away.

Chase and Oliver got out of the pickup and walked over to where Kayden and the others were waiting.

Amy and I stepped out of my Camaro and watchfully approached the group. We stopped about ten yards away, and we all stared warily at one another without a word for a few minutes.

Kayden's eyes glinted and he slid off the front of the truck. "Tallinn," he started. "You're way outnumbered. If you want to give in now, I'll kill you quickly." He looked in Amy's direction eagerly and continued. "I'm not promising the same for your friend here. I've had my eye on her since the first day she showed up at school."

Amy glared at him angrily and her eyes started to flame. "All you'll ever get of me is my teeth on your throat as I rip you in half, you jerk."

I turned to Tiffany. "You don't have to stay with them, Tiffany. You can come over here with us."

She laughed at me and then said with contempt, "I'm looking forward to Kayden killing you, Rurik. Ever since you dumped me for that tramp Mindy."

I stiffened angrily. "Mindy is not a tramp, which unfortunately is more than I can say for you."

She glared at me with anger and her eyes blazed.

"Enough chit chat," Kayden said. He growled and bared his fangs while he and I circled each other.

I was suddenly side swiped by Brett, and I turned to him, snarling. Brett lunged in my direction again, but this time I was prepared. I had faster reflexes than any other vampire except maybe Amy, and I jumped forward and grabbed his throat with my teeth, pushing him down to the ground. He screamed and howled, and tried with desperation to escape. With one swift move I tore his throat out and went after Chase, who was quickly backing away.

Tiffany shrieked, and I turned in their direction just in time to see Amy hit her with such force that Tiffany's head was torn completely off her body. Tiffany's head flew in one direction, while her body twisted horribly and collapsed to the ground. I swiveled with super human speed back at Chase to continue my pursuit, and noticed that Kayden, Oliver, and Ryan were retreating in Kayden's car.

Chase looked absolutely desperate at the thought that they had all deserted him. His face was full of fear, and he slowly backed away. Amy came up to stand beside me, while Chase continued his retreat and shook his head.

"Don't kill me. I don't want to die," he pleaded.

Amy laughed cruelly. "You should have thought of that before you took up with Kayden." Then she leaped on him in an instant. It was amazing how fast she moved. I didn't think Chase even saw her coming until he was flat on his back with her on top of him.

He looked angrily into her face and roared, mistakenly thinking that because she was female that he was more powerful. He smiled with malice and flipped her over in one swift move, then lowered his fangs to her throat.

Amy pushed violently against his body with hers and flung him backwards. It took her only about a half a second to get to her feet and jump on top of him, while he was still trying to comprehend how he ended up flat on his back again. In the next instant Chase was dead on the pavement. It was impressive.

Amy stood up from Chase's body and wiped her face with her hand, and then straightened her dress. She smiled and smoothed her hair back into place.

I had to grin. "Remind me never to piss you off." I looked down the road where Kayden and the others had disappeared to, and sighed. They were long gone, and would no doubt hide out and lick their wounds before returning to fight again.

I dropped Amy off at her house and then headed over to Mindy's. I wanted to see her before I went home to reassure her that we were fine.

Amy and I decided the best thing to do was to leave the bodies and the car where they were in the parking lot. It resembled the aftermath of a gang fight, and with Kayden running away, he would most likely be the prime suspect.

When I arrived at Mindy's house she answered the door and leapt into my arms.

"I was so worried about you." She looked up into my face with concern and tears.

I brushed her tears away and sighed with exasperation. "We only got half of them. Kayden, Oliver, and Ryan ran off."

"What are you going to do now?" she asked.

I shook my head. It was a quandary. I couldn't tell Dad and Mom because of the dire consequences to all of us, even though I knew that they could handle the situation efficiently. The whole mess just kept spiraling out of control.

By the time I got back to my house, I was exhausted. I didn't need very much sleep usually, but I'd been exerting extra energy physically and emotionally for days. I crashed in my bed and didn't wake until Mom was shaking me hours later.

"Rurik, wake up. You're going to be late for school if you don't get with it."

I groaned and rolled over to look at the clock. "Thanks for waking me, Mom. I guess I must have needed some sleep."

She smiled. "Your body is growing and changing so much right now, it's no wonder."

I was sitting at the table eating a quick bowl of cereal when Dad walked into the kitchen. His entire countenance was reverberating with rage he was trying hard to control. Mom was following him, and she looked absolutely horrified.

I stopped with the spoon to my mouth and froze. I knew the shit was about to hit the fan, and that I was that shit.

Chapter Six
Repercussions

Dad walked up to me and stared down into my eyes. His were darker than the blackest night. He said nothing for a moment, and then in a much calmer tone than I was expecting asked, "Busy night?"

I knew that he knew at this point, but admitting it to his face was paramount to saying, "Go ahead and torture and kill me, I deserve it." I still felt justified in my mind for acting the way I had, no matter how wrong it was. So I slowly lowered my spoon to the bowl, tried not to look too terrified, and asked, "What are you talking about, Dad?"

He'd been holding a newspaper in his hand, and in the next instant, his eyes glowed red. He slammed the newspaper down in front of me with such force that the sound echoed around the kitchen, and with so much power that the bowl of cereal in front of me jumped off the table and shattered on the floor.

I instinctively shrank back, and Mom leaped forward protectively.

"Adrian!" she almost shouted. There was real fear in her eyes, and I could tell that she was afraid for me.

Dad turned to her, his eyes still glowing, his brow furiously creased, and yelled, "Carmen, stay out of this! You're not objective right now!"

She backed up a few steps, but her eyes were sparking with anger. "Neither are you," she said very quietly.

Dad stared into her face for a moment, took a deep breath, and nodded his head. Then he turned to me, slightly calmer. "You'd better start explaining, and it better be good." He pointed to the picture on the front page.

The caption read in huge black bold letters, 'Gangs at Local High School?' There was an almost full page picture of the school parking lot with the bodies covered in plastic, Chase's pickup in the background…the exact scene that Amy and I'd left early that morning. I stared down at the picture for several moments without a word.

Dad finally sighed and said in a quiet tone, "You can't deny this, Rurik. One body had the head completely torn off, the other the throat ripped out. There's mention of weird cult drinking rituals, because none of the bodies seemed to have blood in them…probably because they were already vampires." He paused for a moment. "Am I right in my assumptions?"

I looked up into Dad's eyes and slowly nodded my head in agreement. I guess that was the wrong thing to do, because he was instantly over the table and had me against the wall, with his hands on my shoulders staring angrily into my face.

I tried really hard not to cower.

I could hear Mom gasp behind him. "Please Adrian, don't do something you're going to regret later."

"Carmen, I don't need your comments right now," Dad said, never taking his eyes off of mine. I'd never seen Dad angrier about anything. He grabbed me around the shirt collar and hauled me out of the kitchen and down the hall.

I knew where we were going, to the dungeon. We'd had prisoners in there on many occasions over the years. I didn't fight Dad at all. In actuality, I could have beaten him…I was stronger and faster. But he was my dad, and even though I couldn't have done anything differently than I did, I knew that he was also right.

He practically dragged me down the winding stairs and then over to the cell, where he flung me in with such force that I hit the wall on the other side. Then he closed the jail door and stormed up the stairs.

I sat on the bench for hours and no one came back down. I was worried about what Dad was thinking, what he was planning to do with me. I was concerned about Amy and the way I'd involved her in this…she'd only helped me because she liked me. I felt bad now for dragging her into everything. But I was terrified for Mindy. She was probably the most innocent victim in all of this, but she was probably the one who would pay the stiffest penalties, because she was an outsider. I paced back and forth. The waiting was torture…I needed to know what was happening.

Finally, after several hours, Dad and Mom came back down into the dungeon. Mom looked incredibly sad, and Dad was still beyond furious. He walked over and sat on the bench in front of my cell and sighed. "Okay, Rurik. Tell me what happened. And if you leave anything out…and I mean anything…it'll be much worse for you and everyone else involved than if you just come clean right now."

I sat silently for a few moments. I was still desperate to protect Mindy, but everything ultimately revolved around her. I knew I couldn't even begin to explain without bringing her into this.

I took a deep breath. "I just want to start with saying that I'm sorry about how out of control this whole thing got. I…had good intentions when I started, and then everything got all screwed up." I paused and nervously brushed my long bangs from my face, glanced at Mom, then back to Dad. I said earnestly, "Please consider the innocents that were dragged into this. I'm the one to blame for all of it, not them."

Dad's eyes narrowed and he said, "I'm listening."

I sighed. "It all started with Kayden attacking Mindy."

Dad's eyes blackened, but he kept silent and nodded for me to continue.

"He…he tried to rape her. I had to take care of him…I knew he would come back and attempt it again."

"Didn't it occur to you to let the humans handle it? They have laws too, and you needn't have gotten involved."

"No," I said defensively. "You know what that would all entail. Their messed up protect the perpetrator laws. Mindy would've been put through more than she already was, and Kayden would probably have gotten out on probation and tried to retaliate. Then if everything finally managed to go to trial somewhere off in the distant future, he would get a few years in jail and then be out on parole. Basically free to torment Mindy forever. How can you say I should've left it to them?!"

"Mindy is human, and none of your business, Rurik!"

"She's a wonderful, sweet girl, Dad, and just needed a little help."

"So," he said quietly. "You have appointed yourself her protector and helper?"

I stared back at him defiantly without a word. Dad looked into my eyes; he knew…he could tell that I loved Mindy.

"Okay," he said quietly. "What happened next?"

I cringed. This is where it got sticky. All of our lives could hinge on what and how I said the next part. I took a deep breath. "When I got to Mindy's, there was blood everywhere. She'd clobbered Kayden good and he left."

Dad looked like he was impressed with Mindy for that part.

"Um, I caught up with Kayden in an alley. I…I drained him, but…." I stopped apprehensively.

"Go ahead," he said almost gently.

I swallowed anxiously and continued. "Mindy followed the blood trail and found us. She was worried about me, didn't want me to get hurt…or do something stupid."

He sighed. "It's way too late for that."

I frowned. "She saw me with Kayden. She was terrified and ran off. I had to stop her, so I followed after her to calm her down and took her back to her house. But…when I returned to take care of Kayden, the body was gone. I guess his friends found him." I sighed. "He made several students vampires, and Amy and I met them last night to fight."

Dad continued to stare at me for a moment, and then put his head in his hands, closed his eyes, and groaned loudly.

"I just want to say that Amy wanted me to tell you. I wouldn't let her. Don't be too hard on her…she was just trying to help me."

I sat and held my breath while I waited for him to say something. It seemed an eternity, all of our lives held in the balance, while he digested and mulled it over. Finally he looked up into my face, and I didn't like what I saw. His expression was cold, emotionless, and all-business. He would do what needed to be done in the situation, as unfortunate as it might be to everyone involved.

"Dad, please," I said with earnest. "This is all my fault. Don't punish Amy or Mindy. Do anything to me you have to. I take full responsibility." I was desperate, staring at his ominous features.

He stood up, deep in thought. "The paper said that Kayden, Oliver, and Ryan were the prime suspects, so at least the finger hasn't pointed this direction. Yet." He turned to Mom. "I'm going to need your help to hunt down Kayden and the others. Obviously they'll need to be taken care of with no trace ever being found."

Mom nodded; she was the society's most lethal weapon. When she became a vampire, her slayer abilities had only been enhanced. She could kick some serious vampire butt when she needed to.

Dad looked in my direction again. "Mindy's mom works nights?"

I swallowed and nodded uneasily.

"Okay, you're going to call Mindy and tell her you'll be over tonight. We'll wait until then to pick her up…when no one else will be around to witness it."

"What're you going to do with her?!" I couldn't help asking with alarm.

Dad stared at me thoughtfully, with very little emotion. "I don't know yet. She's an outsider and has too much knowledge of our society. There are serious risks there."

"Dad," I said, trying to keep the fear out of my voice. "She won't ever say anything to anyone, I swear."

"You don't know that, and you can't promise it, Rurik."

"I know her!" I practically shouted.

His eyes narrowed, and the look he gave me chilled me to the bone. "None of this would have happened if you had stayed away from Mindy like I told you to."

"At least let me go with you when you pick her up. She's going to be terrified," I begged. "Please, Dad."

"I don't know, I'll think about it." Then he turned around and left the room.

Mom stood and looked at me sympathetically. "I'm sorry, Rurik. I know how much you love Mindy."

"Mom, promise you won't let Dad hurt her. If I never see her again, I can live with it. As long as she's okay." My eyes filled with tears.

Mom shook her head. "I can't promise you something I have no control over." She stared compassionately at me for a moment, and then turned and walked silently out of the room and up the stairs.

I sank back down on the bench. I was very afraid for Mindy. Amy would pay the penalty…but Mindy may die.

#

When Adrian arrived at Mindy's house with a couple of other vampires and knocked on her door, Mindy immediately answered. She smiled widely, expecting to see Rurik, and had surprise on her face that quickly turned to concern as she stared back at Adrian. His eyes were black and menacing, and he wasn't smiling.

"Where's Rurik?" Mindy asked in a small voice. Her heart was starting to nervously pound and she couldn't keep the fear out of her eyes. She knew that Rurik's dad, the ruler of the vampire society, standing at her door with two other vampires, without Rurik, wasn't a good thing.

Adrian's eyes tightened slightly. He was still very angry, but he did feel sorry for this fragile girl standing in front of him. "I need you to come with me, Mindy. You can see Rurik when you get to our house."

Mindy swallowed uneasily. "Is anything wrong?" Then almost with panic, she pleaded, "Rurik isn't hurt, is he?!"

"No, Rurik is fine. But there are some issues that I need to discuss with you and him."

Mindy's heart was pounding in her chest. She didn't want to go anywhere with these vampires, but she also realized that she didn't have a choice. The look in Adrian's eyes told her that this was not a request. "Okay. Can I get my purse and keys?"

Adrian nodded and stepped into the living room with her.

Mindy walked timidly down the hall and came back with the items in hand. She closed and locked the door behind her, and they went over to Adrian's black Audi.

He got in the front to drive, and one of the vampires took Mindy's arm and guided her into the backseat between them. Adrian watched Mindy through the rearview mirror as he drove. He couldn't help having sympathy for her as she sat there with wide eyes full of fear. She almost looked like she was going to burst into tears at any moment.

Once they got to the house, Adrian directed Mindy to the hall by the kitchen and opened the door that led down to the dungeon. He held it to the side, and gestured for Mindy to go in front of him.

"Is Rurik in here?" Mindy asked fearfully.

Adrian nodded his head.

Mindy stepped into the dark, damp hallway and looked around. The walls were old, with rotten plaster hanging in only a few places still. There were small sconces on the murky stone walls with flickering lights in them. She moved anxiously forward while Adrian followed close behind. She was rapidly becoming terrified…this looked like the creepy secret passageway of a castle. If there had been anywhere to run to, she would have. When she came to some stairs, she hesitated and stared down at the dark descending pathway.

"Go ahead, Mindy," Adrian said, almost gently. "Rurik is down there."

She took a deep breath to calm her nerves and headed down the twisting, stone stairs. They descended further and further into the gloomy cavern. When she got to the bottom, it opened up to a large room with tables on one side and jail cells along another. That's when she saw Rurik…he was in one of the jail cells staring in her direction.

#

I heard soft footsteps coming down the stairs to the dungeon and waited. Mindy stepped into the room, followed closely by Dad. Her face was full of fear and her eyes wide.

I stood up and went quickly over to the cell door. "Mindy!"

Mindy ran over, put her hand in, and took mine. "What's going on, Rurik?" she asked in a small, frightened voice.

I stared with trepidation behind her at Dad.

His eyes were very dark and angry still, and his jaw was clenched. He opened the cell door and took Mindy's arm. She looked terrified when he directed her into the cell with me, and then walked out and shut the door behind us.

I put my arms around Mindy and held her next to me. "It's okay, Mindy," I said reassuringly. Then I turned to Dad. "What are you going to do with us?"

To my surprise Dad appeared to be in turmoil. I could tell he was anguishing over his responsibility as the ruler of this country. He shook his head. "You've broken some very serious laws. There needs to be consequences."

I held my arms tightly around Mindy who was now trembling. "I know that. I take full responsibility. Just don't punish Mindy for what I decided to do."

He didn't say anything for a moment and then sighed, his eyes as black as coals. "I'll give you five minutes alone together, and then you'll never see each other again. Ever! Is that clear?"

Mindy gasped and turned to me with sadness, tears running down her cheeks.

"Dad," I tried to protest. "Please don't do this. We love each other."

"Stop it, Rurik! You have other plans for your future. I'm sorry, but you have no choice in this." His eyes were menacing. "I'll be back in five minutes."

Then he turned around and walked out of the room and up the stairs.

I looked into Mindy's face, so sad, so heartbroken. My heart was breaking too. I loved her with everything in me. I put my hands on both sides of her face, brushing away the tears streaming down her cheeks.

"I love you more than anything, Mindy." I leaned down and gently kissed her soft sweet lips. Then I pulled back again, staring at her closely. "I promise that someday we will be together again. Okay?" I didn't know if it was true, but I had to say that to her, to give her hope.

She nodded and tried to smile at me. Her lower lip quivered, her expression crushed. I gently caressed her face and hair. I sighed and brought my lips to hers and kissed her, wrapping my arms around her warm body and pulling her as close as possible. She held onto me tightly and we fervently embraced.

It was the last kiss of two souls whose lives had become intertwined at the heart, who were to be shortly torn apart, leaving a gaping hole in both of our lives. My last moment of happiness, because I knew that without Mindy, I would never be the same, never again be truly happy.

I drew back and looked into her face. Her eyes were soft and smoldering from our kiss and final embrace. I gently bent down and ran my lips over every inch of her face, lightly caressing her skin. She sighed with the ecstasy of our tender love and the agony of our last goodbye.

"I love you so much, Mindy," I whispered into her ear.

"I love you too, Rurik," she answered. "Always."

Then I heard Mom and Dad coming back down the stairs, and they entered the room.   They walked over and opened the cell door.

Mindy glanced at them and then turned to me with panic. She put her arms around me, desperate to stay here, to hold on to our final moment together. "No," she said miserably.

Mom looked incredibly sad, walked over, and took Mindy's arm. "Time to go, Mindy."

Mindy was almost frantic. "No." She turned to me with a pleading look. "Rurik?"

My heart was breaking. This delicate being cherished me so much, but didn't belong in our world and now was going to pay the penalty for having loved me.

My eyes filled with tears. "It's okay, Mindy. I love you."

But she wouldn't let go…Mom had to physically pull her off my arm. Mindy sobbed uncontrollably as Mom dragged her out of the cell and toward the stairs. "Rurik!" she cried, and looked my direction one last time, sadness, despair, and utter hopelessness written in her expression, before Mom towed her out of the room.

I wondered if that would be the last time I ever saw her. If the panicked look on her face would be my final memory of her. "I love you, Mindy!" I shouted one more time, and then sank down onto the bench, completely inconsolable. I put my head in my hands and cried.

After several minutes, I lifted my face to Dad, who was still standing there. His eyes looked pained gazing down into mine, although there was still so much anger in them.

"What are you going to do with her?" I asked wretchedly. "None of this is her fault."

His eyes narrowed and he took a slow breath. "No, you're right. It's yours, and you are going to have to live with your decisions, Rurik. Grow up faster than you were expecting to have to. I told you from the beginning to stay away from Mindy. Your future is with Amy."

"Please…*please don't kill her*."

He stared at me for several moments, and then without a word turned and left the room.

#

Carmen firmly held onto Mindy's arm and pulled her up the stairs. She felt sorry for the poor girl, who sobbed miserably the entire way. When they got to the top, she directed Mindy to the sitting room by the kitchen and sat her on the sofa beside her with a box of tissues while she waited for Adrian. She put her arm around Mindy's shoulder and held her next to her side while the girl shook and cried.

Finally, as Mindy was getting over her hysterics, Adrian walked in.

Carmen braced herself. She knew the laws about humans with knowledge of their society, and what Adrian was required to do no matter what his personal feelings were.

#

When Adrian stepped into the sitting room his eyes were black, and he was very angry. This entire situation could have been prevented if Rurik had just done what he was told to. Mindy sat on the sofa next to Carmen, and he could see that she was terrified and trembling, staring at him with wide eyes. She looked like a deer facing a mountain lion. She'd stopped crying but her eyes were red and puffy, and she clutched a wad of tissues in her hand.

This was one of those situations where he dreaded being in charge of the country, wished he could trade places with anyone right now. A no win situation for everyone involved. He sighed and sat down in the chair across from them. Carmen had an anxious expression, and he could tell that Mindy had gotten under her skin too.

He turned his attention back to Mindy. "Mindy, I'm sorry for everything you got dragged into. I should have trusted my instincts and not allowed Rurik to ever attend a public school." He paused for a moment. "But that is all water under the bridge. The problem is what to do with you now." He lowered his head into his hands and closed his eyes for a moment, and let out a long, deep sigh. Mindy and Carmen stared at him while he sat there saying nothing for several moments. Then he raised his head again to look at them, his eyes coal black and intimidating.

"The law says that you have to die," Adrian said in a deadly tone.

Mindy shrank back in her seat with absolute terror.

"She's just a child," Carmen couldn't help saying.

Adrian turned his furious expression on her. "I realize that!" He cursed under his breath. "This whole situation is such a mess! Too many students have died already!" He looked at Mindy and she was shaking uncontrollably now, staring at him, petrified. He stood up, leaned over, and took Mindy by the arms, and lifted her to her feet until she was only inches from his face. She was too frightened to even cry as she stared back into his frightening visage with wide eyes, took small gasping breaths, and cowered under his grasp. He knew his expression was terrifying. He wanted her to see his horrible vampire side to its full extent.

"I don't know why, but I feel compelled to let you live," Adrian said slowly and carefully.

Mindy went limp with relief. He could hear Carmen let out a breath, and he glanced in her direction. She was looking back into his eyes with surprise. Then he turned all the fury he felt over the whole situation toward Mindy again. "You can never see Rurik or any of us again. And you can never say anything about our society to anyone. Ever! Is that clearly understood?!"

Mindy weakly nodded her head in response…there was no way she could talk right now.

"I mean it, Mindy," Adrian continued in a harsh tone. "If there is ever any question, you will be hunted down and killed. This is your one and only reprieve. Which is more than most humans who have been unfortunate enough to come across our paths get." He stared into her face with a threatening expression for several moments before he turned to Carmen.

"Help Mindy get herself together and take her back to her house. Then you need to organize a few hunters to go with you and eliminate Kayden and the other two. I have to deal with Rurik, which I'm dreading…he has to be severely punished." He looked at Mindy one last time. "Do your best to forget that you ever met any of us, Mindy." Then he smiled grimly at her and turned and left the room.

\#

I sat on the bench in the jail cell in total despair and shock. I didn't want to go on without Mindy. The thought of what was probably happening up there was more than I could bear…the horror, fear, and pain that I was sure Mindy was going through right now. I knew this was all my doing, that I was to blame for her dying. The girl I loved more than life itself. If there had been any way to end my life at that moment I would have. The agony was intolerable.

I heard Dad coming down the stairs, and sat where I was and waited. He stepped into the room and his eyes were dark and angry, beyond anything I'd ever seen. I stared despondently back at him, just waiting for him to say the dreaded words, the ones that would turn my heart to cold, unfeeling stone and stop it from ever beating again.

He sighed. "I let Mindy go. I told her in no uncertain terms if she ever caused any problems, she would be hunted down and killed."

I felt I would pass out as a wave of total relief washed over me. She was alive! "Thank you, Dad," I said in a whisper. "I can never thank you enough."

His eyes were torrents and his jaw was clenched. "You, however, are going to be punished to the fullest extent of the law, Rurik…. Do you understand me?"

My joy at Mindy's survival was short lived at his words. I knew I was about to endure horrible consequences and pain. I nodded my head and looked back into his face soberly and with fear. Nothing in this world was as frightening as my dad could be when he was mad, and right now he was so far beyond that, there weren't words to describe it.

"Three students are dead because of you, and three more will be shortly! Six! Do you comprehend that? You could have ripped our entire society in two with your disobedience. Luckily the evidence didn't point in this direction and can be covered up as gang violence." He sighed. "I know I'm not supposed to show any favoritism, but if you weren't my son, you would die for this." He was so angry he paced back and forth in front of the cell while he talked. "You're not ever going to public school again, or having any contact with any outsiders until your mother and I have real evidence that you've learned your lesson and can be trusted. Is all of this clearly understood?!"

I nodded my head, too afraid to speak. I was shaking with fear.

"All right," he continued furiously, and walked over to the other side of the room and took a large whip off the wall. "Take your shirt off...I have no choice but to flog you."

#

I lay up on my bed in agony, my back raw. Dad had shown me no mercy, and I couldn't say that I blamed him. He was right. All of this was my fault...the six dead students and Mindy being totally heartbroken. I almost wished the punishment had been worse for me with all of the sorrow I'd caused everyone. The pain was severe and I couldn't help writhing, but my body would be completely healed shortly. Most vampires took a couple of days to heal from their wounds; mine and Amy's bodies only took hours, benefits of the new improved model. It hardly seemed fair with the grief I'd caused everyone else. I was sure that was part of the reason Dad had been so harsh with me.

But the anguish I felt in my heart wouldn't go away, the total despair of never seeing Mindy again. At least she was alive; I could be thankful for that. No matter what Dad did to me, I couldn't hate him for letting Mindy live.

Carmen pulled into the truck stop on the outskirts of town with the two vampire hunters. Their contact had told them that a credit card in Kayden's dad's name was used here to buy gas. She went inside while the others waited in the vehicle.

Carmen smiled at the woman behind the counter. "Hi, I'm trying to find my nephew. He's sixteen and ran away from home. We were told he used a credit card that belongs to my brother-in-law to buy gas here. My sister is sick about the whole thing."

The woman looked back at her with compassion, "What did he look like?"

"Well, he's large, six foot, with blond hair and dark brown eyes. He has a couple of friends with him too. Two boys, one has brown hair with blue eyes, and the other is Hispanic."

"Oh, I remember them. They seemed like they were up to no good."

"Did they say anything you might remember about where they were heading, or the direction they went when they left here?"

"Well, two of them left in the car and went south from here, down that dirt road, that's all I know. The big guy…um…your nephew, got into a truck cab."

Carmen frowned. It wasn't good that they were clever enough to split up. "Which way did the truck head?"

The woman shrugged. "Sorry, I didn't notice. We suddenly had a rash of customers and I was busy."

"Okay, thanks for your help." Carmen walked back out to the car to the waiting vampires. "Well, the car headed south down that side street, the woman said.

Unfortunately, Kayden left in a truck in an unknown direction." She sighed and thought out loud. "We better follow the trail we know and take care of those two before they turn any more vampires. Then we'll worry about Kayden."

They left the gas station and proceeded down the small side street. It curved and twisted its way for several miles. There wasn't much out there…an occasional farmhouse or acres of farmland. It went on for hours, and Carmen was starting to think they should turn back and search for Kayden when she saw a car parked at the side of what looked like an old deserted farm silo. They pulled the van over to the edge of the road and stopped under large overhanging trees, then silently got out to survey the area. Carmen grabbed her dagger, and hoped Oliver and Ryan hadn't heard their approaching vehicle already; vampires had excellent hearing.

With the greatest stealth the three of them drew nearer to the large dilapidated silo. It was completely quiet, which wasn't a good sign. They'd probably already heard Carmen and her men approaching. Carmen's senses were on alert, listening for any sound and checking the breezes for scents. She picked up the distinct odor of blood. It grew stronger as she approached the small door that was hanging partially opened and crooked on its hinges. She waved the other two vampires around to another entrance, and watched them disappear behind the building, then stepped cautiously over the towering weeds to the entry.

Carmen quickly entered and glanced about. It was a blood bath. There were three bodies of victims that hadn't just been killed, it looked like they had been tortured first. Red streaks and spatters of blood were everywhere. One of the victims, who had obviously gotten the brunt of their anger, had his throat ripped out. He wouldn't become a vampire, so Carmen stepped over the body and looked at the other two, and then swiftly cut their heads off with her dagger so that they wouldn't turn. She heard a noise, and turned abruptly to see her two hunters entering from the other side.

"No one is here anymore," one of them said.

She sighed. "Help me destroy all of this evidence and we'll track them on foot. Their scent trail will be easier to follow than in a car."

They set off on foot after the slight undeniable odor of the undead. It was a smell that no other creature could discern, not even the most well trained bloodhounds. Only other vampires could smell its lingering gray iciness, indicating the path that another cold, dead being had taken.

Carmen could tell that the two who fled had taken off at a quick pace, and she sped up, leaving her fellow hunters in the dust. She was faster than any other vampire, except Rurik and Amy, and needed to stop Oliver and Ryan before they did any irreparable damage. The hunters would catch up, and it wasn't necessary for them to be with her when she caught the others. She knew she could easily kill both Oliver and Ryan. Her helpers had only been along as back up, and also because she realized that Adrian would always be overprotective of her no matter how lethal of a machine she'd become.

She came to an abrupt stop and stood deathly still, not moving a muscle, not even breathing. There was talking up ahead.

"I think we should circle back and get the car. It'll hide our scent better, and we can cover larger distances quicker," Oliver said to Ryan. Oliver was the thinker of the group. He'd been smart as a human. He looked with contempt at Ryan, who only thought with his senses, what he wanted at the moment. They would've been long gone way before now if Ryan hadn't been so bent on torturing that poor guy in the barn silo. Oliver had thoroughly enjoyed the bloodlust of the whole experience, but it reminded him of his human days and all the bullying he'd received at the hands of others. He finally insisted that Ryan get on with it, drink the man's blood, and kill him. But by then they heard the approaching car and had to take off on foot.

"I don't know, Oliver," Ryan said. "They may be waiting for us back there. I think we should just keep running."

Oliver frowned at him with irritation. "You don't have enough brains to think. Let me do that part, okay? We will silently circle back. No one will ever know we are there."

Just then they heard a noise, and turned to see Carmen streak in their direction. It happened so fast that Ryan didn't even have time to brace himself, or turn to flee. She was on him in an instant and cut his head off with one swift flick of her dagger, and then turned to Oliver.

He jumped back, throwing his hands in the air. "Hey, I don't want any of this! I didn't become a vampire by choice."

"I'm sorry, Oliver, but you still have to die," Carmen said. "You never should have been a vampire in the first place."

"I...I'm very smart. I could be helpful to have around." He was trying to back up while he spoke.

Carmen's blue green eyes narrowed and took on a yellow glint. "Do you know where Kayden went?"

Oliver shook his head. "No, he didn't say. All I know is that he said we could have the car, and he hopped into a truck cab and left." He looked with apprehension at the knife in her hand. "I'll do anything you want...just let me live."

Carmen almost felt sorry for Oliver, but she didn't have any qualms about killing vampires that shouldn't be there. She shook her head. "There's no other way for you."

Oliver lowered his hands and stood resignedly still. "All right." He grimaced. "Make it quick."

Carmen walked up to Oliver while he stared with dread on his face. She suddenly smiled, as if she'd changed her mind, and he breathed a sigh of relief, smiling back. In that instant she reached up swiftly with her dagger and cut off his head. The smile was still on Oliver's face when his body fell to the ground and his head rolled across the grass.

Just then the two hunters showed up and took in the scene.

"Get rid of these bodies," Carmen ordered. Then she pulled out her cell phone to give Adrian an update and see how Rurik was fairing after his punishment. She cringed at the thought, but was thankful she didn't have to witness it. She felt sorry for Rurik, all the pain and the anguish in his heart for losing Mindy. But she felt bad for Adrian too. She knew how much he loved Rurik, and was sure it had been just as torturous for Adrian as it had been for Rurik.

#

I sat at the table and ate a sandwich while Dad looked over his paperwork across from me. I knew he didn't want to leave me unattended for long to make sure I wasn't going to try anything stupid. I didn't see the point. I had no place to run to, and didn't really care enough about anything at the moment, as my mind went continually back to the thought of Mindy and the knowledge that I would never see her again. And I didn't know if I could realistically even do myself in. Vampires had incredible survival instincts, and my body healed extremely fast.

Dad glanced up at me occasionally with an almost pained expression. I knew he felt bad for punishing me earlier.

I shuddered, remembering his absolute fury. But I was completely healed already…my body recovered quickly. And I had to be thankful he'd let Mindy live, and also for the realization that if I had been anyone but his son, I would have gotten much worse.

Suddenly his cell phone rang and he glanced down at the number. "Hello Carmen. What's the news?" He paused for a moment. "Yes…he's all right. No…it was very difficult." He almost cringed when he glanced in my direction, then got up and went over to the back door and stood looking out at the gardens. He sighed. "Being a parent and the ruler is almost impossible at times. Did you take care of Kayden and the others?"

He was silent for a few moments and I listened intently. I could hear some of what Mom said over the phone. It sounded as if she just said that Oliver and Ryan were dead and all evidence destroyed, but Kayden had escaped in a truck.

Dad continued. "I don't think he would come back here. That would be tantamount to asking us to kill him. He isn't that dumb. No…continue your search in the direction you're going, and keep me informed."

My heart stopped in my chest. Kayden wasn't with the others? I knew where he would go. They didn't understand how fixated he was on Mindy. He considered her his property. I went as cold as ice, thinking about him attacking her, of him saying that he couldn't wait to pick up where he'd left off. I had to help Mindy!

Dad was deep in conversation with Mom when I silently got up from the table and walked out of the kitchen to the front door, opened it, and stepped outside into the night.

Chapter Seven
Fugitives

Mindy sat in her pajamas on the bed and stared numbly at the wall in front of her. She was still in shock from everything that had transpired. An occasional tear ran down her cheek, and a sporadic sob escaped her lips. It was impossible for her to imagine not ever seeing Rurik again. The anguish of it cut her heart, as if someone was literally piercing her chest with a knife and carving it away. It was agony. She hugged her arms around herself as if trying to protect her heart against an actual blade.

It was almost morning and her mom would be home soon. She knew her mother would see the horrible anguish she was in, and didn't know what she was going to say to her. She could never tell anyone. The look in Adrian's eyes had been ominous. He'd meant it when he said he would kill her, and she didn't want to put her mom in danger too. She stood up and headed into the bathroom to wash her face.

Somehow she had to go to school and function. At least her friends would be somewhat sympathetic, because they understood how much she loved Rurik. But they would never know the real reason he was gone, and she couldn't ever tell them.

She heard a noise and looked at her clock. It was a little early for her mom to be home, but sometimes she got off from work sooner than expected.

Mindy took a deep breath, trying to put an unemotional face on, and walked out of her bedroom down the hall and into the living room. She came to an abrupt stop and gasped, her hand to her throat, her heart pounding in her chest.

Kayden was standing inside her front door, staring at her, a sinister smile spreading across his face. "Hello, Mindy," he said. "We finally get to finish what we started the other day. You have no idea how much I've been looking forward to this."

Mindy backed slowly away, never taking her eyes off Kayden, who approached threateningly. She knew it was impossible to outrun him, but she had to try. She turned and raced down the hall to the bathroom and slammed the door and locked it. She braced herself against the back wall and listened, terrified.

"Miinnddyyy," Kayden said in a high, mocking voice. "I know you're in there. I can smell your fear and hear your heart racing." He chuckled.

Then the door blasted open with such force, it flew off of its hinges and fell to the floor. Mindy jumped back and screamed. Kayden stood in the doorway and stared at her with anticipation in his eyes.

"Please don't hurt me, Kayden," she said in a small frightened voice.

He smiled widely and slowly walked forward. "You should've thought of that before you hit me in the face with the vase. Turnabout is fair play." His eyes turned dark and menacing, and his face took on an angry, evil expression.

Mindy took a deep breath and tried to kick him hard in the groin. But he was too fast and caught her leg, flipping her onto the floor. Kayden leaned down and grabbed her by the arms and hauled her to her feet. She fought him with everything in her and screamed at the top of her lungs. He dragged her kicking and screaming down the hall to her bedroom and threw her furiously onto the bed. It was with such force that Mindy had the wind knocked out of her. She was so far beyond horrified that she couldn't even move while Kayden advanced on her with a wicked smile on his face.

Mindy stared back at Kayden. She knew there was no way she could fight him, no way to even defend herself against him, so she braced herself for the pain she knew he would inflict on her with pleasure.

He towered over her, looking down for a moment. Then he reached out and hit her cruelly across the face. Mindy immediately tasted blood on her lip. The pain was incredible, and she gasped as tears streamed down her cheeks.

"That's for the vase," he said angrily. Then with real malice in his eyes, he growled, "The rest of this is for choosing Rurik over me."

Mindy screamed and tried desperately to shield herself from Kayden's onslaught.

Suddenly Kayden stopped and turned. Then Mindy heard it too, and looked down the hallway with terror.

"Mindy! Mindy! What's wrong?!" her mother shouted.

Mindy stared with wide eyed panic up into Kayden's face. He smiled at her malevolently and then turned toward the hall. "No!" she shouted. "Run Mom, run!!" Mindy jumped to her feet while Kayden was sauntering out of her doorway. "No, Kayden, come back. Please don't hurt my mom!" Mindy screamed frantically. She leaped on his shoulders and tried to pull him back.

He turned and grabbed her furiously, and threw her into the bedroom. "Wait here!"

Mindy was flung violently across the room and hit her head hard against the corner of the dresser. Everything blacked out in front of her eyes as she heard her mother's bloodcurdling scream.

Mindy was abruptly awakened to Kayden flinging her roughly onto the bed again. She grimaced from the awful pain where her head had hit the dresser. Her hair felt matted, wet, and sticky…she knew it was blood from the wound. She was shaking with absolute terror, which only heightened Kayden's excitement and anticipation. His eyes turned red and glowing, and he stared down into Mindy's horrified expression.

#

I was very afraid for Mindy, and ran faster than I thought I ever could through the trees to her house. I had no idea if I was too late already. Kayden would do terrible, awful things to Mindy if I didn't get there in time to stop him. My eyes got blacker and blacker while I thought about Kayden and what I would do to him if he laid a finger on her. He would suffer beyond what anyone else had ever endured.

When I got to Mindy's house my heart went to my throat. The front door was wide open and there was no sound. The smell of blood was overpowering. I was afraid my worst fears had been realized. I stepped inside and looked down the hall, and saw a woman, who I assumed was Mindy's mom, lying in a large pool of blood. I braced myself for the terrible scene of witnessing Mindy's body while I stepped over her mom's corpse and started down the hall.

Then I heard Mindy scream and sob frantically. "No, pleeaassse!"

I wasn't too late! I raced down the hall to her bedroom, stopped in the doorway, and took in the scene. Kayden was bent over Mindy and was starting to remove his shirt. His eyes blazed and he smiled cruelly. Mindy's face was so far beyond horrified it was heart wrenching to witness while she cowered on the bed and waited for her attacker.

I roared, my eyes turning red with fury.

Both of their faces looked to mine at the same time. Mindy's showed so much relief it was an amazing transformation, and Kayden's went from surprise to rage.

He growled and lunged forward. I stepped away and we circled each other.

"Mindy's mine!" Kayden yelled furiously.

"You're going to die this time, Kayden!" I barked.

He sprang back and forth and I readied myself to charge him. I knew I was far superior. I didn't think Kayden realized that to its fullest, or he would have run away as fast as he could. He mistakenly thought he could take me. When he leaped at me, growling and baring his fangs, I was ready. I easily stepped out of his path, as if he moved in slow motion, and then turned and attacked him forcefully. I had him on the floor under me within seconds. His face quickly went from anger and murder to fear while he whimpered in my clutches.

I smiled while I held him down on the floor. I wanted him to suffer for all the torment and pain he'd caused Mindy. I wasn't in a hurry to kill him. "I'm going to enjoy killing you very slowly, Kayden," I said angrily.

He cowered under me and yelled like a baby.

Then I heard Mindy crying behind me. I'd forgotten she was even there, in my desire to torture Kayden. I didn't want Mindy to see that darker, evil side of me that would enjoy inflicting pain, even if it was on someone like Kayden, who in my opinion deserved it. She'd been traumatized way too much already. I sighed and quickly ripped his throat out.

Kayden stared back up at me with disbelieving dead eyes.

I stood and turned to Mindy, who gaped at me with fear, relief, and shock, if it were possible to have all those expressions on one face at the same time. She was still shaking uncontrollably, and had a large welt on her mouth where Kayden had hit her, and blood was matted in her hair.

I went over to her, took the blanket and wrapped her body with it, and pulled her to me. Mindy burst into hysterical tears. I held her against me, rocking her and talking soothingly into her ear while she cried.

When she finally stopped crying and looked up into my face, I asked gently, "Are you going to be okay?"

She sighed and nodded. I knew she felt completely safe in my arms.

I bent down and tenderly kissed her lips. "Oh Mindy, I didn't think I would ever see you again," I whispered. "I'm so glad I got here in time."

"I never want to be away from you again, Rurik," she said with complete relief in her voice.

I frowned thoughtfully. "We need to leave. My parents will be here soon. If they find us together I don't know what they'll do."

At the mention of my parents, Mindy suddenly looked alarmed. "My mom! She came home when

Kayden was attacking me, and she…she….” Mindy tried to pull away from me to go find her mom.

"Mindy…Mindy," I said as calmly as I could. I held my arms around her tightly so that she couldn't budge.

"Let go, Rurik. My mom might need me." She was starting to get a little irritated at my insistence that she stay where she was, and struggled in my arms.

"No, Mindy," I said softly.

Understanding came into her face and her expression grew instantly crushed; she burst into tears again.

"She died quickly. It didn't look like she suffered." I knew I was lying to her, but why torment her with the truth?

Mindy shook her head back and forth. "No, no…no," she repeated several times.

I pulled her away and gently shook her to bring her back into the moment. "Mindy. If we're going to go, we need to leave now. Do you understand?"

She stared into my face and slowly nodded her head.

"Okay," I said, and stood her on her feet. "Get cleaned up and dressed as quickly as possible."

Still draped in the blanket, she went over to her closet and dresser and grabbed some clothes.

"I'll be out into the hall while you dress," I said.

I stepped outside and surveyed the house…it was a mess. My parents weren't going to be happy when they got there and saw all of it. I sighed. I knew that I'd made my decision to leave with Mindy and never look back…leave my previous life behind and start a new one with her. I wasn't sad at the thought, though. Yes, I would miss life here. But Mindy was my breath and my heart. The total encompassing feelings of joy I felt at having her by my side made everything else pale in comparison.

When Mindy was ready, I stepped back into her room and picked her up. "Close your eyes, I don't want you to see anything out there that might upset you. Okay?"

She nodded and put her arms around my neck, with her head against my chest and her eyes closed tightly. We went silently into the night with her wrapped in my arms. I was able to move swiftly through the trees; carrying her didn't even slow me down.

#

Kayden woke with a start and grabbed his throat, remembering the feeling of his flesh being ripped open by Rurik's razor sharp fangs. He sat up and looked in the mirror, running his hand across his neck. There were no wounds…it had completely healed. He got to his feet and stretched and smiled. If it were at all possible, he felt even better than he had before.

Someone was approaching the house. He could hear them clearly, even though he could also tell that they were silent vampires. Looking one more time in the mirror and adjusting his hair, he slipped out Mindy's window, closing it behind him.

#

When Adrian and Carmen arrived at Mindy's house, the door was ajar and the smell of blood overwhelming. They walked inside and looked around. A woman was lying in a pool of blood on the floor in the hall, probably Mindy's mom. The door to the bathroom was on the floor, ripped off its hinges. They headed down the hallway and into Mindy's bedroom. No one else was there, but there were torn nightgown pieces around the bed.

Adrian surveyed the scene with a furious expression. It didn't take too much to figure out what had happened here. It appeared that Kayden had gotten in and killed Mindy's mom, and then caught up with Mindy in the bathroom and dragged her over to the bed, where he attacked her. The house was deserted now, but Adrian could smell the lingering scents of Rurik, Mindy, and Kayden. He put his hand on his forehead and groaned loudly and closed his eyes. Was this nightmare never going to end?

Carmen sat on the bed and stared at Adrian with worry. "What are we going to do?"

Adrian sighed. "I'll call some men to come over, clean this place up good, and then cause a gas leak to burn it to the ground to destroy any evidence." He sat on the bed next to Carmen and took her hand and looked into her eyes. "For obvious reasons we need to find them quickly."

Carmen nodded her head and tried to hold the tears back. "Rurik's very smart…he'll be hard to track. He has your brains."

Adrian smiled with a wistful expression. "Yes, and your stubborn determination. Not the best combination under these circumstances." He stood up and pulled Carmen to her feet and held her close, and looked deep into her eyes. "Maybe it was impossible to stop this from the beginning. Trying to stop love is like trying to keep the tide back in a tsunami."

Carmen couldn't help smiling. "Nothing deterred us, did it?"

"No, and I wouldn't ever change a thing," he said, and took her hand and led her out of the bedroom. "Let's get this mess straightened out and see if we can find our son."

#

I finally felt like we had covered enough distance to be able to stop and put Mindy on the ground in the shadows next to a gas station, and then surveyed my surroundings. There was an older woman inside that was waiting on a customer. I watched from the darkness until the patron left, and then walked casually inside. The attendant glanced in my direction, but was busy with paperwork behind the counter. I looked around the store for a few minutes before I walked over to the register.

I stared into her eyes with my mesmerizing power, and she was instantly drawn in. She stood in a fog while I leaped over the counter, took the money out of the register, and then easily pried the safe door open with my fingers. When I was finished, I pulled the three security cameras off the wall and crushed them in my hands, and removed the live feed from the machine in the office before going back outside where Mindy was waiting. I handed her a nut bar and a bottle of water, and she hungrily grabbed them. I was going to have to remember that being human, she needed sustenance a lot more regularly than I did.

I found a small motel several miles up the road and checked us in. Once inside the room, Mindy sat on the bed and looked at me with sad eyes. I went over, sat beside her, and took her hand.

Her eyes filled with tears and she tried hard not to cry. "I'm sorry that I've ruined your life, Rurik."

"What do you mean? You're the best thing that's ever happened to me."

She wiped her tears away. "You had your future all planned out before you met me."

"Yeah. A future I didn't want," I said darkly. "I'm not sorry I'm here with you." I sighed and lifted her face to look into mine. "I love you more than anything, Mindy. I'll always be here for you no matter what. I belong with you. Period."

I bent down and kissed her, and she melted willingly into my arms, then suddenly pressed against me with her hands.

"Rurik! Stop!"

It took me by surprise and I sat up. Mindy got quickly to her feet and went to the other side of the room with an anxious expression.

"What's wrong, Mindy?"

She shook her head and burst into tears. "I'm sorry. I thought of Kayden and panicked."

I stood up, walked slowly over to her, and put my arms gently around her. It made me angry that Kayden had hurt someone like Mindy. I knew it would take time to deal with the memories of what he'd tried to do to her. "It's okay, Angel. Kayden's dead. I'm here with you now, and no one is ever going to hurt you again." I took her hand and led her back over to the bed and wrapped her in my arms, cuddling her against me. She relaxed into my warm embrace and drifted off to sleep.

\#

Kayden easily followed Rurik and Mindy's scent. It was as clear as if he were following a lit-up neon sign.

Somehow his senses were even sharper than they'd been before he was killed again. He was an even bigger, badder version of the vampire he used to be. He shrugged and grinned. This was going to be a piece of cake. He couldn't wait to catch up with them and take care of that interfering pain in the neck Rurik once and for all. He went swiftly through the trees until he came to a gas station, and stood outside for a few moments assessing the place. There were a couple of customers inside, and an older woman behind the counter. They would be no match for him.

Kayden sauntered through the front door with a wide smile on his face. "Good morning," he said pleasantly, and walked up to the woman behind the counter.

She eyed him suspiciously. "What do you want?"

"I want to know where the boy that was in here earlier was going. Did he say anything to you?"

The attendant shook her head. "I already told everything to the police. Somehow he paralyzed me. I couldn't move while he helped himself to the money. Must've been some kind of weird hypnosis. I didn't see where he went after that."

Kayden was starting to get irritated at the woman's obvious attitude. "What about the girl?"

She shook her head. "I didn't see any girl."

That infuriated Kayden, and he grabbed the woman and pulled her over the counter. "There was a girl! Pretty, with brown hair and green eyes."

The woman cried, "I didn't see anyone else. If she was here, she was outside."

"Hey!" someone shouted behind Kayden. He turned to see a large, heavyset man with several tattoos rushing over to him. "Let go of the lady now!"

Kayden smiled. "Or what?" He picked the woman up till her feet were dangling, purposely antagonizing the man. The woman screamed loudly.

"That's enough!" the man shouted to Kayden.

Kayden tossed the woman aside and she hit shelves against the wall, knocking candy and chips to the floor. He waved the man closer. "Come on," he taunted. "I haven't killed anyone all day."

The man hesitated, eyeing Kayden carefully.

Kayden snorted with contempt. "I knew you were a coward."

"Someone needs to teach you some manners," the man said furiously, and took a swing at Kayden.

But Kayden was so fast that in the next instant he grabbed the man's fist and pinned him against the floor. The rest of the customers watched with horror when Kayden leaned into the man's throat and drank hungrily, while the man screamed. Then Kayden stood up, his face covered in blood, turning to smile at his terror struck audience. He instinctively knew that he shouldn't leave any witnesses alive.

#

I brushed the hair out of Mindy's face when she started to stir. "Good morning."

She opened her eyes. "Hi," she said bashfully.

"I think we should get moving soon. I'm going to go out and find a car. My mom's an incredible tracker, and it'll be difficult to hide from her."

Mindy sat up and nodded.

"Let's have breakfast before we go. You haven't eaten real food in days, and I need to something too." That was one thing I needed to make sure of, that I didn't get too hungry around Mindy. I figured as long as I wasn't starving that I could control my cravings for her blood.

We sat and ate at the small diner in front of the motel.

I reached across and held Mindy's free hand. "I think we should continue to go south, to the coast. The sunnier it is, the fewer vampires we'll be running into. I'm sure my dad has put out an APB by now for us with the society."

Mindy nodded in agreement, and then asked, "Vampires don't like the sun?"

"Vampires have to avoid the bright sun. It doesn't hurt them, but it does show them for what they are, walking corpses."

Mindy shuddered. "I don't ever want to see that."

"No...you don't," I agreed.

"But..." Mindy looked confused. "I've seen you in the sun and you look fine."

I nodded. "Since Amy and I are half human, we can go out in the sun without showing our true identities. My mom and Amy's mom, Amanda, are the only other vampires that can besides us. That's why it will be easier for us to hide in a sunny climate," I said with a grin.

After we checked out, Mindy waited in front of the hotel for me while I found a car. It was an older nondescript white sedan. I knew we could use it to get to the coast and then ditch it. She hopped in and we took off down the road. Mindy settled against my shoulder and I put my arm protectively around her while I drove. I couldn't help being completely contented with her by my side.

When we got closer to the coast I left the vehicle in a secluded treed area where it wouldn't be discovered easily, and we walked down the highway hand in hand until a truck driver stopped and picked us up.

"Where you kids headed to?" he asked when we climbed into the cab.

I shrugged. "Just wanted to see the ocean."

"Well, I'm going over across the bridge to the island. Does that sound good?"

"Sounds great," I replied. "I'm Rurik, and this is Mindy."

The truck driver smiled widely. "I'm Jerry."

We watched the scenery as it changed from rolling hills to more and more palm trees with sandy vegetation the further south we drove.

"What brings you kids down here?" Jerry asked.

I tried not to stiffen. I could tell he'd been eyeing us carefully and didn't answer.

"I'm not trying to be nosy…you just look a little young to be hitchhiking down the highway by yourselves, that's all." When I still didn't say anything, he continued. "Are you two looking for some work? I have a friend down there that's always hiring. "

I grinned. "That would be great."

"Okay, I'll introduce you to him. He owns a fishing company, and needs help with a lot of different things."

\#

Mindy and I held hands and gazed out the window while we crossed the long bridge from the mainland over to the island. The water was a crystal blue with glistening white sandy beaches. The houses along the shore were impressive, with their large windows and decks facing the ocean.

Jerry drove down a frontage road along the waterfront to the other end of the small island town. There were docks and fishing boats, with row after row of piers and buildings. He pulled up to an alley and stopped. "This is it," he said, and opened the door and hopped out.

We jumped down from the cab and followed Jerry to the end of one of the piers, where there were several boats with fishermen on them unloading fish. Noisy pelicans and seagulls swarmed the area, screeching hungrily for scraps. Occasionally they would swoop in and grab a fish out of one of the buckets, and an angry fisherman would throw things, waving his arms to chase them off. Mindy couldn't help giggling at the birds and the mad seamen.

We walked all the way to the end, where a large middle aged man in his mid-fifties was talking to several fishermen. He wore galoshes and a hat, and had red hair and a thick beard.

Jerry walked up and slapped the guy on the shoulder, and the man turned to grin at him. "Hey, Mack! Long time no see. What've you been up to?"

"Just working, as usual," Mack replied. "Let's get together for a beer later today. Give me a call."

"Will do," Jerry exclaimed. They conversed for a few minutes about supplies that Jerry had on his truck and where Mack wanted them. "Hey, I've got a couple of kids here looking for work, and I know you're always hiring."

Mack turned to really look for the first time, and scrutinized us with his sharp blue eyes. "Yeah, I could use some extra hands. I'm Mack, as you heard. I run this dock, and can always use good wharf laborers."

I grinned and gripped his extended hand. "I'm Rurik, and this is Mindy."

"You look plenty big and strong enough," he commented while he checked me over. "It's not pretty work, but the pay's decent."

I shrugged. "I'm not afraid of work."

He nodded. "Okay." Then he turned his attention to Mindy. "My wife runs a small fresh fish restaurant down at the end of the next pier. Nothing fancy, but the best fish and chips. She could use help in the kitchen."

Mindy nodded and grinned.

"Great," Mack said. "Let me finish with this motley group in front of me and I'll show you two around."

Mindy and I went over and leaned against a post to wait. She nuzzled into my side and I put my arm around her. Jerry waved to us on his way back up the dock when he left. I watched Mack closely while he dealt with the crew in front of him. He had an easy going, natural way about him, and the others gave him respect and admiration. I could instantly tell that he was one of those rare honest souls who saw people for who they were and enjoyed them and life.

When Mack was finished, he came over to where we were waiting and nodded in our direction. "I'm guessing you two could use a place to stay, also."

"Well...we just got in town...," I answered with a nod.

"I know a lady who has a small cottage that she rents pretty cheap for workers. I think her last occupant just left. I'll take you over there after I show you around. Follow me."

Mindy and I fell in behind him. We went back up the dock to the left, where there were more buildings on the water side, then all the way to the end of another pier. A cute little white sided building with blue trim and large windows sat at the end on stilt legs above the water. The freshly painted sign read, Kim's Fresh Fish and Chips. Even though the building had enjoyed years of use, it was well kept and immaculate.

Mack held the door open and we stepped in. A middle aged plump woman looked up from behind the counter, where she was deep-frying seafood, and smiled.

"Kimmy," Mack said affectionately to her. "This is Mindy, and she's looking for work."

Kimmy grinned while she studied Mindy. She came around to the front of the counter and put her hands on her hips. "Hi, Mindy. I could use a little help doing dishes and waiting on customers. Not much pay, mostly tips. How does that sound?"

I checked the place out while we stood there. Several customers were eating at small tables with neat white table cloths, or over at the bar in front of the counter. Most looked like fisherman and seemed to be all right. I wanted to make sure the environment would be okay for Mindy to work in. Kimmy also appeared to be a pleasant person with her smiling face and relaxed demeanor.

Mindy turned questioningly in my direction, and I smiled and nodded. She smiled timidly back at Kimmy. "Okay."

"Great. I'll take you two over to the cottage for rent and introduce you," Mack said. He took off on foot away from the water and up the gradual incline to where rows and rows of tiny houses stood. "Everything here is within walking distance. Makes life easy, and you don't need a car. On weekends with all the tourists, it would take you thirty minutes to go half a mile, so it's much quicker to walk anyway."

We came to a small pink house with white trim, and Mack stepped up to the door and knocked. An elderly lady answered with a frown, but when she saw Mack it immediately changed to a grin. "Mack, what brings you here?"

"Hi, Rosy. I got some kids looking for a place to rent. Is yours available?"

Rosy nodded her head. "Yes, it is." She scrutinized us carefully. "You two look a little young to be down here working and renting a place by yourselves."

Mindy turned to me with concern and I tried not to get defensive. "We're older than we look."

Rosy shrugged. "None of my business. Just seems kids start younger and younger these days. Come with me," she said, and stepped outside.

We went around the side of her small house to the back, where there was a tiny building, not much larger than a big shed. Rosy pulled a key out of her pocket, unlocked the door, and we entered. The cozy interior had a miniature kitchen including all the amenities, and a sofa in front of a fireplace, plus a TV. Against the opposite wall sat a two chair wooden table by a window. There was also a petite bathroom with a shower, tub enclosure, and sink. It was very snug.

"The sofa pulls out into a hide-a-bed, and there's a picnic table outside by the grill. Two hundred fifty a month, which is half what you'll find anywhere else in this tourist trap. Oh, and the laundry is right off my back door, so help yourself to washing your clothes. Just pick up as you go."

"This is perfect," Mindy said. She looked up into my eyes and hers sparkled happily. Little was the optimum word here, but we didn't need a lot of space, and Mindy was pleased. That was all that mattered.

"We'll take it," I replied.

"Okay, you two," Mack commented. "I'll see you bright and early at the dock, five a.m., Rurik. And Mindy, Kimmy gets going at eight in the morning."

I nodded. "Sounds good. We'll be there."

Mack and Rosy walked out. I closed the door behind them and turned to Mindy, put my arms around her, and drew her to me. I couldn't help sighing, I was so contented that she was here with me. "Let's go shopping and buy a few clothes and things we'll need."

"Okay," she grinned.

We walked hand in hand for miles along the rows of cute shops, and went in and out of several of them. We both needed clothes and necessities. I was checking out an old historic anchor in an antique store when Mindy suddenly gasped and I turned to her with alarm, thinking that something was wrong.

"Rurik! Isn't it beautiful?!" she exclaimed. She was over in the corner of the store pointing to a table lamp sitting on a small desk…an ornate porcelain painted angel with golden wings that came up to a point that held the crystal lampshade above them. The angel herself was dressed in a beautiful white flowing gown and adorned with dainty pink roses, with pale green leaves that cascaded from the shoulder down to the ground and then framed her feet at the base. It was an amazing piece of artwork, I had to admit. The angel had exquisitely carved features, with large green eyes, full lips, and a small upturned nose, and her brown hair was shoulder length. It was stunningly similar to Mindy…she could have been the model.

"She looks like you," I had to say.

"No she doesn't. I'm not that pretty."

"Yes you are, Mindy," I insisted. "She has your face." I raised my hand up and touched the delicate skin on her cheek, and smiled down at her. She blushed at my intent gaze and was drawn into my eyes. I had to make myself glance away to break our trance.

Next we went to the small grocery store at the end of our street and loaded up on food before we headed back to our cottage. After putting the things away in the refrigerator and the cupboards, we made roast beef sandwiches and sat down in front of the TV to relax. It wasn't long before Mindy was nodding off in my arms.

I shook her gently to wake her. "Mindy, let's make up the hide-a-bed so you can sleep," I said softly.

After the bed was made Mindy went into the small bathroom to change and brush her teeth. When she returned, she wore a simple, full length flannel green nightgown with a small white ruffle of lace around the collar. She was beautiful. The green in the pajamas really showed off her eyes.

"You're gorgeous," I stated.

She smiled and I pulled her into my arms and kissed her. Her scent was overpoweringly intoxicating, and I held her tightly against me. When I finally let her go, she was breathless and her eyes were warm and smoldering. I knew that I'd better leave now, or I would be sorry.

I took a couple of quick steps away from her and put my hand on the doorknob. "I need to go out. I'll be back later." Her face looked puzzled and hurt, but I turned around and walked quickly out the door, closing it behind me.

I stepped into the cool, salty ocean air and took a few deep breaths. The vampire in me was sometimes frightening when I was that close to Mindy. I'd wanted her again, and not just her flesh. The scent of her blood and the feel of her pulse under my grasp had been almost too much to resist. I desperately craved her blood again.

I stayed in the shadows and moved swiftly toward the bridge. This time of night there was very little traffic when I crossed over to the mainland. I slowed when a car would approach, but otherwise I practically flew down the road, moving toward the hospital in town. I could already smell death inside, and it attracted me…the vampire in me that searched for a sick, or weak, victim. This was the way it had always been. Vampires could smell, or sense, the presence of death. We were kind of the grim reapers of the human world. When someone lay at death's door we would silently come in, unnoticed, and help them to die a little quicker, less painfully than they may have otherwise.

I moved without a sound down the hospital corridor to a room at the end. When I entered there was a young woman lying on the bed. Her breath was shallow and her heartbeat very faint. I walked over and gazed down at her, and she smiled up at me. This was the way it was most times when someone lay dying. They looked for us, expected us, and when we showed up they seemed almost happy and relieved to see us.

I gently brushed my hand across her face and down to her neck and smiled back at her, then turned her head to the side and bent down. My eyes glowed red and my lips became frosty when I placed them against her throat and sank my teeth into her flesh. She stiffened slightly, but didn't fight me. It only took moments to drain enough of her blood to end her life. I didn't take all of it, or she would have become a vampire if I didn't tear out her throat, but took only enough to end her suffering.

My blood craving had been satiated, and I turned and walked swiftly down the hall and back out into the night, nothing more than a fast moving shadow. When I entered our little cottage, Mindy was asleep in the hide-a-bed. I went over to her and stood looking down for a long time, listening to her heartbeat and slow, steady breathing. I had overwhelming feelings of protectiveness for her, for how gentle and vulnerable she was. But the vampire in me desired her too. It was frustrating that I wanted to shield her from the evils of the world, but I was the most malevolent of all the creatures she would ever encounter. I sat at the small table by the window and watched her sleep all night.

#

When Kayden got to the hotel, the scent abruptly stopped. Rurik and Mindy must have left there in a vehicle. He raised his head and screamed his aggravation to the stars. There was no clue to where they had gone. He heaved a sigh and entered the hotel office to get a room for the day, his instinct to stay out of the sun strong.

By evening he was beside himself with frustration. He wandered into the small diner and sat down at the bar.

The bartender eyed him carefully. "You got some I.D.?"

"Just give me a soda," Kayden replied with annoyance. When the bartender sat the drink in front of him, Kayden asked, "Did you see a high school boy and girl in here this morning?"

The bartender shrugged. "I didn't arrive till this afternoon. Ask Marie, she was here." He turned to an attractive waitress across the eatery. "Hey Marie. Did you wait on a couple of high school kids earlier today?"

Marie turned to look at them. She was pretty in an excessively made up way, with lots of makeup and perfume. She looked Kayden over as she walked up. "Yeah. I saw them."

Kayden grinned…he could tell that Marie desired him. "She's my sister," Kayden lied. "Do you know where they went?"

Marie smiled widely at Kayden. "Maybe. I was just getting off my shift." She put her hands on her hips and smiled provocatively. "You can walk with me if you want while we talk."

Kayden smiled pleasantly and nodded his head. He could hardly stand the anticipation as he walked out the door with Marie.

#

Carmen stepped inside Adrian's office and sat in the chair across from him. He looked up at her with anticipation.

"There was a convenience store robbed that night, after Rurik and Mindy disappeared, about three hundred miles south of here. The feed to the tape was completely destroyed, and the safe was pried open by an unknown source. Do you think it might have been Rurik?"

"Sounds like it," Adrian commented.

"The next morning, after the police were there, everyone in the place was brutally killed. Some had their throats ripped out."

Adrian sighed. "That must have been Kayden. He's tracking them. I wonder what happened to keep Rurik from killing Kayden at Mindy's house? It doesn't make sense that he wouldn't have."

Carmen shook her head. "I don't know. Maybe Mindy needed Rurik's attention and Kayden was able to escape." She continued. "There was also a waitress that disappeared at a local hotel, and a car was stolen in the same vicinity."

Adrian perked up a bit. "If we can locate that car, we may be able to find them."

"What are we going to do when we do find them?" Carmen asked with concern.

"I don't know, sweetheart. They've gone through a lot to be together already, and seem determined to love each other. There's no easy answer here at all. We know where Rurik's destiny lies, but love isn't easily thwarted." He got up and came around the desk and put his hand on her shoulder. "Kayden's a loose cannon. We need to take care of this before he does damage that isn't repairable."

"Well, if he continues to follow Rurik and Mindy, Rurik will easily kill him. But we don't want Kayden leaving a path of destruction in the meantime."

Adrian nodded in agreement. "Hopefully we'll find them soon. At least we have a few leads to follow now."

#

I was dressing in the work jeans and shirt I'd purchased the day before when Mindy woke. She sat up and rubbed her eyes.

I sat down beside her on the edge of the bed. "Sorry I woke you. I was trying to be quiet. I'm leaving for work in a few minutes."

She stretched. "That's okay. I feel rested. Do you want to eat something before you go?"

"No," I answered. "I already ate."

She glanced over at the kitchen and didn't see a bowl in the sink, or an open box of cereal. "What? It doesn't look like you ate anything."

I shifted my eyes from hers and didn't answer, not wanting to tell her that's what I had gone out for last night, why I'd left in such a hurry.

But realization came into her expression and her face paled. She said nothing, but I could hear her heartbeat speed up nervously. I put my hand under her chin and raised her eyes to mine, staring into hers carefully for a few moments. There was a little fear there.

I sighed, bent down, and gently kissed her lips. "I love you. I gotta go. I'll stop by the restaurant after I'm done at the docks, okay?"

"Okay, Rurik," she answered quietly, trying to smile at me before I walked out the door.

I couldn't help frowning. It bothered me that there was apprehension in Mindy's eyes that was directed toward me. But in reality I knew she was wise to be afraid of me; I was a hunter vampire, and she was prey.

Chapter Eight
Mack

I got to the end of the dock the same time as two other guys did.

Mack was smoking a pipe and leaning against a post while he waited for us to arrive. "All right," Mack said. "Now that we're all here, we'll get to work." He turned to a big guy in his mid-twenties. "Randall, I want you to take Rurik and Kent and teach them what we do in a day."

Randall smiled and nodded his head toward Mack, and then turned to me and Kent. "Okay, you heard him! Let's get going!"

I immediately didn't like him or his attitude.

We followed Randall down to a couple of fishing boats at the end of the pier. I watched him while we went. I had an in-depth perception about people that I'd inherited from my mom, the slayer side of me, and I didn't like Randall. He was going to cause problems at some point, I could tell. He was large and bulky—not in an overweight way, but more like a linebacker—and had a definite air about him. He was in charge, period.

Once we got to the boats and out of earshot of Mack, Randall turned disdainfully in our direction. "I don't know how either one of you two got a job here. Kent, you're as scrawny as they come. If you make it through the day, I'll be amazed. And you, Rurik. You may have muscle, but I can tell you're too much of a know it all for this type of work."

I gave him a sarcastic grin, but said nothing. I knew by the end of the day I would be running circles around him and not even be winded. Kent stared nervously back at Randall. I had a feeling that Randall was probably dead on about Kent.

The day started with scrubbing down two boats, upper and lower decks. Then we loaded the cargo net, crane bucket, and conveyor on the vessels so they would be ready for the fishermen to take out. Next we cleaned the fishing tables for when the catch came in. Finally we had a small break and sat on benches, waiting for the fishing boats to arrive with their hauls.

Kent looked pretty wiped out already, and the day wasn't even half over. He also was kind of green around the gills from the strong fish odor that hung in the air.

Randall kept eyeing me. I could tell it irked him that I kept right up with him and didn't even falter.

It wasn't long before the boats docked and we were busy unloading the catch and hauling it over to the fishing tables to be cleaned. Then we stacked ice around the cleaned fish to keep it cool until it could be stored. After the cleaning was finished, all of the scrap was shoveled into carts to push to the disposal areas. By this time Kent was practically puking from the smell and slime.

When I left in the afternoon, Randall was glaring in my direction; I'd impressed him, and he didn't like me. "See you tomorrow," I said with a smile. I couldn't help rubbing it in.

Kent was literally dragging, and I didn't expect to see him again. I decided I'd better go to the cottage and clean up and wash my clothes before I saw Mindy. I knew she wouldn't want me anywhere near her with the way I smelled at the moment.

When I stepped inside the small restaurant, Mindy was waiting on a couple of fishermen down at the end of the bar. She looked so cute in her little apron with her hair pulled back. I grinned widely at her and went over to the bar and sat down.

Once she was done with the others' orders, she smiled and walked up to me. "Hi, can I help you, sir?"

I put my hand over hers that was resting on the counter. "Yes, I'm looking for a beautiful green eyed girl who's stolen my heart."

She blushed slightly at my words. "The one who loves you more than anything?" she asked.

"That's the one," I answered.

She laughed suddenly. "I'll be off in half an hour. Do you want something to eat…er…drink…? I mean…." She frowned at me and looked flustered.

I sighed. "It's okay. I'll take a soda." I squeezed her hand.

She turned around and filled a glass at the soda fountain, then turned back to me. She sighed loudly and had tears in her eyes.

"It's all right, Mindy," I said softly, and smiled at her.

I sat and sipped my drink while Mindy finished with her customers, and then pulled her apron off and threw it in the back laundry bag.

"See you at eight tomorrow," Kimmy called to her when we left.

"Okay," Mindy returned.

I took her hand and we strolled back toward our cottage. "How was your first day?" I asked.

"Good. It was fun." She smiled up at me and leaned her head against my shoulder. "And yours?"

"Oh, fine." I bent down and kissed the top of her head.

When we got back to the cottage, I sat close to her on the couch. "Are you doing okay with everything?" I asked.

She smiled and nodded. "I'm fine. But…sometimes I forget that you're a vampire, and then…when I remember, it frightens me. I don't know how to act…and…. I get all anxious."

I put my arms tight around her and hugged her to me. "I won't ever hurt you, Mindy," I said gently. "You don't have to worry about that. I promise. "

She sighed and cuddled into my chest and closed her eyes. I hoped that I could keep my promise to her…that I could control my cravings around her. She was everything to me, and I would rather die than ever harm one hair of her head.

#

Today was Mindy's birthday and she was officially sixteen. I was very content with our existence in the little cottage close to the beach. The dock job wasn't fun, but gave us the cash that we needed, and between mine and Mindy's jobs we had enough to get by on. I could have easily taken what we required, but didn't want to draw any attention to us with illegal activities. I knew that my parents would be watching for higher crime rates or mysterious deaths, trying to locate me. So I worked extra hard at avoiding hunting anyone when I was thirsty, and only took the sick and dying.

Randall and I barely tolerated each other. He hated me because I was strong and never tired. I could outwork him in every category, which made him furious. The harder he tried to surpass me, the madder he got that he couldn't.

I had a surprise for Mindy when she was done with work, and I cleaned up and walked down to meet her. When I stepped inside the restaurant, Mindy was just taking off her apron. I took her hand and we headed out the door. I'd never get use to the way her heartbeat sped up and her eyes sparkled anytime I looked at her or touched her. She was incredible.

"Did you have a good day?"

She nodded. "It was great, and I made some nice tips. Maybe we can go out to dinner tonight."

"That sounds fun," I answered. "But you're not paying…my treat for your birthday." I smiled widely. "I have a surprise for you at the cottage, too."

"Really?!" she exclaimed. She jumped up and down excitedly, like a child.

I couldn't help laughing. "Uh-huh. You can have it when we get there."

"Then let's walk faster…I can't wait." She yanked on my arm to speed me up.

"Okay, okay," I said good-naturedly. She let go of my hand and ran up the hill toward our place.

"I had no idea you could move so fast when you wanted to!" I yelled, and ran after her. I purposely slowed my pace so I wouldn't catch her. She looked over her shoulder and saw me in pursuit, and squealed with delight. I was right on her heels and caught her just as she opened the door and stepped inside. I grabbed her around the waist and gently tossed her on the sofa with me on top. Her eyes were sparkling with excitement, her heart pounded, and she breathed rapidly.

"Oh Mindy, I love you so much." I pressed her lips to mine and kissed her. Suddenly I could feel the vampire in me wanting to take over. I ran my lips down to her throat and growled softly.

She tensed under me. "Rurik." Her voice sounded scared.

I didn't answer and pressed my mouth to her neck, her pulse pounding nervously against my lips. I could feel my excitement mounting. My mouth turned to ice against her flesh.

She started to tremble. "Rurik, don't…please don't."

I loved Mindy more than my own life; I had to somehow stop myself. I clenched my teeth. The struggle inside of me was like a war between angels and demons. I wanted her blood desperately. I lifted my head and growled with frustration, while Mindy cringed under me. I clenched my eyes closed, every muscle in my body taut, and then I quickly stood up and stepped back several paces from her.

She lay where she was, with an expression of absolute horror on her face.

"I'm sorry, Mindy," I whispered. I stood still, just watching her for several minutes while I regained control, and then carefully walked back over to her. "Are you okay?"

She swallowed nervously and nodded her head.

I sat beside her and took her hand. I could feel her pulse still furiously pounding.

She was trying to find her voice. She moved her lips, not saying anything, before finally whispering. "I…I don't understand, Rurik. Did I do something I shouldn't have?"

I sighed and stared down at our hands clasped together in her lap. "No, it isn't anything you did." I brought my eyes back up to meet hers. "Sometimes the desire for blood is overpowering, and it's difficult to control. I'm so sorry I scared you." I stroked her cheek with my free hand and looked sadly into her frightened eyes. "You are such an angel. I don't deserve you."

"Don't say that about yourself," she said quietly.

"But it's true. I have a dark side to me that wants to harm the person I love most in this world."

She put her hand on the side of my face and stared intently into my eyes. "I love you more than anything. We can handle this. I know you won't ever hurt me."

I tried not to cringe…I wished I was as confident about it as she. My vampire side would not be ignored or subdued at times. It was frightening, even for me, who was born the way I was. I hugged Mindy to me and kissed the top of her head. We sat that way for several minutes, and I could hear her heartbeat slowly returning to normal.

After a while she pulled away and looked up into my eyes. Hers were dancing with excitement again. "Where's my present?"

I smiled. She tugged at my heartstrings, she was so beautiful, and kind, and sweet. I stood up and went into the bathroom, where I'd hid it in the bathtub. "Close your eyes."

She giggled. "Okay."

"Ready? Are your eyes closed?"

"Yes," she answered with excitement.

I walked out with her present in my hands and put it on the coffee table in front of where she was seated on the couch. "You can open them," I said quietly.

I'd bought her the angel lamp that she loved at the antique store. She opened her eyes and gasped. They immediately filled with tears. "Oh, Rurik! It's the most beautiful thing ever. I can't believe you got it for me!"

I couldn't help grinning at her enthusiasm. I went over and sat beside her, and she threw her arms around my neck and hugged me.

"You're the most wonderful person in the world. Thank you so much," she exclaimed.

"I knew you liked it that day in the antique store. I put a down payment on it so the lady would hold it for your birthday." I brushed my fingers across her cheek. "She looks so much like you. You're my angel, Mindy."

#

There was a fancy seafood restaurant at the other end of the wharf, so we walked arm in arm down the waterfront. It was a magnificent night with bright stars in the sky, the air cool but comfortable. I was so happy here with Mindy that if we stayed forever, I would be satisfied. She was wearing a light aqua blue patterned flowing dress, with sandals that wrapped around her ankles and minimal jewelry. Her simple beauty took my breath away.

"You look amazing tonight," I softly commented.

Mindy smiled up at me and snuggled into my side.

After dinner we walked along the beach and held hands. The ocean was picturesque, with moonlight reflecting in silver strings of light across the waves. We headed down to the end of the pier and sat on the edge, dangling our feet over.

Mindy leaned her head against my shoulder and happily sighed.

"What're you thinking?" I asked.

"About how happy I am, and that I want to be with you always." Then she gazed intently into my face. "What's it like to become a vampire?"

I stiffened beside her. "Forget it. There's no way I'm ever doing that to you."

"Why not?" She looked at me with surprise.

"Because, you're too nice to be a creature of the night. I don't want you to be like me."

She frowned. "But I want to be with you forever."

I shook my head. "I have a dark side that thirsts for human blood. You don't want to be that way."

"If I can be with you, I don't care," she answered stubbornly.

I stared into her eyes carefully. "Yes, you do, Mindy. You're an angel…there's no way I'm turning you into a devil."

She sighed with frustration and looked out at the distant horizon. "You're not a devil, Rurik," she said quietly. She turned to stare keenly at me. "Do you think I would love a devil? I have better taste than that."

"I think you just choose to not look at that side of me."

She reached up, brushed my bangs to the side, and smiled. "I don't ever want to lose you, and if I have to become a vampire to keep you, I can live with that."

"I can't," I immediately retorted. I stared acutely into her face. "Let's not talk about this now and ruin the mood. We don't have to think about that for years still."

She nodded in agreement. "You're right. We're only sixteen."

We sat on the dock for a long time. It was peaceful and quiet to stare out at the waves, hand in hand with Mindy. After a while I reluctantly pulled her to her feet and we walked back to the cottage.

"This was the best birthday I ever had," Mindy said with sincerity.

When we got back to our place Mindy changed and crawled into bed. I leaned down and kissed her. "I need to go out for a bit."

Her face was sober as I turned and stepped outside; she knew what I was going out for.

I walked silently along the beach. It was so deathly quiet in the wee hours of the morning, my favorite hunting time…the darkest, coolest time of night. The only noise was the gentle lapping of the waves along the shoreline. The only light was the glittering stars overhead and an occasional house glow. In a few hours the place would be buzzing with dock workers and fisherman. The seagulls and pelicans would be screeching and swooping down to the water.

Normally I wouldn't hunt this close to where Mindy and I lived, but I could smell death in the air. It hung like a dinner bell, beckoning me closer. I moved swiftly down to the end of a pier and surveyed my surroundings.

Lying on the sand, under the edge of the dock, was an old fisherman. I'd seen him on many occasions hanging out at the pier during the day while I worked. His face was lined with deep creases from years of the onslaught of sun and salt. He was leaning against one of the barnacled posts, holding his chest and gasping for air. It was apparent he was having a heart attack. I walked silently up to him, and he slowly raised his eyes to meet mine. A knowing look came into his weathered visage. He knew what I was, and why I was there.

Fishermen were a different breed in a lot of ways, still believing in superstitions. Whereas the rest of the modern world had moved on and left the old tales and legends behind for more logical thinking, fishermen knew and understood that there were unexplainable forces at work in the universe. They had on many occasions been out to sea with nothing around but the tempest storms that had a life of their own, and realized it was up to the secrets within the depths of the ocean whether they lived, died, prospered, or went home without any catch at all. Life was not really a game of chance, but of circumstances and fate.

The old man had fear in his eyes as I approached, but there was also a sense of peace and resignation. His life was finished and he had no regrets. He'd lived how he wanted, with the salty air always in his face, the feel of the ocean under him, and the fishing boat rocking and swaying to its nautical music. He would die knowing the thrill of winning against all the insurmountable odds of unknown waters, winds, and storms to bring in his livelihood so that he could go out and repeat the process another day.

I knelt down in front of him and quickly took his lifeblood.

After spending a leisurely reflective night along the coast, I walked casually back up the shoreline while the golden rays flooded over the horizon and glinted across the tops of the waves and the docks. The air was starting to stir with sea birds and laborers already. I slipped back into our little cottage to get ready for the day. Mindy was sleeping peacefully on the sofa, so I changed my clothes and then gently kissed her on the forehead before I left to go to work.

#

Kayden climbed into the cab of the R.V. and smiled at the driver. "Thanks for the ride."

"No problem," the driver replied. "I'm Ed. Where you headed to?"

"Kayden's my name. I'm going down to the coast to do some fishin'." He looked around the inside of the small portable house and turned to Ed with a grin. "This is a great little R.V. A fellow could live out of here and have everything he ever needed."

Ed nodded in agreement. "That's what I do. Been all over this country the past few years." He smiled. "Sometimes it gets lonely. Once in a while it's good to have someone to talk to. That's why I like to pick up hitchhikers. I get to meet some pretty interesting people that way." He paused for a moment and then said, "Tell me your story, Kayden."

Kayden suppressed a snicker. "All right Ed…if you really want to hear it."

#

It was another typical day of hauling nets, ice, and fish. Scrubbing boats and cleaning docks. Randall seemed to be in a particularly sour mood, so I tried hard to avoid him. He kept glaring in my direction hatefully. I could tell he had a real chip on his shoulder about something, and when the day was about over, I found out what it was.

I was arranging a pile of fish netting when Mack walked up to me. "Hey, Rurik. How's it going?"

"Great, Mack," I answered with a grin.

"I'd like you to stay a little longer today so we can talk." Then he turned to Randall. "Randall, you can go ahead and leave."

Randall gave him a bad-tempered look, tossed the bucket he was carrying into the pile with anger, turned around, and stormed back up the dock.

I finished my nets and then went to find Mack. He was enjoying his pipe while he sat on a bench waiting for me. "Have a seat," he gestured, and took a few slow puffs. I sat down next to him and waited for him to speak. "I've been watching you these last few months, Rurik, and you're not your typical teenager."

I didn't respond. I wasn't sure what he was referring to, and I didn't want to jump to conclusions that he knew what I was. I liked Mack and had no desire to harm him.

He took another puff on his pipe. "You run circles around Randall without even trying. You never seem to tire, and are very intelligent. I don't know why you would want to be down here laboring on a dock. I have a feeling you could do whatever you set your mind to. But I know it has something to do with that gal you're hooked up with."

I stiffened a little at his reference to Mindy, but didn't answer.

He could tell I was getting protective of her. "Don't get me wrong, it's none of my business what you two do," he continued. "If you're happy here, I'm glad to have you." He eyed me for a moment with his sharp blue eyes. Mack was a wise old bird, I could tell. The smoke curled up around his face as he exhaled. "I want you to take over Randall's position as the dock coordinator. It's more responsibility, but more money also."

I nodded my head. "Okay."

"It'll cause problems between you and Randall."

I shrugged. "He's never liked me."

Mack grinned. "Jealousy is its own kind of monster." He stood up and patted my shoulder. "I like you, Rurik. You have a job here as long as you and Mindy want to stick around."

"Thanks, Mack," I smiled.

"Come in an hour earlier tomorrow so we can go over all the details of the position. As smart as you are, that's all you'll need."

"All right," I nodded.

I went home, took a shower, and changed to go meet Mindy. She would be happy about my new position, which would mean more money for us. We got by already, but a little extra income would be nice…things wouldn't be so tight.

After changing, I hurried down to the restaurant, a little late since I'd stayed after to talk with Mack. As I approached, I could see Mindy outside waiting for me, already done with work. I bristled as I walked up. Randall was standing next to her and leaning in talking, while she stood against the side of the building. I could see in her face that she was uncomfortable with the situation. Having keen vampire ears, I heard the conversation.

"Oh, come on, Mindy, I can tell you like me. Meet me after work sometime and we'll go out for a drink, or something."

I tried to control my anger while I approached. I didn't think Randall realized that Mindy and I were together because she never came down to the docks…I always met her here.

"I…I already told you, Randall," Mindy was saying. "I have a boyfriend." She was way too nice to be rude to him like she needed to be. Randall would never take that excuse as a no.

Mindy was pressing her back against the wall, trying to keep some distance between them, but Randall was leaning down over her and had his hand beside her shoulder, trapping her where she was.

"I could be your boyfriend," he continued. Then he reached in and touched her hair. "You're very pretty."

She flinched from him, and I could see panic in her eyes. "Stop, Randall!" She tried to squirm around him, and he lowered his arm to keep her from escaping, and laughed.

That was it, I'd seen enough. I was at Randall's side in an instant, and grabbed him by the arm and shoved him back. Neither one of them saw me coming. Randall stumbled back several feet trying to catch his balance, with a surprised look on his face. Mindy looked relieved when she saw it was me.

"Hey!" Randall shouted angrily.

"Get away from her…now," I growled. It took major control to not throw him across the dock.

"What the hell are you doing here, Rurik?!" Randall shouted, recovering his dignity. Then understanding came into his face. "Oh, Mindy's your girlfriend?"

I stood and glared at him angrily without a word.

He turned back to Mindy. "What do you want to hook up with this guy for? He's a freak." Mindy didn't answer. "I'm not joking, Mindy," he continued. "I've seen him pick up things that takes three guys to move. He ain't normal."

I stepped toward him menacingly and he backed away. "I would suggest you leave Mindy alone, Randall. You don't want to piss me off, especially since I'm your boss now."

His eyes turned hateful and he glared back. "You think you're hot stuff, don't you?" He stared at me and Mindy for a moment. "You'll get yours." Then he turned around and stormed up the dock.

Mindy breathed a noticeable sigh of relief. I walked over and took her arm; her heart was pounding.

"Are you okay?"

She nodded, but her eyes filled with tears. I pulled her against me and hugged her.

"He comes here and bothers me when he gets off work sometimes."

"Why didn't you tell me?" I asked her.

"I didn't want you to think I was totally helpless. I thought I could handle him."

"Guys like Randall don't take no for an answer. You're too nice to tell him to get lost or jump off a bridge, which is the only thing he would understand." I looked intently into her face. "Don't ever keep anything like that from me again. I'm here to protect you."

She tried to smile. "Okay."

I took her arm and we headed back to our place.

For the next week I gradually took over running the docks. It required extra time, and I had to go in an hour earlier to handle any paperwork, or unexpected things that would come up. I enjoyed it…it wasn't as mindless as being a laborer, and I was even organizing things that Randall had left undone. I could tell that Mack was fairly impressed with me already.

Randall was a serious problem. He came to work every morning with a bad attitude, and often I could smell alcohol on his breath from the night before. He flung stuff around angrily, and grumbled constantly. I could see things coming to a head between us, and was dreading what the outcome could be. I liked being here with Mindy, and didn't want to mess up our comfortable existence by losing my temper and taking care of Randall the way I was inclined to. So I put up with him as best I could, and tried hard to avoid too many confrontations.

One morning I was at the end of the dock, going over the list for the day, when I heard Randall stumbling toward me. I turned with irritation and waited for him; it was obvious he was still plastered from the night before. I stared at him for a moment while he swayed back and forth on his feet, trying to keep his balance.

I sighed. "Go home, Randall."

He looked surprised. "What?" His eyes narrowed. "Why?"

"Because you're still drunk!" I yelled. "I can't let you work in your current condition…it wouldn't be safe for anyone."

He glared back. "I'm fine."

"No…you're not. Leave."

He stared at me for a moment, and then turned with anger and stomped off.

Unfortunately, he didn't stay gone. I was helping a couple of the dock laborers with bins and nets when Randall came staggering back down to the end of the pier. It was pretty obvious he'd left only long enough to get riled up with more booze. I stood and waited while he approached with a heated glare.

"You...you can't tell me what to do, punk. I'm older than you. I was runnin' things before you ever showed up. You come in here and just think you can take over."

"Randall," I tried to say evenly. "Go home and don't come back till tomorrow. And don't come back at all if you can't show up sober."

He suddenly took a swing at me. Humans were incredibly slow anyway, but the fact that he was trashed and could hardly stand made him that much more so. I grabbed his arm and pushed him to the ground, and glared into his eyes. I showed him the terrifying creature in me while we glowered at each other. He stared back, horrified.

"Go home...you got it?" I threatened.

He nodded, scared to death. I got off the top of him and he scrambled to his feet and backed away. "You're a freak!" He stared at me for another moment and then turned and quickly left.

I couldn't help sighing under my breath; I'd avoided a serious confrontation with him.

The other dock workers looked at me with curiosity. They could see the fear in Randall's eyes, but hadn't been the focus of my glare, so didn't see in me what Randall had.

Mindy and I sat outside under the small covered porch area at the picnic table to the side of the cottage and grilled burgers. It was a pleasant evening, and we held hands while the burgers sizzled on the grill. Mindy was lightly running her fingers up and down my arm, and the sensation was wonderful. I was enjoying the moment with my eyes closed.

"Rurik?" she asked softly.

I opened my eyes. "Hmm?"

"I…I…." She was suddenly a little embarrassed.

"What is it, Mindy?"

She sighed nervously. "I love you. I want to be with you."

"I love you too," I answered.

"I know, but you know…you know what I mean." She blushed. "As lovers."

It took me a little bit by surprise. "Are you sure you're ready, Mindy? I told you there was no rush, and I'm happy for now. Don't feel like you have to just to please me."

She sighed. "I'm still nervous, after everything with Kayden. But I want to be fair to you." Her eyes filled with tears. "I don't want you to do without."

I smiled and squeezed her hand. "I'm not doing without. Having you here with me is amazing. We'll get around to that when you're ready. We've only been together here for a couple of months. We have our whole lives."

She smiled and then leaned her head against my shoulder. "You're the kindest, nicest person, Rurik."

I snorted under my breath.

"You are," she insisted. "All you want is for me to be happy. I could never find anyone to replace you in a million years. You're my guardian angel."

I frowned at her. "There's no way I'm an angel, Mindy."

"You are to me."

"You're delusional," I couldn't help saying.

She playfully hit my arm. "I am not! You've saved me more than once. You're my guardian angel whether you believe it or not."

I snorted again. "They must have really lowered their standards to let someone like me be an angel."

"Stop belittling yourself," she said, almost angrily. "You're the most wonderful person there is."

"Okay," I smiled. "I'm not going to keep arguing with you. But you're crazy." I stood up and grabbed the spatula and slipped the burgers onto the buns. "Ready for a burger?"

She nodded and laughed.

#

After my altercation with Randall, he'd backed off. He came to work every day and gave me angry stares, but avoided getting too close. I could see real fear in his eyes when he glanced in my direction sometimes. He'd started directing his anger and frustrations to one of the new dock workers, Bud. I felt sorry for Bud, but he was large enough to hold his own, and with Randall focused on him, I didn't have to be as concerned about things coming to a head between us.

One gray, cold day, Randall was in a particularly sour mood. Winter was in full swing, and it was miserable a lot of the time working in these conditions. Definitely a low time of year for fishing, but there were fishermen that worked all year, and the docks still had to be maintained. The dock workers all had their hours cut for the winter season, and Randall had been grumbling about that for days. I was the only one who still worked full time, and if it wasn't for me, he would be.

Randall was relentless with his attacks on Bud. It started only verbally, with him berating him about every little thing. Bud did his best to ignore Randall, which infuriated Randall even more, until he was roughly throwing things to Bud and purposefully slamming into him when he would walk by. Finally, Bud had enough, and when Randall ambled by him and hit him squarely on the shoulder, knocking Bud against the wall, Bud grabbed Randall and pressed him to the deck.

Randall immediately took a swing at Bud and the fight ensued. Dock workers and fishermen can be the type to enjoy a good scuffle, and a crowd formed around the two while they grappled and rolled across the dock, swinging and hitting. The bystanders hooped and hollered with excitement; there was nothing more entertaining than a good fight. I let it go on for a few minutes before I decided to intervene…they both had pent up hostilities they needed to vent.

"All right, all right. Break it up now, guys. Time to get back to work!" I yelled good-naturedly.

Bud backed away from Randall and grinned. He had a swollen lip, but Randall was bleeding from a bloody nose. It appeared to be a draw as to who'd actually won. Bud turned to pick up his net that he'd dropped in the fight, and Randall leaped on him with fury, knocking him to the ground and pounding Bud in the face.

I pounced on top of Randall and had to physically pull him back. "I said that's enough, Randall!" I yelled.

But Randall wasn't done and came at me with his fists. I held him at bay with no effort, but was trying hard not to show how easy it really was and let him have a few swings. "Randall! Relax, it's time to get back to work!"

"I'm going to kill you, Rurik," he went on. "I've had enough of you!"

He tried his best to hit me, and I had to practically carry him to the end of the dock and set him down, then shoved him away with force. He went careening away from me and fell backwards, and stared up at me, fuming.

"Go home, now!" I shouted.

"I'm not leaving!" Randall screamed back. "I'm tired of being ordered around by a teenage punk freak!" He stood up and came toward me again.

I shoved him hard and he slammed against the side of the office building on the end of the dock. "Yes, you are! I'm not putting up with your disruptions anymore. You're fired!"

He stopped in mid stride and stared at me with astonishment. "You can't fire me."

I knew there was a gleam in my cold, black eyes. "I just did. Take it up with Mack if you don't like it." I felt total contempt and stood regarding him for a moment, and then turned and left him standing there.

Mack came up to me the following morning when I was going over some of the inventory. "Hi, Rurik."

"Hey, Mack," I answered.

He stood beside me in utter silence, so I turned to observe him. I could tell he had something to say.

"Randall came to me begging for his job back last night."

My eyes narrowed, but I didn't respond. I sighed and just shook my head.

Mack shrugged and continued. "It's up to you. I just thought I should let you know."

"He's a really bad egg, Mack. He causes division and strife among all the other workers. It's not worth having him around."

Mack smirked. "I can't disagree with you. He's always been a lot to deal with." His eyes squinted and he concentrated his gaze on me. "But he's not one to take any sort of refusal gracefully. I would watch my back if I were you."

I nodded my head. "Thanks, Mack. I can take care of myself."

His piercing eyes bore into mine. "I knew that you could, Rurik." The way he said that and the wise look he gave me almost made me think he knew me too well. Then he patted my shoulder. "I'm glad you're running things."

I watched him walk back up the dock to his office. Mack was clever; there was a lot going on behind his casual expression and smile. I would have to be extra careful around him. I hated to have to do anything to someone like him, who was a real joy to be around, just because he'd discovered what I was.

#

It was Saturday morning and I woke Mindy up shortly before I left for the docks. Kimmy liked her to come in early on weekends to help with the food prep since it was their busiest days. Mindy entered the kitchen to get a bowl of cereal while I was standing at the sink washing my plate. I just had to kiss her. She was turned away from me looking in the cupboard when I grabbed her around the waist and quickly spun her in my direction. She gasped, surprised, and stared up into my eyes while I smiled and pressed her against the counter. I could hear her heart beating wildly in her chest, as she flung her arms around my neck to hold on.

I leaned down, softly blowing my hot breath against her throat, and then playfully nipped her ear. "I love you so much, Mindy."

She trembled when my lips brushed against her neck, and then sighed. "I love you too, Rurik. More than anything."

I brushed her hair out of her eyes; it was still a little disheveled from sleeping. "See you after work."

She smiled and I turned and walked out the door.

\#

Mindy was in the back closet of the small restaurant getting some linens to set up the tables for the next day. It had been a long day. Most Saturdays she was able to leave early, but they'd been swamped with customers since that morning. Her feet hurt, and she couldn't wait to put them up and cuddle with Rurik. She smiled at the thought. He was everything to her. It seemed she could hardly go an hour out of the day without thinking of him. Life down here was pleasant and simple. She could happily stay here with Rurik forever.

Suddenly she heard Kimmy's panic-stricken scream. Mindy's heart went to her throat and she raced out of the back to the dining room and stopped short. Her blood pounding in her ears, her face went white as a sheet. This had to be some kind of horrible nightmare, she thought.

Kayden was standing in the middle of the dining area. His eyes were red and glowing and he smiled in her direction, showing his horrible, long fangs.

Kimmy lay on the floor, unconscious.

"Hello Mindy. It's been too long," Kayden said with a malicious grin.

Mindy couldn't speak, or move. She was dumbstruck with horror and stood where she was and quaked.

Kayden frowned. "Don't you have anything to say to me after all this time?"

She shook her head back and forth in slow, jerky movements. This couldn't be happening. "You're dead. You're not here."

He retorted sarcastically, "Of course I'm dead. I'm a vampire."

"But…but I saw Rurik kill you when you were a vampire. You're supposed to be dead," she insisted.

Kayden walked slowly forward. "Well, I hate to break it to ya, but I aint dead."

Mindy backed slowly away from him and continued to shake her head, her eyes wide and frightened. Kayden reached out and grabbed Mindy's arm, and she screamed with terror.

"Shhhh…," Kayden said, and reached out with his other hand and stroked her hair. "I really missed you, Mindy. I've been looking for you for months."

Mindy stared up into Kayden's blood red eyes with fear.

Kimmy suddenly moaned and was starting to stir. Kayden dragged Mindy over to where Kimmy lay on the floor. He had murder in his eyes while he stared down at Kimmy.

"No! Kayden, please don't hurt her!" Mindy pleaded.

Kayden laughed and bent down to Kimmy.

Mindy was desperate to save her. "I'll go with you. Just…just let her live. Please."

Kayden turned to Mindy and smiled cruelly. "Okay," he said. "If you come with me willingly I won't kill her."

Mindy hesitated and stared down at Kimmy, who was stirring again, then back up into Kayden's evil expression. She was frozen with fear. The thought if leaving here with Kayden was so far beyond frightening it was paralyzing.

"She's starting to come to. Make up your mind, Mindy." He put his foot over Kimmy's head and glared at Mindy. "Now," he said in a deadly tone.

"Okay, okay. Don't hurt her," Mindy quickly answered.

Kayden smiled smugly and yanked Mindy to the front and out the door. They went swiftly up the pier. Mindy had to run to keep up with Kayden, who was practically dragging her along. By the time he stopped in front of a small R.V. Mindy was panting for breath. Kayden opened the side door and shoved her in, then stepped in and closed the door behind them.

#

Mindy had called earlier and said that Kimmy needed her to stay till closing. It was just starting to get dark when I left to meet her. I walked down to the end of the pier to the small restaurant, enjoying the scenery along the way.

Even with the heavily overcast sky the ocean was amazing; midnight blue with hints of brilliant green that swirled down into its shadowy depths. When the sun was bright overhead the water resembled more of an aqua that you could look right through, sometimes all the way to the glistening sand at the bottom.

As I approached the front door, I sensed something was very wrong. I braced myself and then burst inside. Kimmy was trying to get up off the floor. She had a large bump and cut on the side of her head, and when she finally stood, stumbled around, disoriented.

I quickly went over and took her arm. "Kimmy, what happened?!" I asked with alarm.

"Oh, my head," she groaned with her hand on her forehead.

I sat her in a chair at one of the tables and looked around the room. "Where's Mindy?"

Kimmy glanced about, as if finally aware of her surroundings. "Mindy? I…I don't know."

"What happened here?" I asked a little more forcefully.

"I was cleaning and…a young man came in. I didn't even look up…just saw him out of the corner of my eye. I was busy…it had been a hectic day." She paused for a moment and tried to formulate what happened next. "I said, 'sorry, we're closed,' and then he grabbed me from behind. I screamed and he hit me over the head. That's the last thing I remember till now. I figured he wanted to rob the place." She looked at me with confusion. "Where's Mindy?"

I was rapidly getting more concerned. "I don't know. I'm trying to find that out from you. What did the man look like?"

She rubbed her head again. "I…I didn't see him very well. He was tall, very young, in his teens, with blond hair and dark eyes…almost black, I think, and mean-looking. About your size."

My heart went cold, and I looked a little more carefully at my surroundings. I tested the air and picked up the slight odor of a vampire. It was familiar, but peculiar at the same time. It resembled Kayden, but there were differences that I couldn't quite discern. "Kayden," I said, more to myself than to her.

"Who?" Kimmy asked.

It couldn't be though. He was dead. I looked thoughtfully into Kimmy's eyes. "I don't know for sure, but this could be very bad." I stood up and went quickly to the door.

"Where are you going?" Kimmy asked.

I didn't answer, and walked out the door and up the pier. The scent was strange. It didn't quite seem like vampire, and didn't exactly smell like Kayden. None of it made any sense. I knew that I'd killed him. He was dead when Mindy and I left her house months ago to come out here.

#

Mindy sat at a small table in the R.V. and anxiously watched Kayden at the wheel while he drove. She couldn't believe that it was really him. Half of her expected to wake up from the worst, most realistic nightmare she'd ever had. Her hands and feet were tied tightly so she could hardly move. Tears streamed down her face.

The clouds were starting to break up in the sky, and the sun came out for a split second before disappearing again. Mindy stared at Kayden with horror. The back of his head had, in that instant, briefly become a decayed, rotten skull. Her eyes widened while she watched a large patch of sun on the road in front of the R.V. She didn't want to see what she'd glimpsed a few moments earlier, but couldn't turn away. Transfixed with dread, Mindy stared straight ahead, her heart furiously pounding as the sun burst brightly in through the windshield and hit Kayden with clarity.

His arms became skeletal, and his head turned to a skull again with loose, rotten, hanging skin, the hair stringy and sparse. Mindy screamed at the top of her lungs and Kayden turned to grin widely at her, his face a horrible skull with sunken, dead holes for eyes. Mindy felt like she would pass out from absolute fright when the light just as quickly disappeared, and Kayden's features became normal again.

They drove for at least an hour before Kayden pulled off the main highway and onto a back road. The vegetation was thick and the road narrowed. Mindy's heart was in her throat when the vehicle came to a slow stop. Kayden turned off the engine and then spun in his chair, anticipation in his face. He stared silently at her for a few moments before he got up and walked back, bent down, and untied the ropes on Mindy's hands and feet.

There was a sudden deafening crash and everything splintered around Mindy. She screamed and was tossed through the air, landing hard on the ground. She shook her head, trying to get her bearings. She stared in disbelief at what was left of the R.V. Pieces of fractured fiberglass lay strewn for yards around her. The contents looked like nothing more than a pile of rubble. There was a horrendous growling noise behind her, and she turned to stare with wide eyes.

Rurik and Kayden were circling each other, fangs exposed and eyes glowing a horrible blood red. Kayden had become the frightening skeleton again. His horrible features illuminated in the bright light.

Mindy rose to her feet and backed away. She was completely relieved that Rurik was there. Now Kayden would die.

#

I'd had to use all of my concentration and tracking abilities to follow Kayden and Mindy. It was easy up until they got in the vehicle and drove away. The only thing that saved me was the fact that it was a very old vehicle and was emitting lots of carbon dioxide. Otherwise I never would have been able to distinguish it from the others on the road. I followed for hours. I knew as long as Kayden was driving that he wasn't hurting Mindy, and hoped that I could catch up with them before they stopped. I tried hard to keep my mind focused on the scent, and not think too much about Kayden and what he would do to Mindy.

The trail turned off the main highway to a back secluded road. There was no other traffic at all, and I knew Kayden wouldn't have to drive too far down this road before he would want to stop. I quickened my pace. Suddenly I saw the vehicle pulled over to the side of the road and raced forward. I didn't even slow down when I reached it, and crashed through the flimsy shell of the old R.V. The pieces exploded around me like a bomb. I saw Mindy fly backwards and land hard on the ground. She looked unharmed, so I turned my attention to Kayden.

He had a moment of shock that instantly changed to fury, and glared at me, his features hideous and decayed in the bright overhead sunlight. We growled, and circled each other a few times.

"Rurik!" Kayden shouted. "This is the last time you'll interfere in my plans!"

"You should be dead, Kayden!" I yelled back. "I don't know how you survived, but this time I'll make sure you die!"

Kayden laughed loudly. "You don't get it, do you, Rurik? You did kill me."

I stopped and stared at him with disbelief. "Then how are you here?"

He shrugged. "I don't know, but I feel even better than I did before. You're the one who's gonna die. Then Mindy will be mine forever."

I growled. "There's no way you're ever laying a finger on her again." I stepped confidently forward. I knew he didn't stand a chance against me, because I was the most powerful creature on this planet.

Kayden looked concerned at my confidence, and backed away. We circled each other, and then he lunged at me. It took me by surprise how fast he was…faster than any other vampire I'd ever come up against. I didn't move out of his path quickly enough, and his claws raked my side from my shoulder all the way down to my leg. I yelled with anger and pain and turned on him with my fangs bared. I sunk them into his neck, but he promptly twisted away from me and escaped, leaving a sizeable gash across the side of his throat.

We stepped back to catch our breath and resize our opponent.

The sun faded behind a cloud again and Kayden's appearance became normal. I didn't understand why he wasn't as easy to kill as he should have been. He growled and leaped at me.

I stepped swiftly to the side, but he was able to sink his claws painfully into my chest. I grimaced and lunged back. We fell to the ground and rolled together, snapping and growling. He equaled all of my maneuvers; I couldn't seem to best him no matter what I tried. My strength was actually starting to falter. But I could see in his face that he was tired too. I surged with new energy and pushed him forcefully back.

Kayden staggered away several feet and then came toward me again. He leaped at me, pushed me to the ground, and brought his fangs down to my throat. I struggled with all of my might, but couldn't budge him. He grinned and sank his fangs into my flesh. I fought him with everything in me. I thought I was going to die.

"No!" I heard Mindy shout. She jumped on Kayden's back and put her hands around his head. She clawed at his eyes and he turned furiously from me to her. He had her under him in an instant, and hit her several times before I was able to pull him off her. One of his eyes was gouged out from Mindy's fingernails, but I watched with horror and amazement as it instantly grew back.

Kayden saw the incredulous look on my face, and laughed. "I told you that you couldn't kill me, Rurik. I'm indestructible."

"We'll see about that," I answered determinedly, and flew at him. In a split second I had him on the ground with my teeth in his neck. He yelled from the pain and pushed me off. I came at him again, more determined than ever. It was time to end this. I leaped on him and pummeled him repeatedly with my fists. He tried to shield himself from my onslaught while I hit him with everything I had in me.

Kayden was quickly getting battered, and was suddenly desperate to get away. He shoved me hard and I hit a tree several yards back. Then he jumped to his feet and ran off into the brush.

I wanted to pursue him, but when I turned to glance at Mindy she was still lying on the ground where Kayden had left her. She had several gashes across her face from Kayden striking her, and there was blood on her mouth. "Mindy!" I shouted, and rushed to her side. I lifted her into my arms and cradled her against me.

She held onto me tightly and sobbed, burying her head in my chest. We stayed that way for several minutes. I finally pulled away and took my hand, lifting her face to mine. She was still trembling and her eyes were as large as saucers.

"Are you okay, Angel?" I asked gently.

She nodded her head and wiped her tears away with her hand. "I thought you were going to die, Rurik. I thought Kayden was going to kill you."

I sighed. "I'm fine, and he's gone now." I lifted her to her feet and put my arm around her waist.

We walked slowly back down the road the way I had come. The dark was creeping in and Mindy was very tired, so I picked her up and held her in my arms so that I could go back to our cottage faster. When we got there, Mindy took a shower and put her pajamas on. She snuggled into my side, slowly relaxing from the harrowing day, and drifted off to sleep.

I called Mack once Mindy was sleeping soundly to make sure Kimmy was all right after her encounter with Kayden. Mack said she was, just bruised and scared.

They'd filed a police report. I feigned ignorance about any knowledge of Kayden and said I'd left to find Mindy, who had been scared and run off. I hung up, relieved that everything had turned out okay. It could have ended so much worse.

I stared down at my sleeping angel and thought about Kayden. Somehow he'd become as powerful as me. It didn't make any sense. The only thing that made any sense was my venom. Every part of me was stronger and faster and better. So it stood to reason that my venom would be superior too. Somehow it had turned Kayden into a creature of the night that was more powerful than other vampires. Almost as powerful as I was. And it seemed that killing him had only made him even stronger than before. I was going to have to make sure he was really dead the next time, or he may come back more indestructible than me.

Mindy slept for a long time before she finally woke. I was sitting over at the small table when she started to stir. "Rurik?" she called.

"Over here," I said behind her.

She turned to look at me. "Oh," then smiled. "Hi."

I grinned. "Hello, Angel." I walked over to her and sat down and took her hand. I tenderly caressed the soft skin on her arm. "Are you going to be okay?"

She nodded. "But I already told you, you're the one that's an angel," she smiled. "My guardian angel."

I shook my head. "You're unreal. There's no way that I'm an angel. You, on the other hand, are the definition of one." I bent down and kissed her lips. She stared up into my face with such love and trust it was an almost overwhelming feeling.

"You want to eat something?"

She nodded and we both got up to raid the fridge. After looking through the shelves, we decided to make B.L.T.'s.

I couldn't help sighing heavily, and Mindy looked up at me from her plate. "What?"

"We can't stay here," I said with sad realization.

"It's Kayden, isn't it?"

"Yeah. He ran off, but he won't stay gone for long, and I don't want to put Mack and Kimmy in any more danger. I have to make sure he's permanently dead next time."

Mindy's eyes filled with tears. "I'll miss it here. And Kimmy."

"I know. Once Kayden's dead we could probably come back."

That brightened Mindy's unhappy mood, and she smiled. "Really?"

"Uh-huh," I said. "Let's go to work, and then we can pack and leave tonight. Don't say anything to Kimmy. I think it's best if they know nothing about it."

"All right," Mindy agreed.

When I left for work, Mindy was getting ready for her day. I pulled her to me and hugged her. Her eyes sparkled. "I'm making your favorite for our last night here. Since you got a raise I decided to splurge and get some steaks."

I grinned at her. "Sounds delicious. Rare for me."

She laughed. "I knew that about you."

I pulled her close and looked deep into her eyes. "Maybe we can have a nice romantic evening together before we hit the road," I said with meaning.

She blushed at the thought. "All right."

"I love you." I leaned down and whispered softly into her ear.

She sighed with contentment. "I love you, too."

I had a great day at work anticipating the evening's events, and couldn't wait to have Mindy in my arms forever. There were no doubts in my mind that she was the love of my life. She called and told me that she'd gotten off a little early and was going to meet me back at the cottage. I was in a fantastic mood as I walked up the hill to our home. I went around the side of the small pink house in front of our cottage and stopped dead in my tracks. My heart went to my throat.

"No!" I yelled, and took off at top speed for the door.

Parked beside the grill on the side of our little cottage was an Audi...my dad's Audi.

Chapter Nine
Discovered

I burst through the front door and stopped. Mindy was sitting on the couch with Dad next to her, and Mom was seated at the small table behind them. Mindy's expression was that of terror while she sat there with Dad's arm wrapped around her shoulder. Mom's face had concern and relief all at the same time at seeing me.

Dad was beyond angry. His eyes were coal black with firestorms at the centers, his brow furiously creased. I was very concerned for Mindy.

"Come in and sit down, Rurik," Dad said in a relatively calm tone.

I stepped into the room with hesitation, closed the door, and sat in the chair across from the couch. I glanced from Dad back to Mindy. She was trembling and barely holding in the tears.

I took a slow breath. "Dad," I whispered, "please don't do anything you'll regret."

Dad's eyes glinted angrily. "Did you think you could just hide down here forever?" he asked quietly. "That we wouldn't eventually find you? What were you thinking, Rurik? I would really like to understand."

I was desperate about the way he had his hand wrapped around Mindy's shoulder, only inches from her throat. With one quick flick of his wrist, he could quickly kill her.

"I…we…um…." I was having a hard time forming rational whole thoughts in my brain at the moment.

"Spit it out!" he yelled.

Mindy cringed and I flinched.

"We…love each other, Dad." I answered quietly. "We just wanted to be together." Tears were rolling down Mindy's cheeks. I was desperate to hold her. "It's okay, Angel," I said. "Everything will be fine." I shifted my eyes to Dad's. "What are you going to do?"

"We are all going to get in the car and go back home," he answered.

"Then what?" I couldn't help asking.

He didn't answer and stood up, holding onto Mindy's arm.

Mindy suddenly turned toward me with a troubled expression. "Rurik…my angel." Mindy wanted the lamp I'd bought for her birthday.

"Can we please bring Mindy's angel lamp?" I asked.

Dad stared at me darkly, and then opened his mouth to protest when Mom stepped up. "Of course," she said, and picked it up off the table.

Mom drove and Dad sat in the back with me and Mindy. He never took his arm from around Mindy, and watched me without wavering. I knew he knew I was more powerful than him, but also that there was no way I would try anything with Mindy in danger. It was a long drive back up the coast, and after a while Mindy, try as she might, couldn't keep her eyes open any longer. It had been a harrowing few days for her, and she nodded off. It wasn't long before she was sleeping with her head resting against Dad's shoulder. I noticed him glancing at her occasionally while she slept. She really did look like an angel. His hard expression even seemed to have softened slightly.

"Have you seen Kayden these last months since you left?" Dad asked.

I nodded. "He showed up here the other day and took Mindy. I followed his trail and was able to get her back, but he was so strong that I couldn't defeat him."

Dad's eyes narrowed. "Are you saying he was as strong as you?"

"Yeah, he was. I don't know why. The only thing I could think it might be is that my venom made him more powerful than normal. I'm sure that I killed him at Mindy's house, but somehow he came back stronger than ever. He ran off while I was helping Mindy."

Dad let out a slow breath and stared at me ponderingly. "We need to find and destroy him completely before he tears open our society and exposes it to the rest of the world." His expression turned furious again. "I keep hating to reiterate what I've already said. But if you had left Mindy alone from the beginning we wouldn't be in this situation now."

I nodded but kept my mouth shut. I didn't want to rile him anymore than he already was…especially with Mindy in such close reach.

Mindy woke with a jolt when the car slowed down in the drive in front of the house. We all got out and Dad directed us inside and to his office.

I went over to Mindy and sat beside her. She took my hand in hers…she was still so scared. I reached up and tenderly touched her face. "Don't worry. Everything will be okay." I tried to reassure her, even though I had no idea whether it would be.

"All right," Dad said, interrupting. "First we have to decide what to do about Mindy."

My heart went to my throat at the dark expression on his face, and I wrapped Mindy in my arms protectively.

"Couldn't we just keep her?" Mom piped up.

"What?" Dad asked.

"Couldn't we just keep Mindy?"

"She's not a lost pet, Carmen," he answered dryly.

"I realize that," Mom said indignantly. "But she has nowhere else to go. Her family is all dead, and the authorities think she is, too. There wasn't much left of the house after the fire. We obviously can't just let her go free…she knows too much about our society."

"The smart thing under the circumstances would be to get rid of her. Like you said, no one knows she's here," Dad returned grimly.

Mindy cringed back and her eyes widened even more.

"No!" I couldn't help yelling. "It's not her fault. Her only crime has been loving me."

Dad gave me a dark stare and was silent for several minutes, deep in thought. He got up from his desk and paced back and forth around the room while we all held our breaths. I had my arms tightly around Mindy, and she shrunk back against my chest.

Then he turned to me with vehemence. "This is ultimately your doing, Rurik," he said. "Whatever happens with Mindy is because of your actions!"

My heart stopped in my throat. I thought he was deciding against letting Mindy live. "Please don't—" I started.

He held up his hand to silence me and sighed. "You have a destiny with Amy, and you're going to fulfill it. Do you understand? If I let Mindy live it's only with that idea. You and her were never meant to be. Got it?!"

I breathed a huge sigh of relief and nodded my head.

Then Dad turned to Mindy. She stared back at him with terrified eyes, and he said, almost gently, "Mindy, you have been unwittingly dragged into our world, a place that you never belonged from the beginning. The law demands that you die." He paused meaningfully.

Mindy shook uncontrollably in my arms.

"But we are not without compassion. You're a very nice girl. All I can offer you is a life here in our custody, with maybe the possibility of becoming a vampire at some point. Otherwise you'll work for us in some fashion. Is that acceptable to you?"

Mindy looked completely relieved that she wasn't going to be killed, and nodded her head.

Dad turned to Mom. "Give Mindy the room down here at the end of the hall. It's close to the kitchen and the library. Rurik and I need to continue this discussion." Then he turned back to Mindy and said, "If you ever try to leave or cause problems, you'll be taken care of. Is that completely understood?"

Mindy took a deep breath and said quietly, "I understand, Mr. Tallinn. I won't."

Mom came over, took Mindy by the arm, and guided her out of the room. Mindy stared into my face one last time before they left the room. My heart went out to her…she still had so much fear in her eyes. Mom closed the door behind them and I turned back to Dad, and braced myself for what I was sure was coming.

He stood for several moments without a word. "Rurik," he finally started. "You've broken just about every law on our books this last year. I really don't know what I'm supposed to do with you."

"I'm sorry, Dad. I...I just wanted to be with Mindy. To protect her. I love her."

He slammed his hand down on the desk furiously. "That is not an excuse!" he yelled.

I jumped back in my chair at his sudden outburst.

It took him a few moments to calm down before he asked, "Is there any possibility that she's pregnant?"

"What?" I asked. "No."

"Are you sure?"

"Positive," I said with certainty. "Mindy and I haven't ever had an intimate relationship."

He stared at me with disbelief. "You expect me to believe that you've been down there with her for almost a year and you two haven't ever done anything?"

"Yes."

"How is that possible?" he asked.

"Because I love her. I want what's best for Mindy, and it wasn't best for her to have a physical relationship yet."

He seemed genuinely surprised. "I'm proud of you for having that attitude, Rurik. It takes a lot of maturity to put others' needs before your own."

"That's what true love is all about, isn't it?" I asked flatly.

He sighed. "Well, that will make this part a little easier for both of you then. I'm sorry this is so painful, but you and Mindy are to be nothing but friends from now on." He looked carefully into my eyes. "Can you do that?"

"I can do anything that I have to for Mindy," I answered quietly.

"Good. Because that's the only way she's staying alive." He paused before he said, "Okay, we're going to go down to the dungeon for your punishment. I'd hoped that when I flogged you the last time that you'd learned your lesson and I would never have to repeat it." He walked over to the door and opened it, and stood to the side and waited for me. "Some learn quicker than others."

My heart was in my throat as we walked down the hall, and then into the passageway to the dungeon. I was beyond terrified, but reminded myself I could endure anything as long as I knew Mindy was to be spared.

#

I was up in my room lying on my bed, hating my dad at the moment. I was in misery from the flogging, and tears rolled unchecked down my cheeks. There was a soft knock at my door. I figured it must be Mom, seeing if I'd survived. I sat up and wiped the tears off my face.

"Come in," I said quietly.

The door opened and it was Mom, but Mindy was also with her. Mindy looked at me sadly when they walked into the room. Mom came over and brushed my tousled hair out of my face with sympathy.

"I'm sorry, Rurik," she said softly. "But you know the laws, and your father was very generous with you, compared to the punishment you could have received."

I flinched back from her hand. "He has no feelings at all!" I couldn't help stating with anger.

Her expression was sad. "You know that's not true. He let Mindy live, despite the logical decision being to kill her. And your father loves you very much."

I let out a deep breath of frustration. I knew that what she said was true, but all of the pain I felt at the moment was overwhelming. Not just the physical pain, but the emotional turmoil of living the rest of my life without Mindy in my arms. Never having her soft warm kisses against my lips again, never holding her tender body to mine...never consummating our love for each other. That was the part that was too painful to deal with right now.

"I'll leave you two alone to talk...I know you have a lot to say to each other," Mom said with compassion.

I nodded despondently to her and she walked out the door and closed it behind her. Mindy came over and sat down on the edge of the bed beside me and took my hand. She glanced at my back and grimaced at the welts and cuts. "I'm so sorry, Rurik," she said as the tears spilled down her cheeks.

I squeezed her hand. "It's okay, Mindy. I'll be fine in a few hours...my body heals fast." I continued with sarcasm, "I think that's part of the reason Dad doesn't show me any mercy." I cringed from the pain, then sighed and looked deep into her eyes. "The part that's killing me right now is never having you in my arms again." I reached up and softly touched her face.

She closed her eyes and melted against my hand, and sighed heavily. Then she took my hand in hers and brought it up to her lips and gently kissed it. "I love you so much," she whispered. She opened her eyes and looked into mine, and tried to smile. "At least I still get to be in your world."

I shook my head. "This is all so wrong. You belong to me, Mindy. It's not fair that our love can't be."

I stared deep into her eyes and leaned in and kissed her, long and with passion. I knew it would be our last kiss ever, and I wanted to savor it. The memory of it would have to last forever. She melted into my arms. I didn't want to ever let her go, but after several minutes I reluctantly pulled back and stared into her soft, smoldering green eyes.

"I can do anything I have to…to keep you safe. You're everything to me," I whispered.

Tears continued to stream down Mindy's face while she stared back into my eyes. I stood up and went over to my closet and got a shirt. I grimaced when I put it on; even the softest material was painful. "Let's go downstairs and get something to eat. I'm hungry, and I'm sure you're starving."

"Yeah, I'm pretty much famished," Mindy agreed and tried to smile, wiping her tears away.

We sat at the table and ate a sandwich and potato chips. It was nice to still be able to interact with Mindy. Not only did I love her with my whole heart, but she was also my friend. I was thankful that we could still enjoy that. We chatted and laughed while we ate.

Dad walked into the kitchen and stopped in front of the table. Mindy immediately stiffened. She was smart enough to realize that he was the one who decided whether she lived or died at any moment. I felt bad for her; living with that hanging over her head was not an easy thing. We waited silently…he obviously had something to say.

His expression had relaxed and the furious anger was gone. I couldn't help breathing a sigh of relief.

"I think that we'll hire a private tutor for Mindy. Obviously she can't go back to a public school…everyone around here believes she's dead. It's been a year since what happened with Kayden."

"Dad, I can teach her. You don't need to hire a tutor. And then when she's ready she can take her G.E.D." I noticed Mindy perk up at the idea.

He frowned. "I'm not sure I want you two spending that much time together."

"It'll just be studying," I reasoned. "Besides, if you hire a tutor, it could get sticky with the idea that Mindy isn't supposed to even be here."

"You're right about that," he agreed. "It would be better not to involve another human in this fiasco if we can avoid it. If things go wrong we don't want to have to end up killing half this town again." He turned to Mindy while he was considering everything. "From now on your name is Mindy Brian. Your last name is no longer Brown. All right?"

"Okay, Mr. Tallinn," Mindy answered quietly.

"Mindy, you don't have to call me Mr. Tallinn. Adrian is fine." He sighed. "I'm sorry for all the fear we've caused you. As long as you do as you're told, you don't have to be afraid. No one is going to harm you."

She nodded, and her face looked relieved at his words.

He smiled at her, and then said to me, "She can use your school books from the high school, and we'll figure out a good schedule."

"Okay, Dad," I answered.

He left the room and I grinned at Mindy. It would be nice to be able to study together.

#

Adrian went down the hall to the sitting room and found Carmen on the sofa by the fireplace. He walked up and put his hand on her shoulder.

Carmen looked up at him and smiled wistfully. "Sometimes I still miss being human. I sit here by the fire and I can feel its warmth, but I don't need it. I don't get cold like I used to, no matter what the temperature is." She laughed at herself. "Listen to me. I used to hate the cold, now I miss it." She reached up and put her hand on Adrian's. "How're you doing?"

"I'm okay, sweetheart," he answered. "But this entire situation should've never happened."

"Mindy's very sweet," Carmen stated. "I remember being human and the fear I felt about being around vampires. It's too bad she was dragged into our world this way. I feel sorry for Rurik too. He really loves her."

Adrian's eyes grew dark and angry. "He's to blame for this whole mess."

Carmen sighed. "Don't be too hard on him. He's just a kid in love."

"In love with the wrong person. I don't know if it's a good idea to have Mindy and Rurik this close to each other, but I couldn't just kill her either."

"No, Rurik would never forgive you if you did."

"I had Charlie put keyed locks on Mindy's door. I hate to treat her like a prisoner, but in a lot of ways she is. And I don't want Rurik to be able to have easy access to her room."

"That's probably a smart thing to do. At least for a while, until we can make sure they are both moving forward and adjusting."

#

That evening we all sat in the living area and watched a movie. Normally I would've had Mindy snuggled against me on the sofa, but I knew Mom and Dad wouldn't allow it. So I sat next to Mindy, but didn't even dare to touch her hand. It was torture…I could literally feel the electricity from our closeness, and not having contact was unbearable. I glanced over at my parents and they were sitting together holding hands. Mom had her head resting against Dad's shoulder. It was so unfair. At one point I saw Mindy turn briefly to me, and she had tears in her eyes. She was in as much agony as I was.

Once the movie was over, Mindy stood up and stretched. "Well, I should get some sleep."

Dad stood up also. "All right, Mindy." He hesitated briefly, and then said. "I need to lock your door once you're in your room, so I'll walk with you."

"What?!" I couldn't help exclaiming. "Why?"

Dad looked at me darkly for a moment. "There's no point in leaving anything open to temptation, Rurik."

I sighed. I hated that Mindy was being treated this way. I stood up and looked down into Mindy's eyes for a moment. The longing in hers was apparent. I wanted to embrace her and kiss her badly. I had to touch her, so I reached out and took her hand and squeezed it. Her eyes softened slightly at that simple contact; I could tell she appreciated it.

"Goodnight, Angel," I said gently.

She smiled. "See you in the morning, Rurik."
Then she turned around and walked out of the room, with Dad following her.

#

For the next week Mindy and I did her lessons together and would hang out to eat, or watch movies. But Mom and Dad made sure we were never left alone no matter what we were doing. It was frustrating that I couldn't even touch Mindy's hand, let alone kiss her. I could tell it was weighing heavily on her too. Her eyes weren't sparkling and happy like they used to be…most of the time she just looked sad.

Dad and Mom were still searching diligently for Kayden, but it seemed after his altercation with me that he had vanished into thin air. And there were no unexplained or violent deaths to give away his whereabouts. There wasn't anything else to do but wait for him to surface again.

On Saturday, Mindy and I were sitting at the table eating breakfast, and Mom was doing the dishes at the sink when she suddenly turned to us cheerfully and said, "By the way, the Ravens, Tony, Amanda, and Amy, are coming over today to hang out for the weekend. Won't that be fun?"

I tried hard not to cringe and I saw Mindy's face blanch. I hadn't seen Amy in almost a year. I knew she missed me. We'd always gotten along, minus a few minor disagreements here and there, having known each other since we were born. But right now she felt like the enemy.

She was the one that my parents considered me betrothed too. The one I knew that I would end up marrying whether I wanted to or not to keep Mindy alive. I glanced at Mindy and her face had turned completely pale, and she lowered her head to stare at her cereal.

#

We stood obediently in the foyer when the Ravens arrived. Mindy looked straight ahead with a blank expression while Tony, Amanda, and Amy walked in.

Amy took one look at me and grinned, leaping into my arms. "Rurik!" she exclaimed. "I missed you so much! I'm glad you're back." She hugged me tightly and planted a kiss right on my mouth.

I pulled away from her and made myself smile back. "It's good to see you, Amy." Then I turned toward Mindy. "You remember Mindy."

Amy looked at her with barely veiled hate. "Oh yeah…. Hi, Mindy."

Mindy smiled politely, but she could sense Amy's hostility.

Amy grabbed my arm possessively. "Let's go up to your room."

I turned to Mindy as Amy drug me along. "You coming, Mindy?"

Mindy nodded her head and fell in behind us. Her eyes were incredibly unhappy…it was breaking my heart.

We played a few games and then ate dinner. After that we watched a movie with our parents. Amy sat practically on top of me and held onto my arm. It was so unfair that my parents didn't care if Amy hung on me, but if Mindy got too close Dad would give me a dark look.

After the movie was over, Mindy stood up to go to her room to sleep, and Dad immediately got to his feet to follow her. When she walked out of the room with Dad, Amy turned to me and said loudly. "Thank goodness she finally left. I haven't had five minutes alone with you since I got here."

I gave her a sour look, got up, and walked out of the room.

"What? What did I say?" Amy asked and followed after me.

"Nothing," I said with irritation. "I'm just not in a very good mood these days."

Amy followed me upstairs, and we sat on my futon. She looked into my eyes. "Rurik, why did you run off with Mindy? I really missed you."

I sighed. "I don't want to talk about her with you, all right?"

She pouted for a few minutes, then said. "I don't understand the attraction there when you have me."

I lifted my head and stared at the ceiling. "Please Amy, don't. This is hard enough right now, okay?"

She put her head against my shoulder and played with my hand while she held onto it. After a few minutes she looked back up into my face. She always did have the most amazing turquoise blue eyes, like a bottomless ocean. She stared up at me longingly, and I knew she wanted me to kiss her. I could feel myself being drawn into her eyes. I glanced away and sighed.

"What's wrong, Rurik?" she asked. "I can tell you want to kiss me."

"I just need some space right now." I looked down at her again and frowned.

"I can help you forget her, Rurik. You know I can. We both have the same mesmerizing abilities. Think how magical we'll be together."

I stared into her face for a moment. She was right, there was a part of me that wanted to kiss her. But it would have been for all the wrong reasons. I stood up and walked over to the other side of the room, and turned to look at her. "I won't do that. It isn't fair to either of you."

"You and Mindy were never supposed to be. We're going to get married and have children together. Forget her, Rurik."

I sighed with frustration. "You don't understand. I love her. I can't just forget that."

"Why?" she asked with a puzzled expression. "She's human, inferior…she's just food."

I looked at her crossly. "Don't say that about Mindy! She's warm and sweet and good."

Amy snorted. "She doesn't belong here. She'll just end up dead."

I glared. "Mindy has me to protect her, and don't you forget that. No one is ever going to hurt her."

Amy folded her arms across her chest in a huff and stared back at me, but didn't comment.

We sat silently for a long time, neither one of us breaking the silence. I reluctantly went back over to the futon and sat down.

After a while Amy took my hand in hers. "Rurik," she said softly, and gazed up at me with her beautiful blue eyes. She leaned in close to my face and put her arms around my neck to kiss me.

I pushed her away. "Amy. Stop it," I said with irritation.

She smiled slyly and took my arm. "It's okay. I know you want to." Her eyes had become liquid pools of green and aqua, warm and entrancing. I knew what she was trying to do, pulling me into her mesmerizing stare, because I was the same lethal creature she was.

I shoved her away more forcefully and stood up. "I said stop it!" I shouted.

Her face instantly turned dark and angry. Her eyes became torrid flames. "You're a fool, Rurik." She got to her feet with anger. "You'll be sorry for pushing me away. Mindy will never make you happy." Then she turned and stormed out of my room, slamming the door behind her.

I was glad when the weekend was over and Amy was finally leaving with her parents. I turned to Mindy after the door was closed. Her face was a picture of total relief to see Amy leave. My parents were standing right beside us, so all I could do was give Mindy a melancholy smile and then walk back to the kitchen to find something to eat.

#

Adrian stepped into the living area where Mindy was sitting with her pile of books, going over homework that Rurik had put together for her. She glanced up at him, and then quickly wiped her eyes. It was pretty obvious she'd been crying.

Adrian walked over and sat on the sofa beside her. "How's everything going, Mindy?"

She nodded her head and tried hard to smile, but it seemed impossible at the moment. "I'm okay, Mr....I mean, Adrian," she answered quietly.

He looked into her eyes. Mindy couldn't help noticing how much like Rurik he was. He had the same incredible eyes and dark features. "Anything you want to talk about?" he asked.

She sighed. "I just miss my mom," she said as a few fresh tears rolled down her cheeks. "And...my house...and everything."

Adrian put his arm around her and hugged her to his side. "I'm sorry this is all so difficult for you."

Mindy burst into tears at his sympathetic words, and buried her head in Adrian's chest and cried. He held her close for a long time until she'd finally stopped crying.

She tried to wipe her face a little. "I'm sorry," she said.

He stared at her pensively. "It's all right."

She tried to smile again. "I really appreciate you letting me stay here with you. I know that you didn't have to."

"That's true, but it isn't your fault you were dragged into our world. We have...." He paused for a moment, trying to search for the right words. "Vampires have the ability to mesmerize their prey. It's very easy for Rurik, or another vampire, to win the affections of a human. It's in our makeup." His eyes turned dark and angry. Mindy couldn't help being a little nervous at his changed features. "Rurik never should have turned his charms toward you in the first place. It was wrong, and he knew it from the beginning. Now we all have to deal with the consequences."

His expression suddenly lightened again, and he smiled. "I can see his attraction for you, though. You're a very sweet girl, the opposite of our dark side." He sighed and patted her hand. "Eventually you two will get over this infatuation. There is someone out there for you also, Mindy. I know your first love seems like it's the end of the world when you break up, but it isn't. You'll see."

Mindy watched Adrian walk out of the room. It didn't feel like infatuation to her. She realized that they thought she and Rurik were too young for real true love, but in her heart she knew that's what it was. There would never be anyone again for her. Rurik owned every little piece of her heart. Now there was nothing but a sharp stabbing pain where her heart used to be. But right now, just being in Rurik's world was enough to keep her hanging on with the tiniest bit of hope that somehow, someway they might be able to be together. As long as there was one single thread, she would never give up.

#

"Rurik! Rurik! Where are you?!" Mindy sounded desperate, panic stricken.

I ran out into the maze. "Mindy!" I yelled.

"Rurik, don't leave me. Help!"

I ran as fast as I could toward her frantic pleas, but never got any closer...her voice was always far off in the distance. The maze twisted and turned in strange new directions. I'd played in here since I was small, but now I couldn't seem to find my way around. There was a thick gray mist that flowed down the paths in front of me, sometimes completely obscuring my view. I was running in circles. No matter which direction I went, I ended up at the same dead end.

The night was eerie and quiet.

"Mindy!" I shouted. "Mindy! Say something!"

There was nothing but silence. I pushed my way through the hedging, and it clawed at my shirt and scratched my arms. I could hear the faintest crying in the distance, and fought my way past the grasping twigs and underbrush. Finally I came to a clearing and could see Mindy at the other end. Fog swirled around her feet, and she was deathly pale. She had on a long flowing white gown that was covered in her blood. She held her middle and stared at me with sad, accusing, frightened eyes.

"It's too late," she said in a monotone, unfeeling voice. "I called you and you didn't come. It's too late, Rurik."

"No!" I yelled. "It's not too late. I can save you Mindy." I ran across the field with desperation.

She stared into my eyes and tears rolled down her cheeks. Shaking her head, she backed away.

"Stop, don't leave!" I yelled.

I scrambled as fast as I could toward her, until I was only a few feet away. I tripped and fell at her feet, and looked up into her face.

"Goodbye, Rurik," she said sadly. "I will always love you."

Then she vanished.

"No, Mindy! Don't leave me!!" I woke myself up shouting, and sat up with a start.

The dream had been so heart wrenchingly real. I couldn't get the images out of my head and had to make sure Mindy was okay. I knew better than to go down the stairs to Mindy's door, so I slipped silently out my window and around the side of the house. I stopped in front of Mindy's bedroom window and peered in. She was tossing and turning in her sleep. It looked as if she were having a nightmare, and tears ran down her face.

I tapped lightly on her window a few times.

At first she didn't stir, and then she opened her eyes and looked around the room, wiping the tears away. I knocked again and she turned to me. Her expression was blank while she tried to wake from the dream, and then she realized it was me.

She jumped quickly out of bed and came over and opened the window. "Rurik, what're you doing out here?" she whispered.

I studied the window. "Pull the tabs down in the corner and lift the screen off."

She grabbed the edges of the screen and did as I asked, then set it carefully on the floor by the window. I slipped silently through and put my arms around her. She sighed and snuggled into my embrace, and we stood there and hugged tightly for several minutes. It felt so incredibly good to have her in my arms again. I sighed and looked down into her face. She was staring up at me with all the love and tenderness that I had desperately missed.

I bent down and pulled her in firmly, pressing her body to mine, and kissed her. I didn't ever want to stop. When I finally pulled back she was breathless, and I took her hand and led her over to the bed. We sat down and I held her close.

"I've missed you so much, Mindy," I whispered in her ear. "It's been torture to have you so close and not be able to kiss you." She sighed with contentment. "Are you okay? It looked like you were having a nightmare when I peeked in the window."

She shuddered and nodded her head. "I have them every night. Horrible dreams about never seeing you again, about dying and you aren't there to save me."

I hugged her tighter. "I'll always be there for you. I promise. I love you more than anything."

I pushed her down onto the bed and leaned over her. I stared into her loving, trusting eyes. "You're everything to me, Mindy," I whispered. I caressed her arms and face and looked tenderly down at her while she melted against my touch. I desperately wanted all of her, but I knew that would be stupid with my parents in the same house. So I kissed her passionately. I held her in my arms and caressed her body with my fingertips. She trembled under my tender caress, her heart beating wildly. I could tell she wanted me also. It was almost agony for us to be this close and not be totally one, but it was ecstasy at the same time. Finally I sighed and stood up to leave.

She sadly gazed into my face.

"I'd better go. I don't want to put your life in danger."

She sat up and nodded unhappily.

I went over to the window. "Put the screen back on after I'm gone. I love you, Mindy."

"I love you too," she answered softly.

I smiled at her one last time and then slipped out her window into the dark.

The next morning when I got up and went down to the kitchen to get a bite to eat, Mindy was already sitting at the table with her bowl of cereal. Mom was over by the sink, emptying the dishwasher. They both looked my direction and smiled. Mindy blushed slightly, remembering our passionate kiss last night and our intimacy.

I winked at her. "Good morning," I smiled, and headed over to the cupboard to get a bowl.

Mom looked at us both curiously but didn't say anything. I hoped she hadn't notice the exchange between Mindy and me.

After sitting at the table and pouring my cereal, I glanced at Mindy again. She was noticeably brighter than she'd been in weeks. I knew it was because of our time together last night, and I realized that Mom and Dad were very observant and we'd better be extra cautious. It wasn't long before Mom left the kitchen to go do a few things and we were actually left alone.

"I really enjoyed being with you last night, Mindy," I whispered into her ear.

She blushed again. "I did too."

I sighed. "I don't want to put you in danger. We better not try that again."

Her expression was instantly crushed. "I need to be with you, Rurik. I don't care."

I shook my head. "I couldn't stand it if something were to happen to you because of me."

Her eyes filled with tears. "I'm not alive when I'm not in your arms. Please don't shut me out."

I looked at her without saying anything. I knew exactly how she felt…she was everything to me. But having her sitting there in front of me, even though we couldn't touch, was better than not having her at all.

I shook my head. "I'm sorry, Mindy, but you're too important. I can't risk it. Dad will kill you."

A few tears spilled down her cheeks, and I put my hand over hers and squeezed it. Just then Dad walked into the room and gave me a dark look. He didn't like me holding Mindy's hand, and I quickly pulled mine back. I could hear Mindy's heart beat speed up nervously at Dad's entrance. She knew that he would take care of her if he needed to, no matter how fond he was of her.

#

Amy watched the man from the shadow of the trees. His clothes were old and torn, and he wore a large hat on his head to hide his features while he placed newspapers on the ground behind the bush. She could see that his beard was long and shaggy from lack of proper grooming, which made him appear older than his mid-thirties. He was muttering to himself while he lay down on the make-shift bed of papers, and then reached over and covered himself with another layer to keep out a little of the dampness and cool night air. Amy smiled and licked her lips with anticipation. He would be asleep shortly, and never wake up.

Just then a quick blur enveloped the man. He opened his eyes, startled, and was about to scream, but the shadow covered him swiftly and bent down to his throat. The man was dead in an instant.

Amy, infuriated, stepped out of the trees and hastened over. Whoever this vampire was, he was going to be sorry that he'd taken her meal. "Hey!" she shouted crossly.

The bent figure turned to look at her and stood up. She was staring into the face of Kayden. They both gawked with shocked expressions for a moment, and then Kayden smirked. "Well, hello beautiful. What a nice surprise running into you here."

Amy put her hands on her hips. "Kayden, you slime. You stole my dinner."

Kayden laughed. "I didn't see your name anywhere on his throat."

Amy took in an angry breath. "I ought to lay you out right here." She grinned suddenly. "In fact, I'd probably get some kind of reward for bringing your body into the society. Everyone's been searching for you."

"You and what army?" Kayden asked haughtily.

"I can whip you without even trying."

"I would like to see that," Kayden challenged with a cocky smirk.

Amy grinned; she couldn't wait to put this overconfident jerk in his place. Her eyes glowed red as they circled each other. Amy leaped toward Kayden, but he was amazingly fast and easily moved out of her path.

"I didn't know you could move so fast," Amy commented with surprise. She lunged at him again and they fell together and rolled across the ground, growling and snapping. No matter what Amy tried, Kayden stayed right with her. She couldn't seem to get the upper hand. Kayden flipped her over and held her wrists tightly. She struggled with all of her might, but Kayden was too strong. She glared up into his eyes.

Kayden grinned with arrogance. "I'm still waiting, Amy."

Amy growled with frustration and struggled under him. "Get off of me!"

Kayden's eyes narrowed. "I'm not sure that would be smart."

"I just want to talk to you. I promise not to try anything."

Kayden stared down into Amy's face for a moment doubtfully, and then gave her a wicked grin. "For a kiss."

"What?!" Amy retorted irately. "There's no way I'm kissing you."

Kayden shrugged. "Suit yourself. I'm comfortable enough to stay here all night." He repositioned his body over hers and leaned on his elbow, smiling, and said, "You know, you might like it if I kiss you."

"Ugh!" Amy exclaimed. She tried repeatedly to push him off her but he wouldn't budge, and only grinned wider with amusement at her futile efforts.

She stared back up into Kayden's face, breathing heavily with frustration. She could tell by the expression on his face that he was enjoying this way too much. "All right," Amy finally said with resignation. "I'll kiss you.

But don't get any ideas. That's all you're ever getting. Got it?!"

Kayden grinned, nodded his head, licked his lips eagerly, and bent down to Amy. He took his time and kissed her fervently. He finally pulled back and stared down into Amy's surprised expression with a smug look. "I told you you'd like it." He rolled off her and stood up, taking Amy's hand and helping her to her feet.

Amy smoothed her hair into place and tried to regain some poise. She had liked Kayden's kiss, but would rather die than admit it to him. She cleared her throat. "I think we may be able to help each other."

"How do you mean?"

"Rurik's ruining his entire future over that stupid human, Mindy. He has a destiny with me that he continues to deny. I think if Mindy were out of the way, he would come to his senses and want me again."

"Mindy's mine," Kayden said possessively.

Amy smiled coyly. "If I helped you to get Mindy away from Rurik and convince him that she's dead, you could have her all to yourself. Rurik would quickly forget about her with me around. Then Rurik and I can be together."

Kayden thought about it for a moment, and then beamed. He liked the idea of having Mindy all to himself. "Okay," he agreed. "But how do we make Rurik believe that Mindy's dead?"

Amy frowned, wrinkling up her cute nose. She knew Rurik was as clever as her, and wouldn't be easily fooled. "Leave that part up to me. I'll think of something."

#

The next several weeks went quickly but painfully by. I didn't dare get close to Mindy again, and even though it had been absolute ecstasy at the time, it seemed to have festered the wound of our separation. A slap in the face of the reality that we couldn't, under any circumstances, consummate the love we had for each other. Mindy was growing more and more withdrawn and quiet, like a withering flower. She was slowly slipping away from life, and I was starting to get very concerned for her. I always knew that she was too delicate and fragile a creature for our dark world.

My parents made sure that Amy came over regularly, which didn't help Mindy's mood any. Often, Amy was cruel and uncaring toward her. Amy knew where my heart was, even though I refused to talk to her about Mindy. She chose to take her frustrations at my lack of love for her out on Mindy. It was all I could do to be civil to Amy these days, and Mindy finally had enough of Amy's relentless verbal onslaught and spent most of the visits by herself in her room. The entire situation was just waiting for one small incident to push it over the edge one way or another.

One weekend when they were visiting, Amy, Mindy, and I were sitting out on the back porch while we grilled hamburgers. Mindy sat over on a bench staring off across the yard lethargically, while Amy sat next to me, holding my hand and rattling on about inconsequential things.

I kept glancing over toward Mindy.

She had really faded in the last few weeks, and just seemed like an empty shell of the person she used to be. She would look at us occasionally, but her expression was completely emotionless. Where she used to look at me with pain, sadness, or love, now there seemed to be nothing at all. She couldn't have been dying any more physically than if someone had stabbed her through the middle. It turned my heart cold as ice to see her this way.

Amy noticed me continually glancing at Mindy with concern, and she was getting more and more insistent to have all my attention. Finally, she couldn't stand it any longer and turned my head to hers, wrapped her arms around my neck, and kissed me forcefully.

Now, I know without a doubt that I had no feelings for Amy these days except irritation, but that didn't change the fact that she was a very alluring creature. She was made to lure in men, and to mesmerize them into submission to her wants before she killed them…like a black widow spider would do to its mate. I was the same type of creature as she was, but was not completely immune to her charms, any more than she was to mine.

The excitement and the flames of the kiss took me off guard, and I pulled her to me and kissed her back. It was only momentary before I realized her intentions and pushed her away, but it was long enough for her to have felt my passion toward her, and for Mindy to have seen it, too.

"Stop it, Amy!" I yelled. I turned to look at Mindy, and she was staring at me with a crushed expression on her face. She got quickly to her feet and raced toward the patio door. I jumped up and caught her arm,

"Mindy!" I said with alarm. "Wait, don't leave."

She turned to me with anger. "I'm not going to sit out here and watch that, Rurik!" she shouted.

"It was nothing, Mindy, I swear. You know that."

Tears were spilling down her face. "It didn't look like nothing."

"Well, how do you like that? I'm nothing!" Amy piped in. She got to her feet and stood next to Mindy and glared back at me. "There's no comparison between me and this…this…sub creature," she said in reference to Mindy.

Mindy gasped and I stared irately into Amy's face. "You'd better watch what you say, Amy."

Her eyes were sparking with fury. "Why? I'm not going to let you ruin your life for some tasty human!"

I let go of Mindy's hand and turned heatedly to Amy. "You will apologize to her right now."

Amy pushed up on her tiptoes and stood her ground against me. "There's no way I'm apologizing! She doesn't belong here and never has. You're mine, Rurik!"

"I'll decide for myself who I choose to be with, or to love…is that understood?!" I unleashed all of my frustrations and rage on Amy, and she suddenly looked concerned and stepped back.

"Rurik!"

We turned and Dad was standing at the entrance to the patio door, his eyes very black and angry. "What's going on here?"

Amy smiled slightly in my direction and I glared at her. "Just a disagreement, Dad," I tried to say evenly.

He stared at all three of us for several moments, not saying anything. Mindy was almost shaking with fear from the rage Amy and I had directed toward each other, and now at Dad as he stood there glowering at us.

"I don't want to hear any more arguing, is that understood?"

We all nodded our heads obediently. Then Dad turned to Mindy. "Mindy, I think you should take your food and eat in the living area, by yourself."

Mindy looked crushed at his words and nodded her head. She glanced sadly into my face, and then pulled her hamburger off the grill onto her waiting plate and walked silently back inside past Dad.

I stared after her. "Dad, this wasn't her fault," I said quietly.

"It doesn't matter, Rurik. Amy's right. Mindy is the outsider, and needs to realize her place."

I clenched my jaw with anger, but I knew better than to argue. It was only his grace that was allowing Mindy to be here alive at all. I turned away from him and put my hamburger on my plate, and went back to the kitchen table and sat down to eat. Amy came in and sat next to me with a smug smile on her lips. I wanted to wipe it off her face so badly right now.

Mindy went directly to her room after she ate, and didn't come out again.

I was desperate to see her, to make sure she was okay. I waited till Mom and Dad were out hunting and snuck through my window and down to Mindy's. I peeked in and could see her sitting on her bed, staring off at the opposite wall, still in her clothes. She wasn't crying, just staring blankly ahead.

I tapped on her window and she turned to me, startled. She came over and opened it.

"Please go away, Rurik," she said quietly.

"I'm not leaving, take the screen off."

She looked at me stubbornly. "No."

"Mindy, I love you, and only you. Please remove the screen," I implored. "I can easily rip it to shreds, but that'll be a little difficult to explain to my parents."

She shook her head. "There's no point," she said sadly. "It doesn't matter that you love me and I love you. We will never be together."

"Don't say that."

She didn't answer back and stared at me with no emotion.

"The thought of being in your arms is the only thing that keeps me going through all of this."

"Ugghh!" she said with frustration. "Stop it, can't you see you're killing me?!"

I looked sadly into her face. "Yes…yes, I can see that. That's what worries me. You're my angel and deserve happiness, and it seems that I've brought you nothing but misery and suffering. I am a devil."

She sighed and her eyes filled with tears. "Don't say that about yourself. You'll always be my guardian angel, no matter what."

I couldn't help grinning slightly. "And you're still delusional. Please let me in, Mindy. I love you."

Tears spilled down her face as she stood there staring back into my eyes. Finally she sighed and removed the screen. I was inside in an instant and had her in my arms. "Oh Mindy, it has been such torture to not be able to hold you," I whispered.

She melted willingly into my embrace, and I kissed every inch of her face as I carried her over to the bed. I had to have her, and I knew she wanted me desperately too. I lay her on the bed and she looked up longingly into my eyes. She was trembling with anticipation while I removed my shirt and then leaned down to unbutton her top. She gasped under my touch as my fingers worked their way lightly down the front of her blouse.

Suddenly the door to her room burst open, and Dad stood there with such ferocity on his face I knew we were about to die.

Mindy screamed at the top of her lungs and cowered back on the bed while he slowly walked into her room. His black eyes were fixed on her, and murder was in them.

"Dad, no!" I yelled. "Stop!"

Chapter Ten
Carnival

Mindy cowered against the headboard as Dad purposefully approached her. I stood where I was beside the bed, transfixed, while the horrible scene unfolded in front of my eyes. Mom was standing at the entrance to Mindy's room with a stunned look on her face.

Dad was focused on Mindy, his eyes lethal and black, his brow furiously creased.

"Dad. Don't do this," I pleaded.

He didn't even glance my direction, and continued his deathly advance.

"Adrian, think about what you're doing," Mom whispered.

Dad walked up to Mindy, grabbed her wrists, and lifted her toward his face. His eyes were glowing an evil blood red. His lips curled back over his fangs. Mindy whimpered and cried, staring back into his horrible expression.

I was desperate; I couldn't let this continue. "Dad!" I yelled. "Please stop!"

It was as if he didn't even hear me. He growled ferociously and bared his fangs. I realized this was it, he was going to kill the girl I loved more than life itself. He brought Mindy's neck to his mouth and placed his lips against her flesh as she trembled with terror.

I flew at him in an instant, and Mindy was knocked back against the opposite wall. Dad and I landed on the floor with me on top of him. I bared my teeth and growled. He looked momentarily surprised, then roared back.

Mom leaped forward. "Stop! Rurik, Adrian! No!"

"Carmen, stay out of this!" Dad yelled furiously.

Mom stepped back and stood against the wall, tears running down her cheeks. She knew one of us was about to die.

I knew it would be Dad.

We rolled across the floor together, growling and snapping in a furious, all-consuming rage. It was the fight of dominance, the instinct of the younger offspring to usurp the leader's throne. It had been the same for thousands of years. The winner took everything, and the loser would die. Dad was an extremely powerful vampire, and it wasn't as effortless as I'd thought it would be. We struggled for several minutes, but it soon became apparent to both of us that I was the superior creature. I was, after all, of the prophesied new race. A knowing look came into Dad's face as I backed him against the wall and held him. We both knew this was it. I could hear Mom crying softly behind me and my heart went out to her, but I could not allow Dad to harm my chosen mate, Mindy.

Dad and I stared into each other's eyes for a few moments, and then I bared my fangs and growled. Dad didn't cower, whimper, or protest as I lowered my teeth to his throat. He had been a formidable leader, one of the greatest, and would die with dignity.

"Rurik stop!" Mindy suddenly yelled with alarm behind me.

"Stay back, Mindy!"

She put her hand on my shoulder. "Rurik," she said evenly. "You can't do this. He's your father."

I turned to look at her with surprise. "He just tried to kill you."

She nodded. "I understand that, but you can't kill your dad. I won't let you do that for me. It's wrong."

I gazed at her for a moment, taken aback at her generous heart, and then looked at Dad.

He was staring intently into Mindy's eyes as if he was seeing her really for the first time, the woman that she was. This fragile human creature that he was about to snuff out, who was suddenly defending him.

"Please, Rurik," she said gently. "I love you. I can't let you kill your dad for me."

I was willing to protect Mindy at all costs, against whoever was a threat. But Mindy was my completely selfless angel. Her act of forgiveness toward Dad was unfathomable, and it stunned me to my very core. I slowly nodded my head to her, and loosened my grip on Dad's shoulders. I stepped back and we all stood and faced each other. Mom ran over to Dad and took his arm, then they walked out of Mindy's room and left us standing there.

I felt as if I'd been holding my breath, and let out a huge sigh. Mindy was shaking in my arms. I held her against me, pulled her over to the bed, and we sat down.

I wasn't sure what this meant, where we went from here. Dad and Mom had left the room without a word. I'd only been interested in protecting my true love, but I knew everything had changed. After several minutes, digesting what had just transpired, I sighed and stood up, then took Mindy's hand and pulled her to her feet.

She looked questioningly into my face.

"We have to go see my parents," I said quietly.

She held my arm tightly while we headed out of her room, and down the hall to the living area where they were sitting. Dad watched us walk in without a word, with very little expression on his face. Mom was sitting next to him, holding his hand. She still looked extremely upset from the incident. We stopped, facing where they were seated on the sofa, and stared silently into each other's eyes for a few moments.

Dad eyes narrowed slightly while he studied me. "What's your plan, Rurik?"

"I...I don't know," I said hesitantly.

"It's obvious that I can't make you follow my rules anymore, so what're you and Mindy planning to do?"

"I hadn't really thought that far...are you kicking me out?"

Mom grimaced beside Dad and turned to him. She didn't want me to go.

"No," Dad stated matter-of-factly. "I would never do that. You're my son and I love you." He paused. "But...you can't stay here in this house unless you plan to follow our rules."

I protectively put my arm around Mindy's shoulder and pulled her next to me. "I won't ever let anything hurt Mindy," I said with conviction.

Dad sighed. "Well, it's obvious you have chosen her as your mate."

I nodded and looked into Mindy's eyes. She smiled back at me. "I would die to protect her. But...I don't want to leave like this."

Dad continued in a serious tone. "I won't have you usurping my authority. I realize you're more powerful than I am, and it was bound to happen. But I'm still in charge here…is that clear?"

I nodded.

His expression was somber. "Okay. I can't deny that you and Mindy truly love each other after everything you've been through to be together. And I can't ignore the fact that Mindy is an incredible young woman." His eyes softened. "I have you to thank for my life, Mindy."

Mindy smiled shyly. "You're welcome, Mr.…I mean Adrian. But I don't think Rurik would've really killed you."

Dad looked into my eyes knowingly. He and I both knew that if it had come to it, he would have died. Mindy, being human, didn't totally understand the lethalness of the vampire side to us, but neither one of us commented.

"If you both decide to stay here I have some serious ground rules for you."

"Okay," I said. "Let's hear them."

He paused for a moment. "Have a seat." He gestured to the sofa across from them and Mindy and I sat down, still holding hands.

"You aren't even seventeen yet. Pretty young to be as serious as you are about each other."

"That doesn't change the fact that we love each other, that it's real."

"I realize that," he answered. "I appreciate the fact that you've waited until now to get intimately involved." He paused. "I would like for you to wait until you are married at this point."

Mindy blushed slightly at the turn the conversation had taken.

I squeezed her hand. "A lot of people don't these days, Dad."

"I know, Rurik. But as I have said from the beginning, you aren't a lot of people. You're a powerful and dangerous predator, and I'm trying to avoid heartbreak here by cautioning you to take it slowly. And I feel strongly that sort of intimacy requires commitment."

"We've already known each other for a year," I answered.

Dad sighed. "I can't make you wait, but if you want to stay under my roof, you have to."

I looked into Mindy's eyes and she smiled shyly back.

"One more thing," Dad said. We turned to look at him. "I won't allow you to get married until you are eighteen."

"That's over a year away still!" I exclaimed.

Mom smiled. "A year goes by very quickly; before you know it you and Mindy will be grown."

I groaned. Another year seemed like an eternity to me.

"It'll just give you that much more time to get to know each other, Rurik. It's very important who you decide to spend the rest of eternity with."

"I'm not ever changing my mind about Mindy," I stated defensively.

"We aren't going to try and make you," Mom said. "But it's important to take it slowly. And it won't hurt you both to wait till you're married. I did with your father, and I was older than you."

I sighed and turned to Mindy. I wasn't going to make these important decisions about our future without her input.

She smiled and squeezed my hand. "I would really like to stay here and get to know your parents better, Rurik. I think it's important to follow their wishes."

I smiled back at her, and gently caressed her cheek with my fingers. "You're way smarter than your years, Mindy." I turned back to my parents. "Okay, we'll stay, and wait to get married…on one condition."

"What is it?" Dad asked with a cautious tone.

"I don't want Mindy to be treated like an outsider anymore."

Dad stared into my eyes silently for a few moments. And then he nodded and turned to Mindy with a smile. "Welcome to the family, Mindy."

She smiled back at them both. "Thank you Mr. and Mrs.…I mean Adrian and Carmen."

We all stood up, and Mom walked over and put her arms around Mindy and hugged her.

"We're happy that you are going to stick around," Mom said.

I looked hesitantly into Dad's eyes as we stood facing each other. I knew things had changed between us, that I was no longer the kid to him. I'd become a man, and commanded respect for my new position. I held out my hand tentatively for him to shake.

Dad smiled at me and grasped my hand in his. Then he pulled me to him and hugged me.

I couldn't help a few tears escaping my eyes, and I had to wipe them away while Dad and I stepped back. Then Mindy and I walked out of the living room together.

Once we were in the hall I grabbed her so quickly it startled her, and she gasped. I picked her up around the waist and twirled her in circles above my head. She giggled happily, and put her arms around my neck and gazed down into my eyes. I sighed and leaned her against the hallway wall, and let her slowly drop until her soft lips came down to touch mine.

Then I hungrily kissed her. When I finally pulled back and looked into her eyes, they were sparkling and happy again.

#

Adrian and Carmen watched Mindy and Rurik leave the living area hand in hand. Carmen sighed. "How are we going to explain all of this to Tony, Amanda, and especially Amy?"

Adrian shook his head. "I don't know, sweetheart. Trying to keep Rurik and Mindy apart was paramount to trying to halt a train. We're all are just going to have to deal with and live with the consequences of their love."

"It doesn't make sense that he isn't in love with Amy. Maybe he's not the one from the prophecies after all," Carmen said.

Adrian shook his head. "No…he definitely is."

Carmen looked questioningly into Adrian's face.

"When we were fighting, Rurik was so powerful and strong. I've never experienced anything like it. He has no idea about his full potential yet."

Carmen leaned her head against Adrian's shoulder. "I was so scared when I thought one of you was going to die."

Adrian smiled grimly and leaned down and kissed the top of Carmen's head. "I was pretty alarmed myself. I had no doubts that Rurik was going to kill me. He's a force to be reckoned with. Trying to rein him in and keep him under control is all we can do right now, until he realizes his place in the society."

Carmen looked up into Adrian's eyes. She could see the obvious respect and admiration that Adrian had for his son.

#

It was nice to hold hands with Mindy, and even give her quick kisses occasionally, to be open about our feelings for each other and not worry about Mindy's life. My parents respected Mindy and my relationship, and Dad no longer treated me like just a child.

It had been a week since the incident, and Mindy and I were in the kitchen, eating breakfast and holding hands while we laughed and chatted, when my parents walked in. They both seemed very somber, so we stopped mid-conversation and turned to them when they sat down at the table.

I could tell by Dad's eyes that he had a serious topic to broach.

"What's up?"

He smiled. "You're as observant as your mother, and always know when something is on my mind." He paused briefly, then sighed. "Tony, Amanda, and Amy are coming over for the weekend tomorrow."

I felt Mindy stiffen beside me. She'd been being treated badly by Amy for months. She had the definite attitude that Mindy was the intruder and that I belonged to her. Mindy turned to me with concern on her face.

I squeezed her hand. "It's okay, Angel." Then I asked Dad, "So…what's the plan?"

Dad sighed and shook his head. "Well, obviously, we're going to have to explain to them that things have changed."

I nodded my head in agreement.

Dad's eyes grew more serious. "I don't expect any of them to be happy about it. We have all planned from the beginning that you and Amy would eventually marry."

I didn't respond while I digested that.

"This could cause division between our families. I hope not, but I can't blame them if they're angry."

Mindy looked at all of us with concern. "I...I'm really sorry to be such a problem."

I sighed. "It's not your fault, Mindy. I love you, period, and you're who I'm going to spend my life with. They'll just have to learn to accept it."

Mom didn't look happy at all. She and Amanda had always been best friends.

"Okay," Dad said, getting up from the table. "Just wanted to prepare you for the fireworks this weekend."

They left the room and I stared into Mindy's face. She looked so glum. "What are you thinking?"

"I cause you nothing but problems with your family."

I frowned at her. "Don't ever say that. You are my happiness, my angel. Okay?" She tried to smile, and I leaned in and kissed her lips. "I love you, Mindy, more than anything. Things change. Who's to say the prophecies haven't changed too?"

#

When the Ravens arrived Mindy stood close to me, and I held her hand tightly and squeezed it to encourage her. Amy immediately took my other arm. She gave

Mindy a dirty look when she noticed us holding hands, and her eyes narrowed with suspicion.

Dad shook Tony's hand, and then said, "Okay, let's all go into the living area to talk. I already explained that this was going to be a weekend of meetings, and there're some important issues we need to discuss and get cleared up right away." He glanced briefly at me and Mindy when he said that, and Amy stared at us warily again.

When we stepped into the living area, Dad directed Tony, Amanda, and Amy to sit on the opposite sofas from the four of us. I could feel Mindy stiffening noticeably beside me, and her heart sped up nervously. Amy was still staring with contempt in our direction. I think she was starting to comprehend what was going to transpire shortly.

Dad took a deep breath and leaned forward in his chair. "There're going to be some unexpected changes of plans to our future." He paused while Tony and Amanda stared at him, and Amy's eyes grew darker and more furious by the second. Dad hesitated for a moment, and then said, in as calm and even of a tone as possible, "Rurik and Mindy are going to be getting married."

Amanda gasped and Tony's normally calm blue eyes instantly became dark, angry seas. Amy sat perfectly still, shock plainly written across her face, trying to grasp the concept. I watched her features contort into several different expressions while she processed the information, and then she leaped to her feet.

I instinctively sprang to mine also, along with everyone else. I could see the furious rage on Amy's expression, and it was all directed toward Mindy. Mindy pressed herself into the back of the sofa where she was still sitting, her heart pounding with fear.

Amy could snuff Mindy out in about half a second. Her eyes turned red and glowing.

"Don't even think about trying anything, Amy," I said meaningfully, my eyes starting to flame. "Mindy's my mate."

"This is beyond ridiculous!" she yelled. She turned to Dad and Mom. "How...how can you allow Rurik to marry that...that—?"

"Amy!" I yelled furiously. "Stop now before you say something you'll regret!"

Amy turned back to me, and behind the rage was confusion and hurt. I had a moment of regret that I'd caused her pain. She'd been my childhood consort and friend forever; it wasn't my desire to upset her. She stared at me silently for a few moments, and then spun on her heels and stormed out of the room.

Amanda looked completely baffled while she stared at all of us. Then she shook her head and headed after Amy.

Tony was the only one left standing across from us, and he was anything but happy. He stared into Dad's eyes accusingly for a few moments before he spoke. "I don't understand any of this, Adrian," he said quietly. He glanced down at Mindy briefly. She was pressed as far back against the sofa as she could possibly get. She looked terrified. Then Tony fixed his eyes back on Dad. "This is not acceptable. It has always been understood that our children would marry."

Dad sighed. "I understand that, Tony, believe me. I did everything in my power to separate Rurik and

Mindy, but their love for each other is strong. Rurik has chosen. I have to respect that."

"No," Tony said coldly, shaking his head. "You didn't do everything in your power." He looked down at Mindy and his eyes were deadly. I'd never seen Tony look so lethal. "That girl should have been killed a long time ago."

Mindy gasped and I stepped between Tony and Mindy, my eyes smoldering red coals again. "She's my mate, Tony, and I will defend her to the death."

Tony stepped menacingly closer, and I prepared myself to fight him.

Dad moved forward. "Get back, Tony. Rurik will kill you if he has too."

Tony looked questioningly into Dad's face, and he understood. He could see in Dad's eyes, without Dad having to say it, that he would not stand a chance against me, that he would die if he didn't back down. Tony turned to me with new eyes and deference. He nodded his head and retreated.

"Okay," he said carefully. "I have to respect your position, Rurik, I don't have a choice. But…," he continued angrily, "Don't expect any of us to like it or accept Mindy. Ever!" With that he turned and walked quickly from the room to find his family.

Dad closed his eyes momentarily; I could see the relief wash over his face that no one had ended up dead. Mom was visibly shaken and upset. Dad glanced at me without a word, and then turned to Mom and put his arm around her shoulder. "Let's give them a bit to digest this, and then we'll go and talk with them." They went out of the room arm in arm.

I shifted my focus to Mindy, who was still sitting on the sofa with the same horrified expression on her face. I sat down beside her and took her hand. She stared at me with sadness and fear.

"I am so sorry," she said with tears in her eyes.

I pulled her to me and hugged her. "It's okay, Mindy. They'll soon see the wonderful person that you are. Dad and Mom already really like you."

I kissed the top of her head and sighed. I knew that Mindy would be in mortal danger constantly, and that I would always have to be on guard with her life. I felt Tony and Amanda would eventually get to know her and accept her, and hoped that Amy would come around too. But there would always be vampires in the society that would never accept Mindy as long as she was human. She was inferior in their eyes. She didn't belong in our world, and they would feel the need to kill her...to right this wrong.

#

The following week I told Mindy to be ready for an evening out. I was excited about all of the plans I'd made, and sat impatiently on the sofa in the living area to wait. I'd told her that she needed comfortable walking shoes and a jacket, in case it was chilly.

When Mindy entered the living area her face had eager anticipation written all over it. She was so much like a child when she was excited about something, and her emerald eyes danced happily when I stood up and took her hands. I stared into her face with all the love in my heart and knelt down, still holding her hands in mine. Her eyes widened and started to fill with tears, anticipating what was going to happen next.

"Mindy," I said softly. I pulled a small case out of my pocket, opened it, and held it out to her. I looked into her eyes and asked, "Will you marry me?"

She was speechless as she stared lovingly into my face for a few silent moments, then nodded her head, tears spilling down her cheeks. She wiped her face and said, "Of course I will. I love you."

I smiled widely, and couldn't help breathing a sigh of relief. Even though I knew Mindy loved me, I'd had a moment of doubt when I thought, what if she really didn't want to marry me after all, now that she knew me better? I was darkness to her light. For everything good, kind, sweet, and gentle that she was, there was a side to me that was the complete opposite.

I stood up from my kneeling position and pulled her to me. Her face shone with adoration as I drew her into my arms and kissed her. She melted into my embrace and sighed.

I held Mindy's left hand out and took the engagement ring from the box, slipping it on her finger. She studied it happily. There was a big center stone with a halo of smaller diamonds around the large one. The band was a double row of pave set diamonds.

"This is the most beautiful ring I've ever seen," Mindy exclaimed.

I was pleased that she liked it so much. "It's one of a kind…designed only for you," I said, and lifted her hand up to my lips, gently kissing it. "Are you ready to go?"

She nodded her head enthusiastically and we headed out the door.

Once we were in the car, Mindy turned to face me. "Are you going to tell me where we're going?"

I smiled mysteriously. "No. You'll see soon enough."

She wrinkled up her nose and tried to frown, but it came out more as a smirk. Being too happy to scowl, she ended up laughing instead.

I laughed back. "You're a goof."

Mindy put her head against my shoulder while we drove down the highway. It wasn't too long before the bright flashing lights were visible in the distance, and she sat up and studied them intently as we got closer.

"A carnival!" She leaned over and hugged my arm. "This is going to be so much fun!"

I pulled into the parking lot, and when we got out she took my hand and dragged me along, jumping up and down like a kid.

"Come on, come on!" she said with excitement.

"Relax, Mindy," I smiled. "We have hours. It's open all night tonight."

"I know…it's just that I didn't get to do stuff like this very often. My mom never had extra money. I'm so excited."

"I'm glad you like my gift."

She nodded. "And this one too." She held her hand out with the ring on it.

I took her hand and grinned. "That rings looks so good on you. It belongs there." I turned her to me, and stopped in the middle of the parking lot and pulled her close. "Like you belong to me," I whispered softly, and kissed her lips.

She pushed away, laughing. "Everyone's looking."

I glanced around. "No one cares, Mindy. Except maybe that clown over there." I gestured behind her and she turned to look. There was indeed a clown on the other side of the lot who was staring our direction.

Mindy shuddered. "I hate clowns."

I laughed. "What's to hate about clowns?

"I don't know, they're just creepy."

I couldn't help grinning with amusement. "Clowns are creepy? They do tricks in circuses, and hand out balloons to kids. But I, on the other hand, who am a vampire and drink your blood, am not creepy at all."

She shrugged. "So?" she said in defense of her position.

"So? That's your reasoning?" I asked.

She sighed heavily, stopped in front of me, and looked up. "Stop it. You're not creepy, and you're not a devil. I don't care what you say about yourself. You'll always be my guardian angel."

"And you will always be delusional," I said, and bent down and kissed the bridge of her nose. Her heartbeat immediately sped up. I smiled playfully and wrapped her in my arms. "I hope this carnival has a long, dark tunnel of love so I can get you alone for a few minutes."

She blushed slightly at the thought, and took my hand and dragged me toward the entrance. "Come on. We have to ride everything in here."

"Okay, okay," I said good-naturedly.

#

I laughed. "You're acting like a five year old. Haven't you ever been to a carnival before?"

Mindy's eyes danced with excitement. "A long time ago. What's wrong with having fun?"

I shook my head, "Nothing. I think we've gone around this entire place twice now."

"No way," she stated.

"Uh-huh…what haven't we done yet?"

She held her map out and pointed. "The Ferris wheel, and this whole section back here."

"I'm all up for the Ferris wheel. And the tunnel of love, so we can be alone again." I leaned in and mockingly chewed on her neck.

She giggled and smiled up at me. "What about this other section? There's a funhouse, freak house, and a haunted house."

I wrinkled up my face. "Sounds too scary for me."

She playfully hit me. "Now who's being the goof? You're not afraid of anything."

I shrugged. "I just didn't think you'd want to do anything creepy."

"I like being scared."

I grinned. "Is that why you like me so much? I could easily be more frightening if you want." I crouched down in front of her, and then suddenly growled and sprang, grabbed her around the waist, lifted her above my head, and spun her.

Mindy squealed with excitement. I gently placed her on the ground again, and she smoothed her disheveled hair and tried to calm her breathing and heart. "You know what I mean. I don't want to be really afraid…just pretend."

"Just teasing you, Angel. If you want to go, I'm more than happy to go with you. Let's do the Ferris wheel first, though."

"Okay," she answered, and pulled me in the direction of the huge spinning, psychedelic wheel.

I hugged Mindy close against me, and we looked out across the landscape while we sat in the gently swaying seat with the light cool breezes blowing across our faces. The carnival music, laughter, and screams were muted and distant up here. It was remarkable all that we could see as we spun slowly around the huge circumference...the entire carnival, the parking lot, and even the highway in the distance.

"Wow, everything's amazing from up here," Mindy said with awe.

I put my arm around her and hugged her to my side. "We should've done this first. Then we would've seen where everything in the park is."

Once we stepped off the Ferris wheel, we headed in the direction of the carnival houses. There was an overhang with dead trees at the entrance to this section of the park, and the sign was old, faded, and worn. Mindy instinctively tightened her hold on my hand and snuggled closer to my side while we walked down the dimly lit path. I grinned and wrapped my arm around her shoulder; maybe this would be fun after all.

We came to the haunted house first, and an attendant dressed like a clown gestured for us to take our seats on the slowly moving conveyor of carts that went by. I could hear Mindy's heart speed up nervously when we entered the darkness. It was what you would expect with lights, and noises, monsters and fog. When we exited I couldn't help grinning at Mindy, who was obviously a bit frightened.

"What?" she asked.

"You're scared."

"Just a little," she said in her own defense. "It wouldn't be exciting if it wasn't a teensy bit scary."

Next on the path was the freak house. We walked through and looked at an assortment of abnormal creatures. Some were obviously birth defects of different animals, like the two headed snake and turtle, or the cat with three faces. Others looked like bones that had been glued together in weird shapes by someone with a twisted sense of aesthetics to resemble what was left of some monster. It was interesting, but very strange.

Last for this section was the funhouse. A small line of people was waiting to get in, and while we stood there, we realized it was because they were only allowing one person in at a time in two to three minute intervals.

"I don't know if I want to go in by myself," Mindy said nervously.

"Why? I thought you liked to be frightened," I teased.

She frowned at me, not appreciating my humor at the moment.

I shrugged. "We don't have to go. I don't care."

She shook her head. "No, we have to," she said with determination. It seemed as if she couldn't pass up even one ride, like she was afraid of missing out on something.

"Are you sure?" I asked.

She nodded apprehensively. "Yeah, I can do this." More to convince herself than me.

"I'll be right behind you, Mindy. If it makes you feel better, wait for me once you get inside and I'll catch up." I put my arms around her waist and pulled her back against my chest. "I'm sure we could find something interesting to do in a dark, creepy funhouse," I whispered in her ear, and nibbled her neck.

After several more minutes it was finally our turn. The attendant was again one of the eerie clowns dressed in circus attire with all the make-up, including a large red

bulbous nose. But it was done in a way to be disturbing.
His eyes had black circles around them, and the painted
mouth turned down instead of up. His teeth were
sharpened to points, and when he talked and smiled it
looked more like an evil glare.

Mindy stared at the clown nervously, and he
grinned back and then pushed her through the door to the
funhouse. She turned to look at me anxiously one more
time before disappearing into the darkness. I heard
sinister laughter and music drifting out from behind the
closed doors while I waited impatiently for the clown
from hell to let me pass. I was concerned for Mindy…I
didn't want her to be too frightened. I suddenly heard her
blood curdling scream from inside, and it took all of my
willpower to not just push my way in. I knew that
making it scary was supposed to be part of the fun, but it
sounded like a desperate, panicked scream from Mindy to
me.

#

Mindy stared back at the closing doors and Rurik's
face one final time, and then entered the room. It was
dark and twisting, like a maze, but there were florescent
lights and paints spattered everywhere. The music was
incredibly spine-chilling, and she slowly walked forward
while things pulled at her feet, making her jump and
flinch. She wove through the blackness, her heart
pounding in her chest. Several times she ran right into
the wall in front of her, not realizing that it turned. Rurik
would be so much better at this. He could see perfectly in
the dark, Mindy thought to herself. She heard strange
shuffling behind her, and then in front. Someone was in
here with her.

"Rurik?" she asked softly. "Rurik, is that you? If you're trying to scare me, stop it. I'm nervous enough already."

She stopped and listened, but no one answered. She continued forward again and came to a maze of mirrors lining the turning paths, and making it impossibly confusing as to which direction to go. Some of the mirrors made Mindy look long and hideous, or short and squatty. There were gruesome clown masks on the walls that eerily watched the passersby. More than once she came to a dead-end and had to turn back the way she'd just come. She was practically in tears, and trying to not get hysterical. This wasn't any fun; she should have just listened to Rurik and not gone in here.

"Rurik?" she said again in a hushed, strained voice. "I'm...I'm just going to wait for you here...okay?"

She heard the shuffling noise again, and listened in the darkness. Mindy swallowed nervously and stared around the area. The mirrors reflected her frightened expression; the evil clown masks mockingly smiled back.

"Please hurry, Rurik," she said quietly, more to herself than anyone. "I'm scared."

"Mindy," a voice murmured in the darkness.

"Is that you, Rurik?" she whispered back.

"Mindy," it said again, louder. She didn't recognize the voice as Rurik's, but it sounded threatening. How did it know her name?! Petrified, she took off at a run, racing through the twisting maze as fast as she could. She slid and stumbled around the sharp corners, tears of fear blinding her vision. She came abruptly to a dead-end, and skidded into the mirror at the end so hard that it cracked. She was utterly panic stricken.

"This isn't fun anymore!" she yelled.

Then someone laughed from around the next corner; it was ominous and hair-raising. Mindy got goose bumps up and down her arms, and she backed against the mirror and waited. Her heart was pounding furiously, and she watched with wide, frightened eyes while a sinister looking clown walked around the corner. He stood at the opposite end and stared at her. Mindy was horror struck when it slowly and menacingly approached.

The clown gazed down into her terrified eyes for a moment and then smiled, exposing its long fangs. His eyes turned an evil blood red, and Mindy screamed at the top of her lungs.   Cowering against the mirror behind her, she stared with dread up into the clown's face towering above her.

The vampire clown wrapped his arm behind her waist and held her against the mirror behind her. He stroked her cheek lightly with his cold fingers, and leaned his head down to kiss her. When his icy lips met hers the room swam around, and she had a sickening familiar feeling that she'd been here before. He kissed her demandingly, and then pulled back and grinned wickedly.

"Mindy!" It was Rurik's voice this time. "Mindy! Where are you?"

Mindy's heart leapt. "Over here!" she yelled back.

The evil clown growled under his breath and glanced quickly in the direction of Rurik's voice. He looked down at Mindy one final time, hesitated briefly, and then disappeared into the black maze and was gone.

In the next instant Rurik appeared out of the shadows and was at her side. "Are you okay?" he asked, and took her arm. "What happened, Angel? Why are you shaking?"

Mindy looked up into Rurik's face with total relief. The horrible clown almost seemed like a mirage that wasn't real now that it was Rurik standing in front of her. But she could still feel the clown's calloused mouth against her bruised lips, and the strangely familiar feeling that she'd had. She suddenly felt faint and her knees went weak. She tried to move her lips to speak, and was finally able to utter, "I…I think it was Kayden. He was here." Then she collapsed into Rurik's arms.

Chapter Eleven
True Love

Amy sat impatiently waiting on a bench at the edge of the park in the cover of trees. She surveyed her surroundings carefully and noticed the figure approaching. She sighed. She didn't want to be seen here by anyone, especially with Kayden.

He stopped in front of where she was seated and stared down at her. "Hi, gorgeous. Have you come up with a plan? It's been weeks. I was starting to think I just needed to handle this my own way."

Amy glared crossly at Kayden. "If you can't control yourself and stay away from Mindy until the time is right, you'll ruin everything. I heard about your little stunt at the carnival the other day."

"I have been hiding in the shadows long enough," he stated angrily. Then his eyes glinted with pleasure at the memory. "It was just a little taste of Mindy's and my future. It didn't cause any harm."

Amy snorted with irritation. "You could have messed up everything. Don't do it again."

Kayden's eyes narrowed hatefully. He didn't like being told what to do. If he didn't need Amy to help him get Mindy permanently away from Rurik, he would show her who was really the boss. But he made himself smile instead. "How much longer do I have to wait?"

Amy sighed at his impatience. He may be as strong as Rurik, but he still had the same small brain as always. But she knew that she needed Kayden's help to pull off getting rid of Mindy so she could be with Rurik. That way Rurik would never suspect she was involved, and it would all be Kayden's fault. "Not very much longer. Don't worry. I've come up with a good way to convince Rurik that Mindy is dead, and he will never know that she isn't. Then you can have her all to yourself."

Kayden liked the thought of Mindy with him where she belonged. "So…what's the plan?"

Amy smiled with anticipation. She couldn't wait to be the one to console Rurik after he thought that Mindy was dead.

Kayden's eyes glistened with anticipation and excitement after he'd listened carefully to Amy. "That's a brilliant plan."

"I know," Amy commented with confidence. "Rurik will believe that Mindy's dead when her blood is all over the deck of the boat."

Kayden chuckled. "I wish I could be there to see the look on his face."

"He'll be devastated when I tell him that you killed her and then tossed her in the water." Amy had only a momentary qualm at the thought. "But…I'll be there to comfort him." She smiled. "I'm so much prettier and smarter than Mindy, it won't take him long to forget all about her."

"How do you know he won't just want to come after me for revenge?" Kayden asked. "I would."

Amy shrugged. "I'll convince him that you're dead, and that I threw your body over the side of the boat too."

"Will he believe you?"

"Why wouldn't he?" Amy asked.

"Well, I'm very powerful. It's not like you could easily kill me."

Amy wrinkled up her nose, deep in thought. "Yeah, that's true. We'll have to think of some way to make it believable."

#

Mindy and I sat on the sofa in front of the T.V. snuggled together. I had my arms protectively around her waist while she leaned back against my chest. My chin rested on the top of her head, and I could smell the delicate scent of vanilla still lingering from her shampoo. I couldn't resist softly running my lips over her hair and down to her neck, and then nibbling on the curve of her throat.

She giggled and trembled. "It gives me chills when you do that." She turned her head and stared up into my face. It was great to see the sparkle in her eyes again…they were dancing and happy.

I sighed with contentment. "I could sit here forever with you in my arms."

Mindy's eyes softened and she put her hand against the side of my face. I turned my head and kissed her hand, and then sensed someone and glanced up.

Amy was standing in the doorway staring at us.

Mindy followed my gaze and pulled away from me a little.

"Do you need something, Amy?" I asked.

Amy shook her head. "No," she mumbled, and then turned around and walked out of the room. I stared at the empty doorway where she had stood for a few moments, and then turned my attention back to Mindy.

"I don't know, Amy," I said with doubt. "It's not like Mindy is exactly comfortable around you. You haven't been very nice to her from the beginning."

"That's why I want to do this," Amy tried to convince me. "She's going to be your wife, and we need to all get along. Your parents really seem to like her, and…and maybe I just need to get to know Mindy a little better. Spend some time with her."

I sighed. "You'd see that Mindy is the sweetest, most wonderful person, if you'd just give her a chance."

Amy shrugged. "There must be something special about her for you to like her so much. Think how nice it'll be for Mindy to be pampered. Besides, your mom is going to meet us at the spa."

"Mom isn't going to dinner with you and Mindy?"

"I want to spend some time with Mindy by myself. We can eat and chat…you know, girl talk. That way she'll see I'm okay."

It would be nice if Mindy and Amy could get along, and maybe even be friends. It was worth a try. I knew Mindy would be fine with Mom there. And Amy knew better than to not be nice to Mindy, or she'd have me to deal with.

"All right," I agreed reluctantly.

#

Mindy was very excited about the spa. She'd never been to one, and looked forward to it all day. She was sitting in the living area waiting for Amy to arrive, and I sat down beside her and took her hand. Her eyes were bright with anticipation.

"Are you going to be okay?" I asked. For some reason I wasn't as happy about this whole idea as everyone else seemed to be.

"Of course, Rurik. It'll be fun."

"Yeah, I guess," I said with doubt.

She laughed. "It's a girl thing to do. You wouldn't understand. Amy said we start with a massage, and then body wraps, facials…and we get our nails done too!" She was practically bubbling with excitement at the idea.

I hugged my arms around her. "I'm more concerned about your dinner with Amy, and you being alone with her."

Mindy shrugged. "She's just trying to be nice. Get to know me better…that's all."

I sighed. "If she's mean to you, or you feel uncomfortable…at all…call me and I'll come get you. Okay?"

"I'll be fine," she insisted, and leaned in and kissed my lips. "Don't be so chicken."

I grinned. "Okay. I won't."

Just then the doorbell rang and Mindy jumped up, ran over, and opened the door. Amy was standing in the entrance, smiling.

"Hi, Amy," I said. "Come in."

Amy stepped into the entry, and I walked over and put my arms around Mindy's waist. "Have fun. Call if you need anything."

Mindy nodded her head and smiled, wrinkling up her cute nose. "I will."

I turned to Amy and looked at her a little more carefully. "Take care of Mindy."

"We'll have a great time. Won't we, Mindy? Don't worry, Rurik. It'll be a blast," Amy commented, and they walked out and got into Amy's car.

I watched them drive down and around the corner before I finally closed the door and went into the living room and sat down. I didn't know why I felt so uneasy about this. I sighed, I knew I was overprotective of Mindy, but she was so delicate and fragile.

#

"This is really nice," Mindy said, and put another forkful of pasta in her mouth.

Amy smiled and nodded. She was enjoying her plate of cannellini also. The food here was excellent. She glanced at the time on her phone. Kayden was going to meet them at the dock in about thirty minutes. Everything was going as planned so far.

"I'm glad we're getting to spend a little time together. I know you and Rurik have been best friends forever, and I just want you to know that I really love him. That I'd do anything for him," Mindy continued with sincerity.

Amy looked into Mindy's eyes and could tell she meant it. There was so much love in her face when she even spoke of Rurik that it was obvious the girl would die for him. Amy had a twinge of guilt, and pushed it to the back of her mind. Rurik belonged with her, the prophecies even said so. Mindy was the interfering intruder.

"He couldn't have chosen a nicer girl," Amy commented.

"Thank you, Amy. I...I know that you weren't happy about him and I getting together at first. But I hope that we can eventually be friends."

"Yeah, me too," Amy answered absently.

"You're so beautiful. Honestly, I don't know why Rurik likes me rather than you."

Amy smiled. She'd had the same thoughts many times over the last several months. She sighed…they said that love was blind. "You're very pretty too, Mindy."

"Not like you," Mindy returned honestly.

Amy had another moment of regret at what she was going to do shortly to Mindy. Give her to Kayden. He was cruel and mean. It would really be kinder to kill Mindy rather than let Kayden have her. But she'd promised Kayden already, and he assured her that they would go far away and never bother them again as long as he could have Mindy. She reminded herself to keep her eyes on the prize… Rurik. She glanced at the time again; just wanting to get this over with. Then she grabbed the bill to pay it. "We should go down to the end of the dock and watch the sunset. They're awesome here. We have time before we're meeting Carmen at the spa."

"Okay," Mindy agreed, and grabbed her jacket before following Amy out to the docks behind the restaurant.

The colors in the sky were changing to oranges, reds, and pinks, with hints of turquoise as the sun set into the ocean.

"Wow! It's so pretty reflecting off the water," Mindy exclaimed.

Amy nodded and looked out across the horizon. She could see the boat in the distance slowly approaching. Kayden would get there about the time the last rays were fading. A couple was standing across from them holding hands and watching the colors fade into blues and grays. Amy hoped they would leave shortly; it could be tricky to get Mindy on the boat unnoticed otherwise.

The stars were starting to magically appear in the sky overhead. They lit up one by one, as if they were being flipped on by small switches. A few lone strands of silver glinted across the ocean and then quickly faded into dark blue. Amy glanced at the couple again and saw that they were heading back down the dock away from them, so she took Mindy's arm and held it tightly. The boat was approaching the end of the dock. Mindy glanced up into her face.

"Act casual and don't scream, Mindy," Amy said with menace, the centers of her eyes flickering with red coals.

Mindy's expression turned to alarm looking into Amy's suddenly threatening features, and then she stared out at the boat that was now pulling up alongside of them. She gasped and put her hand over her mouth.

Kayden was standing on the edge of the deck, grinning.

"No," Mindy whispered. She started to shake and tried to pull away from Amy's grasp.

"Don't fight me," Amy barked. "Get on the boat."

Mindy cringed from Amy's clutches, and stepped off the dock onto the deck of the boat. Kayden was waiting and took her arm. Then Amy stepped on behind Mindy, and Kayden turned the boat around and they sped off.

Mindy sat on the small bench and shook, tears streaming down her face. She was terrified. Kayden was in a great mood, manning the steering and whistling. He would occasionally glance at Mindy, and her heart would leap to her throat again. She turned to look at Amy, who was staring at her with no expression on her features at all.

"Why are you doing this?" Mindy asked in a small frightened voice.

Amy snorted. "You have never belonged to Rurik. He's always been mine. Once you're out of the way, he will be again."

"But he loves me, and I love him. Doesn't that matter?"

"He'll forget you. He's essentially immortal, like me, and you're only human. You're just a phase he's going through. You're right, Mindy. I am so much superior to you in every category. I can't figure out what it is that he likes about you."

Kayden cut the engine and the boat came to a slow stop.

Mindy looked at him, terrified, and turned to Amy for one final plea. "Please don't do this, Amy. You'll break Rurik's heart. If you care about him at all, how can you do this to him?"

Kayden reached down, grabbed Mindy's arm, and hauled her to her feet. "Enough talking. I've been waiting for you for months, Mindy. Soon you'll be all mine."

Tears streamed down Mindy's face.

Amy watched them while Mindy trembled with absolute terror in Kayden's cruel grasp. She felt qualms of guilt again about letting that despicable vampire have someone as nice as Mindy. But she pushed those thoughts out of her mind. Soon Amy and Rurik would be together. "Let's just get this over with, Kayden," she snapped impatiently. "I want to be back on shore before Carmen starts wondering where we are."

"Okay," Kayden said, and held Mindy's arm out.

Mindy tried to pull away. "What are you going to do?!"

Amy walked over. "We have to make it look like you died, so we need some of your blood."

"No!" Mindy exclaimed, and tried to yank free of Kayden's grasp.

Amy held Mindy's arm out to her sharp fingernails and hesitated. She couldn't quite bring herself to do it staring back into the girl's horrified features.

"Come on," Kayden said angrily. He stared at Amy for a moment with contempt, and then took Mindy's arm. "Never mind, I'll do it!"

Mindy winced while Kayden painfully ran his fingernails across her arm in a couple of quick strokes. Blood immediately started flowing from the razor sharp wounds. She sobbed while Kayden held her arm out, dragged her around the deck of the boat, and let the drops splatter until there was an impressive amount of blood. Then he let go of her arm and Mindy quickly retreated over to the bench, holding her arm to her side with a cloth Amy gave her to stop the bleeding.

Kayden turned to Amy and took a menacing step toward her.

Amy's eyes narrowed. "What are you doing? You need to take Mindy, get in the raft, and leave."

Kayden smiled wickedly. "Not until I make it look like you and I fought," he growled, baring his fangs.

Amy backed away. "This wasn't part of the plan. Leave before I have to hurt you."

Kayden smiled and then lunged. "If you return without so much as a scratch it'll be obvious that this was a set up. You need to be wounded so Rurik will believe you."

Amy growled and ducked out of his path, her eyes red. "Back off, Kayden! Or you'll be sorry."

He shook his head. "No way. Rurik needs to be convinced so he doesn't ever come looking for me or Mindy." He leaped on Amy and sank his fangs into the side of her throat. She screamed and flung him off her. He careened backwards several feet before catching his balance. They circled each other again and then crashed together. Amy ripped Kayden's entire side before he was able to grab her arm and rake it with his claws. He flipped her over onto the deck, held her down, and repeatedly hit her.

"Stop it!" Amy yelled. She struggled with all of her might, but couldn't get free of his clutches.

Kayden was out of control. He grinned widely and continued his assault. He'd had enough of Amy's bossing him around. Now she would see who was really in charge.

Amy took the repeated dizzying blows; the pain was incredible. She realized that if Kayden didn't come to his senses she was going to die. No matter how she fought, she couldn't free herself. Suddenly Amy heard a loud crack, and Kayden stopped in mid swing with a stupefied expression and turned to look behind him.

Mindy was standing there holding what was left of an oar that she'd hit Kayden over the head with. It was broken in half, and Mindy held onto the small handle with a death grip. Her angry expression turned quickly to terror as Kayden's furious rage now fixed on her.

Kayden growled and leaped on top of Mindy.

Amy sat up and shook her head, trying to return to her senses, and saw Kayden was relentlessly attacking Mindy. Mindy tried to protect herself as best she could, but she wouldn't survive much longer, and Kayden didn't appear to have any intentions of stopping his onslaught.

"Kayden!" Amy shouted, getting to her feet. "Kayden, stop it! You're going to kill her!" She pulled on his shoulder, trying to get him off of Mindy.

Kayden shoved her back furiously. "Get away from me! Mindy's mine now!"

Amy couldn't let this continue. Mindy had just risked her life to save her from Kayden's cruelty, and now he was going to kill her. Amy leapt on top of Kayden and sank her fangs into the back of his neck. He growled with rage and turned on her. They rolled across the deck of the boat, smashing the bench and everything else in their path.

Mindy leaped to her feet and barely got out of their way as they rolled in her direction. The noises they emitted were deafening and terrifying. Mindy stood as far from them as possible, and watched the fatal fight with absolute horror.

Amy and Kayden's limbs were so tightly wrapped around each other it was hard to distinguish where Kayden ended and Amy began. They sank their claws and fangs deeply into each other's flesh. Suddenly they rolled over the side of the boat and splashed into the ocean, sinking into its murky depths.

Mindy's heart pounded furiously, waiting for them to emerge. After several minutes she carefully peered over the side of the boat. The water was still churning were Kayden and Amy had disappeared into its murkiness.

Mindy took a tentative step closer and stared into the black ocean, slowly and carefully leaning down toward the surface to get a closer look. She held her breath and bent forward over the side, peering intently into the dark liquid.

A hand reached up in a split second, grabbed her arm, and yanked her off the boat and into the water. Mindy screamed while she was hauled into the cold ocean and its darkness, swallowing a mouthful of salt water. She was totally submerged and staring into Kayden's glowing red eyes and evil smile. Mindy pulled furiously against him, but he held her fast. She was rapidly losing oxygen, and struggled with all her might. Her lungs felt like they were going to burst, but Kayden still held her just below the surface of the water. She could see that it was only a matter of inches above her head to desperately needed air. Her body screamed for oxygen. She could not hold her breath any longer.

Suddenly Kayden released her and pushed her up. She gasped and sputtered, filling her aching lungs with fresh air.

Kayden surfaced beside her, grinning with malice. He pulled her back into the boat and Mindy lay where she was, too exhausted to fight or even move.

Once Mindy had finally caught her breath again she sat up and looked around. "Where's Amy?"

Kayden shrugged. "She's gone. I guess she decided that she didn't want to fight me anymore and left." He grinned. "You're all mine now, Mindy."

Mindy swallowed fearfully at his demonic glare, realizing that she was at the mercy of this evil vampire.

She was out here on this boat with him in the middle of the ocean, and no one was around for miles.

He grabbed her arm, hauled her to her feet, and into the raft that was tied to the boat. Then Kayden untied the raft, started its small engine, and they swiftly sped away.

#

I paced with agitation around the living room. I just couldn't sit down and relax. Mom had called a few minutes ago and said that Amy and Mindy were late getting to the spa. She reassured me that everything was all right and that it was probably just traffic. I sighed. I knew this had been a bad idea. I should've trusted my instincts and never let Mindy go. After pacing furiously in circles for five more minutes, I couldn't stand it any longer. I pulled out my cell phone and called her number for the umpteenth time.

It immediately rolled over to her message, and I cursed under my breath. I'd told her several times to make sure that it was fully charged so that I could reach her at all times. I growled to myself, grabbed my keys to the Camaro, and rushed out the door. I really did hope that Mindy had just been irresponsible and forgotten to charge it, but somehow I knew that wasn't the case.

My phone rang and I looked hopefully at my cell. It was Mom.

"Hi, Rurik. I called Amy's number and it's turned off also. Dad and I are heading over to the pier where they had dinner. We'll meet you there."

"All right, Mom," I tried to say in an even tone. But inside I was in turmoil. It seemed way too big of a coincidence that both Amy and Mindy would forget to charge their phones.

#

Mindy stared up into Kayden's evil face with dread. There was no one to save her from what Kayden would do to her now.

Suddenly and without any warning something came up underneath the raft with force, and Mindy went sailing through the air, screaming. She hit the ocean with a painful thud, and then treaded water while searching the area, trying to comprehend what had just happened. She saw Kayden several feet away surveying the waves, looking for some sign of what had caused their boat to capsize. All at once his head ducked under the surface of the ocean and Mindy was alone. She stared around her in the swirling water for several minutes, constantly turning in every direction, waiting with nervous anticipation for something to happen, wondering if she was to be pulled under next.

Without warning Kayden flew out of the water and landed with a splash on the other side of her. Then Amy surfaced and grabbed his throat with her claws. Kayden growled and Amy tightened her hold. He was becoming desperate to get out of her clutches and clawed at her, trying to get away, his face red, his eyes bulging out of their sockets. Amy only tightened her hold, her expression horrible, with teeth pulled back exposing her fangs and eyes glowing an evil blood red. She didn't even resemble the gorgeous girl that she was. All the rage she felt at Kayden was apparent in her features while she concentrated on her one goal.

Kayden screamed hysterically, but Amy ignored his pleas, tightening her grip around his throat. He started to gurgle, his wind pipe completely cut off until he couldn't even shriek out anymore. Then his head literally popped off his shoulders and bobbed up and down in the water.

Mindy gasped and shuddered. It was the most horrendous thing she'd ever witnessed.

Kayden's body sank into the depths of the ocean, while his head continued to bob for a few moments before it sank too.

Mindy stared into the black water where he'd disappeared. The ocean was almost calm while she gawked nervously around her. Amy had vanished and there was no sign of anyone. Mindy noticed the raft in the distance and started to swim toward it.

Suddenly Amy emerged above the waves by the raft, took hold of the rope, and hauled it over to where Mindy was. Amy climbed in and then held her hand out to Mindy.

Mindy hesitated only for a moment before she took it, too exhausted to fight anymore, and lay in the bottom of the boat, trying to get her breathing and heartbeat back to normal.

Amy stood over Mindy, her features beautiful again. She was no longer the hideous creature who'd killed Kayden. "Are you okay, Mindy?" Amy asked, and sat down on the small seat beside where Mindy was lying.

Mindy stared silently back at Amy, not knowing what Amy was planning to do with her.

"I'm really sorry," Amy continued. "I…I don't know what to say. I was overcome with jealousy about how Rurik loves you and not me." She shook her head in disgust at herself, and tried to smile. "I just couldn't see why. I'm so much prettier." She looked into Mindy's face thoughtfully. "Rurik kept telling me how beautiful you were. I didn't understand. There's beauty that's way bigger than just physical. Yes, you are very pretty, Mindy, but you don't compare to my beauty. You aren't a vampire and perfect like I am. But what Rurik was talking about was your heart." Her eyes filled with tears. "I'm so sorry. You're a very sweet, wonderful person like Rurik kept telling me. You risked your life for me, even though I brought you to Kayden so I could be with Rurik."

Mindy sat up and stared back at Amy. "It's okay, Amy. You saved me."

Amy shook her head. "No…no it's not. Kayden would have done unspeakable, horrible things to you, and I didn't care. I just wanted Rurik."

"But you came through in the end," Mindy reasoned. "You didn't have to come back and save me from Kayden. You did the right thing."

They heard the noise of a motor boat approaching and stared in that direction. Rurik was speeding toward them, with Carmen and Adrian also onboard.

Amy tried to smile at Mindy. She sighed. "Too little too late. I will pay for this. The least they'll do is flog me. I'll probably be executed."

Mindy frowned. "But you killed Kayden."

Amy sighed, and with a serious expression said, "It doesn't matter. We have laws, and there are never any exceptions."

#

When I pulled up to the pier Amy's car was still parked out front, and Mom and Dad were hurrying over.

Dad looked at me grimly. "They were last seen getting on a boat at the end of the dock with a large man with blond hair."

"Kayden," I immediately replied with alarm.

We raced down the dock and grabbed a speedboat that a couple were just stepping out of.

"Hey!" the man yelled. "What do you think you're doing?!"

I didn't have time to be nice or explain. I turned to him and showed my fangs, my eyes glowing red. "We're taking your boat!"

The man stared back with absolute shock and horror.

"Is that okay?" I asked in a quiet tone.

He nodded furiously and backed away from us. We jumped into the speedboat, I turned it around, and we sped away.

"Rurik," Dad said disapprovingly. "Was that necessary?"

"I didn't have time to be nice," I answered.

Dad didn't say a thing, only frowned at me and shook his head.

We searched the waves for any sign for several minutes. I was getting extremely agitated, and then saw a small raft up ahead. I could see Amy and Mindy on board. I breathed a sigh of relief that they were still alive. When the boat approached I could tell that they were both wounded, and Mindy was still visibly shaking and upset as she stared back at us with wide eyes.

As soon as the boat was close to the raft, I cut the engine and jumped across to where Mindy and Amy were. I wrapped Mindy in my arms. She had tears in her eyes, she was so relieved to see me. There were several bruises on her face, and large gashes across the inside of her arm. "Are you okay, Angel?"

She nodded while tears poured down her cheeks.

Dad stepped over, took Amy by the arm, and escorted her across to the motor boat while I helped Mindy. Mom wrapped Mindy in a blanket, and we sat down on the bench together.

"What happened here?" I asked, and looked from Amy back to Mindy.

Mindy glanced nervously to Amy, but didn't answer.

Amy sighed. "It's my fault. I...I took Mindy out here so that Kayden could have her. So she would be out of the way, and...you would want me again."

"What?!" I shouted, leaping to my feet. My eyes turning red with fury.

Amy stared back at me sadly. "I just wanted you to love me the way you love Mindy. I'm really sorry."

I had Amy on the floor of the boat in half a second, my hands around her neck. She stared up at me with sadness and fear. "You're sorry?! That's it? Like that's supposed to excuse this?!"

Amy's lower lip started to quiver and her eyes filled with tears, but she didn't even fight me.

I tightened my hold on her; I was beyond furious.

"Rurik! Stop!" Dad shouted. "We'll take her back, and she'll be punished according to our laws."

I glanced at Dad. I knew he was right, but I didn't care at the moment. Mindy could have been killed.

Amy was trembling and crying. She stared with resignation into my frightening expression.

Mindy reached out and put her hand on my arm. "Stop, Rurik. Amy saved me from Kayden and killed him."

I turned to stare at Mindy. "After she brought you out here for him. She deserves to die."

I fixed my red glowing eyes on Amy again. Amy shook but didn't try to defend herself at all. "I…I'm really sorry, Rurik. You're right, Mindy is an angel."

I concentrated intently on Amy until she started to moan, unable to budge from my trance.

"Don't do this, Rurik," Mom said in an even tone. "You know the laws. Amy deserves a hearing."

I ignored them all and kept my fixed eyes on Amy. Her eyes were as large as saucers now while she lay there transfixed by my gaze. We both knew she couldn't last too much longer.

"Rurik, please stop!" Mindy said more forcefully.

"Stay out of this, Mindy!" I yelled back.

"No," Mindy said gently. She took my face in her hands and turned my eyes away from Amy and onto her. Then she screamed and threw her hands up to her face and cowered back from me. I realized that she had just taken on the full force of my dark stare.

I pulled her to me. "I'm so sorry, Mindy. I didn't mean for that to happen."

Mindy shook and cried in my arms for a long time. She sat silently beside me while Dad drove the boat back to shore. I helped her off the boat and to the house, but she never said a word. I tucked her into her bed and sat with her while she drifted off to sleep.

I stayed beside her and watched her toss and turn in her sleep all night. I was very worried for her. My fixed stare could kill a vampire; a fragile human didn't stand a chance.

When Mindy woke in the morning I was still sitting there. She opened her eyes, looked up at me, and smiled.

I breathed a sigh of relief. "Hello, Angel." I gently stroked her cheek. "Are you feeling better?"

She frowned, but nodded. "I'm all right."

"I'm so sorry, Mindy. What were you thinking when you pulled my gaze from Amy? You could have died."

She sighed. "I couldn't let you kill her, Rurik. She's your friend, and...and she did save me from Kayden."

"After she brought you out there for him," I pointed out. Then said callously, "We have laws, and she broke them."

"You've broken them in the past too," she reminded me. "I know that Amy really is sorry; give her another chance." Mindy sat up and looked imploringly into my face.

I sighed. "You really are too good. Amy's been mean to you for months. She wanted you dead, and was going to give you to Kayden. That evil creature would have tortured you and enjoyed it."

Mindy smiled, put her arms around my neck, and leaned in. "But she didn't, and she did save me," she said tenderly, and kissed my lips with her soft, warm ones. "Please...."

I sighed. I knew that I would never be able to resist my angel. Somehow, in her gentle trusting way, she was able to subdue the beast in me like no one else could. And had even gotten to Amy, who'd just wanted her out of the way. I wrapped my arms around her and pushed her back onto the bed while we kissed. When I looked down into her face, her lips curved up into a smile, and her soft green eyes sparkled with happiness.

I couldn't help grinning. "You're absolutely adorable, Mindy. How can I ever say no to you?"

THE
   END

About the Author

Born in Washington state; C. S. Wolfe went to the University of Texas on an art scholarship and majored in art and literature. She also has a Commercial Art degree from North Valley Occupational Center in Mission Hills California and was a successful self-employed artist painting murals and commissioned works of art.

She has always loved classic vampire and monster movies, romance, and horror novels. Her writing and characters are an exciting mixture of those elements.

She lives close to her daughter in a beautiful city near the ocean, where she enjoys writing and painting in her studio/office. Her website where you will find her artwork and latest books in the Fire and Ice Vampire series is www.FireandIceBook.com